Home for the Summer

Suzanne Snow writes contemporary and uplifting fiction with a vibrant sense of setting and community connecting the lives of her characters. A horticulturist who lives with her family in Lancashire, her books are inspired by a love of landscape, romance and rural life. Her first novel in the Thorndale series, *The Cottage of New Beginnings*, was a contender for the 2021 RNA Joan Hessayon Award and she is currently writing the Love in the Lakes series for Canelo. Suzanne is a member of the Romantic Novelists Association and the Society of Authors.

Also by Suzanne Snow

Welcome to Thorndale

The Cottage of New Beginnings
The Garden of Little Rose
A Summer of Second Chances
A Country Village Christmas

Love in the Lakes

Snowfall Over Halesmere House
Wedding Days at Halesmere House
Starting Over at Halesmere House

Hartfell Village

Finding Home in Hartfell
Christmas at the Home Farm Vets
Home for the Summer

Home
for the
Summer

SUZANNE SNOW

canelo

First published in the United Kingdom in 2026 by

Canelo, an imprint of
Canelo Digital Publishing Limited,
20 Vauxhall Bridge Road,
London SW1V 2SA
United Kingdom

A Penguin Random House Company
The authorised representative in the EEA is Dorling Kindersley Verlag GmbH.
Arnulfstr. 124, 80636 Munich, Germany

A CIP catalogue record for this book is available from the British Library.

ISBN 978 1 83598 370 6

Printed and bound in Great Britain by Clays Ltd, Elcograf S.p.A.

Look for more great books at
www.canelo.co | www.dk.com

To Becca and Nicky, with love.

Chapter One

For Cassie McLeod, the prospect of a weekend in Hartfell with her closest friend Pippa was usually a happy one. Their teenage daughters Isla and Harriet were almost inseparable despite the miles between them, and her son Rory wasn't alone in craving the wide-open spaces of the Yorkshire Dales after the confines of London. Cassie, too, found solace and strength in being outdoors, and her days didn't feel complete if she hadn't walked at least a mile or two. Between the demands of her career and the children, time to herself was in short supply, though she didn't really mind as it gave her less time to think. Less time to dwell on life before her husband Ewan had passed away so suddenly after a cycling accident two and a half years ago, and left his family and friends bereft.

But this May half-term holiday promised to be a difficult one, and Cassie was secretly looking forward to it being over. Not because she wanted to hurry back to London, but after the overnight stay in Hartfell, they would head further north to help her beloved parents-in-law move out of their home. She pressed a hand to her temple as she drove, pulsing with the beginnings of a headache, uncomfortably aware she was sidestepping conversations if they included any mention of Pippa's younger brother Raf. She and Pippa generally shared everything, and Cassie hated this new deception and having to hide her feelings from the person who knew her best.

Formerly the drummer with his dad's legendary rock band Blue at Midnight and Ewan's best friend, Raf had invited Cassie, Isla and Rory out to Australia for the final leg of the band's global retirement tour last November. It had been an exceptional and exciting experience, and they'd loved every minute, despite missing Ewan. Raf had been a wonderful support since Ewan had passed away, and for Cassie the holiday had been the perfect distraction after Pippa and Harriet had moved to Yorkshire last summer.

Her phone on the passenger seat flickered with a notification and she pulled a face at the sight of the home screen. She seriously needed to update the wallpaper. The image was one Isla had chosen, a selfie of the four of them on the beach in Australia. In between gigs, Raf had escaped the band and driven her and the children up the coast for a couple of days, and they'd had a wonderful time snorkelling, swimming and chilling out.

But the new tension between them was her own fault. If he hadn't found her on their last night in Queensland, sitting beside the pool at their beachfront house, then he might never have hung around to make sure she was okay. And he wouldn't have hugged her in the way she was so used to from their years of friendship, one which reached back decades to when he and Pippa had moved into the North London street where she'd lived with her parents. A hug which had quickly become something else entirely. The memory of how she'd felt in those moments still made Cassie go cold and then hot every time she thought of it. So now she did her utmost not to think about Raf, or what had occurred between them. At least he wouldn't be in Hartfell this weekend, so she didn't have to worry about bumping into him.

But it was getting ever more impossible to prevent anyone close to them, most of all her children, from suspecting that anything was amiss between her and Raf. He came and went from their home when he was in town much as he always had, and she usually had an excuse ready if there was any possibility that she might be left alone with him.

She'd managed to clear her inbox in preparation for the few days away. Officially she worked full-time hours across a four-day week as head of public relations for a small group of luxury hotels, dividing her time between home and an office in Mayfair, north of the river from their house in Putney. There were still days when she relished the rapidly changing dynamics as she and her team sought new ways of placing the hotels at the forefront of those searching for luxury and home-from-home comforts. Others she found draining, work sapping her energy until she felt barely fit enough to throw together a meal once the children were home from school and whatever extra-curricular activities they had on.

They'd set off for Hartfell in good time and Cassie was thankful they were almost there, the motorways behind them. She stole a glance at her children slumped in the back seat. It had been worth Isla's grumbling about the early start, and at least they would arrive in time for lunch, one Pippa was hosting to welcome a new artist to her gallery in the village. Cassie smiled at the sound of Billie Eilish escaping Isla's single ear bud. Isla always made her presence felt without even trying. It wasn't that she was disruptive or difficult; she was simply unmissable. Cassie often thought that her daughter had inherited this characteristic from her own mother, who'd been a successful model in her day. Rory, two years younger than Isla at thirteen, had long learnt to ignore his sister when he wanted some peace, and Cassie guessed he'd been watching cycling videos on YouTube before he'd dozed off.

Isla's passion for horses was undimmed by living in the city, and she planned to spend most of her time in Hartfell with Harriet and the two ponies who lived at Home Farm with Pippa and her partner Gil. One of the ponies, Flo, whom Harriet had rescued last Christmas, was due to give birth any day, and both girls were desperate for the foal to arrive this weekend. Isla spent most of her Saturday mornings volunteering at a city stables in return for rides.

Cassie was getting used to Isla's growing independence as her daughter approached the end of Year Ten, meeting her friends and making her own social arrangements. Rory, meanwhile, was desperate to take his new gravel bike out this weekend, a treasured birthday gift from his grandparents and another precious link to his dad. Cassie, driving along pretty lanes narrowed by lofty hedges thick with new green leaves and punctuated by clumps of stone walls swathed in moss, ignored the familiar squeeze of anxiety when she thought of him riding it.

Her mind turned to lunch instead, trying to recall what Pippa had mentioned about the new artist. He was a sculptor, apparently a very successful one, whose work was highly collectable. A relieved sigh escaped as she left the familiar sights of the village and turned into the entrance of Home Farm. The farmhouse, built centuries ago from local stone, which gave it a creamy hue between mullioned windows, sat securely on her left, the pony paddock to her right. Further on, the drive curved towards the house before it turned towards the vet practice that Gil ran. Cassie pulled up and turned off the ignition, the children waking instantly and flinging open the doors to escape.

She spotted Pippa, Gil and Harriet, plus their family dogs Lola and Maud, crossing the back garden to greet them, and she waved merrily before going to the boot to retrieve a couple of bags. Harriet was first to reach the gate, and she and Isla squealed as they embraced. Rory crouched to cuddle the dogs leaping excitedly around the three teenagers' legs. Cassie stretched, grateful for the warm spring sunshine welcoming them. Even the air here was different, so fresh and clear, and her shoulders began to loosen. The girls linked arms and hurried towards the stables and the vet practice across the yard as Gil hugged Rory, and Pippa found Cassie.

'Cass, it's so wonderful to see you! It's been weeks.' Pippa's arms went around her as the dogs weaved between their legs, and Cassie melted into the familiar embrace. However much they caught up online, nothing could compare to being together. 'I'm so pleased you've made it in time for lunch. I can't wait for you to meet Jago.'

'Jago?' They separated, and Cassie's mind snagged on the name as Pippa took one of the bags. Her phone beeped again and she frowned at the new notification, one from a colleague. 'Oh yes, your new artist. Sorry, I'm still not quite in holiday mode yet.'

'Work?' Pippa understood the demands on Cassie's time.

'Of course.' She sent her an apologetic look. 'I'm sorry, it looks as though I'll have to schedule a meeting later. Something's come up with an influencer from Paris who's staying next week. She wants to arrive twenty-four hours ahead of schedule, which will require some readjustments.'

There was often a call she needed to make, or an email requiring an urgent response. But her boss was understanding too, and she couldn't mind the interruptions too much because the company was flexible when it came to her family commitments. She could lead the meeting from here and hoped her children wouldn't mind yet another mini absence. Unlikely, seeing as Isla would be off somewhere with Harriet, and Rory probably out cycling with Gil, who was kind enough to ride with him whenever they came up. Raf rode with him too, and Cassie was grateful that both men looked out for Rory the way they did.

'So you haven't looked Jago up?'

'No, sorry. It slipped my mind and we were on the road early.' Something in Pippa's tone had Cassie shooting her a loaded stare. 'Why do you ask? You sound suspiciously casual.'

'No reason. We're just seven for lunch, and as it's such a gorgeous day, I thought we'd eat in the garden. Gil's made the most divine rhubarb and ginger cheesecake. He's really getting into baking and we're all...'

'Pippa, what are you up to?' Cassie wasn't deceived; they'd known each other too long. She caught Pippa's arm, halting them as Gil helped Rory unload his bike. A startling new thought arrived, and she gasped, her voice a muttered hiss. 'You're not seriously trying to set me up? Are you?'

'Of course I'm not. But he seems very nice from what I've seen so far. No subterfuge, I promise.' Pippa squeezed Cassie's hand, concern flaring in her gaze. 'Isla told Harriet you were thinking of dating again, and

Harriet mentioned it to me because she thought I already knew.'

'Oh, hell.' Cassie's face stung as it reddened. 'It was just a throwaway remark when Isla caught me at a bad moment. She said she and Rory would understand if I wanted to date someone else, as she didn't think I'd want to be single forever. That their dad would understand.' A tear slid down her cheek, and she swiped it away. 'I googled what apps were out there for someone like me, and very foolishly signed up to one for dating after bereavement. I told Isla and Rory because I felt it was only fair they knew, and I didn't want it to be some big secret I was keeping from them. I haven't done anything with it yet. I'll probably delete my profile.'

'Don't do that, at least not yet,' Pippa said kindly. 'Maybe it's a good thing, a sign that you're ready to meet someone new.'

Cassie shrugged. She wasn't about to reveal to Raf's sister that she'd only signed up as a means of distracting herself from thoughts of him. It was laughable really; she and Pippa used to have crushes on pop stars all the time, and now she was in the thick of another one. It would pass, she told herself determinedly, just like all the others.

'I'm sorry I didn't tell you. It was one of those things I thought I should tick off my list. You know, moving on and all that.'

'Oh, Cass.' Pippa clutched her arm, throwing Rory a smile and waiting for him to wheel his bike past. 'You know there's no time limit or a to-do list? You don't have to date just because you think you should. And if you do want to date someone, then that's absolutely fine too. You're way too young to spend the rest of your life on your own if that's not what you want.'

7

'I don't really know what I want. Except our old lives back.' Cassie found a tissue and blew her nose; she carried them everywhere. 'But how the hell do I even begin trying to date someone else?'

She was thinking of Raf again, their time in Australia and the perfect few days he'd arranged for her and the children. The relief of being held by someone she trusted and already loved as a friend. The thought of a stranger, someone she'd picked on an app, understanding her so completely seemed so far out of reach as to be impossible.

'Maybe you start by keeping your expectations realistic. Remind yourself there's no pressure to search for the perfect match, and that you can date and have a nice time without it having to be anything more complicated.'

'By realistic, you mean low.' Cassie pulled a face and they laughed. 'I've never done this before. How many people meet their future life partners on a Scottish beach when they're both teenagers?'

'Just the lucky ones,' Pippa said softly. 'Please promise me you'll be careful and follow due diligence before and during any dates? Check them out first and make certain someone knows where you are.'

'Of course I will. It's like buying something on Amazon, all that swiping. Ordering up people like pizza.' That made Pippa laugh again, and Cassie shook her head. 'If I actually do find a decent date, you, Isla and Rory will be the first to know. There's no point in having someone in my life if it's not going to work.'

She flushed guiltily. Raf was a traveller who roamed the world, and Pippa despaired of him ever settling down. 'And seriously, how many middle-aged men are going to want a widow approaching perimenopause, plus two bereaved teenage kids? I wouldn't take me on.'

'That's because you don't see what the rest of us do when you look in the mirror. You may not take after your mother in many ways, but you can at least thank her for that. And there will be someone, just give it time. Maybe he'll be a person in a similar situation, and he'll understand because he's already been through it.'

'Yeah, maybe,' Cassie said wryly, linking arms with Pippa as they made for the house beyond the terrace. 'And maybe it's just not for me and I'm better on my own.'

It struck Cassie that Pippa's decision to include her in this lunch maybe meant that her friend somehow knew about her and Raf. And if so, was Pippa thrusting Cassie in Jago's path as an attempt to make sure her best friend and her brother didn't make any more stupid mistakes? And worse, had Raf confessed and enlisted Pippa's help to keep Cassie at bay? To make certain there would be no repeat of what they'd done, not that she wanted such a thing. But Cassie's mind constantly tugged her back to thoughts of him in Australia, those moments alone beside the pool, his eyes questioning and somehow still certain right before they'd...

'Cass? You were miles away.'

'Sorry!' she replied hastily. 'What were you saying?'

'Just that whatever you decide, I'll support you.' The door to the kitchen was open, and the dogs charged past Pippa to crash into their beds, raising their heads in hopes of treats. 'You're the most wonderful mum and simply brilliant at your job. And you're always checking in with everyone else, so it's about time you put yourself first for a change.'

'Thanks, Pippa, I really appreciate it.' But putting herself first always led to daydreams of Raf and what Cassie couldn't have. She couldn't be the one to come between brother and sister, and force either of them to choose. 'Not much has changed in here since last time, then.' She smiled as she looked at the decades-old beige cupboards and scuffed worktop.

'No, the builders are still busy with the practice and then they'll start on the house.' Pippa rolled her eyes. 'I can't wait to have a proper kitchen again. I'm convinced that old range is going to pack up any minute, but Gil says it'll go on forever.'

'He's probably right.' Cassie eyed the dark blue range; it must have seen thousands of meals prepared in this room. 'So tell me a bit more about Jago, then. It wouldn't hurt to be prepared.'

'Agreed. So he was born in the Dales and decided to come home when his marriage ended. Two grown-up daughters, and I'm pretty sure he's single. And *very* easy on the eye. If I wanted to be picky, his hair could be shorter.'

'I was thinking more about his work,' Cassie said drily as Pippa put down the bag and removed a tray of prepared vegetables from the fridge. 'Not so much his personal credentials.'

'Ah.' Pippa's laugh was an unabashed one as she set the tray down. 'Well, he describes himself as an observer, one who's deeply fascinated by the natural world and our connection with it. His work aims to make sense of that connection while striving to maintain the mystery of what we can't, or don't, see for ourselves. He still shows with a gallery in London and thought it would be nice to expand his reach closer to home. I can't tell you how happy I am he chose us, Cassie. It's huge for the gallery, and we're planning a launch in July. I'd love you to come.'

'I will if I can,' she promised, hauling a bag over each shoulder ready to cart upstairs. The summer holidays seemed ages away, and she had family plans to make for those six weeks before then. 'I'll run and freshen up, then put me to work. I'm here to help.'

'You're also here to relax for a few hours before Galloway and helping Fiona and Gordon pack up the house,' Pippa remonstrated mildly. 'So enjoy it, please. Everything's under control.'

'Thank you.' She still hadn't quite got her head around her parents-in-law's move and the loss of the home in the Scottish Borders she loved like her own. Upstairs in the guest room, she dropped the bags onto the double bed and unzipped one.

'Mum? *Mum?*' There was a knock before the door flew open and Rory charged in, his face pink. Cassie's heart softened at the sight, aware of the ever-present sadness for her children and the gaping void Ewan had left in their lives. Rory looked so like his dad, the same scattered freckles and chestnut-brown hair, the matching determination in his smile, which had carried Ewan from a farmhouse in Galloway on a journey to becoming one of the finest neurosurgeons in the country.

'What's the matter?' She held out a hand, more in hope than expectation. He was well on the way to becoming a young man, with a voice that had broken and fuzz emerging on his face. She and Isla were navigating the road to womanhood together, and it was another level of hurt that Rory couldn't do the same with his dad.

That brought Raf to mind again, who did all he could to step into the breach and had recently helped Rory choose his first razor. No matter how things were between them, she was endlessly grateful for his care towards her children, especially Rory. She hugged Isla and Rory whenever they would allow it, reminding them every day how much they were loved, something she'd learnt from Ewan and his family, not her own.

'Have you seen my jersey, the green Endurance one Raf got me?'

Cassie swallowed. There he was again, popping up in conversation. She wondered if Raf was also planning to help her parents-in-law move out of their home. They looked on him almost as another son since those childhood holidays stretching back to their teenage years. She touched her forehead, trying to smooth away the nagging headache. Not that she could escape him in London either. Raf lived in his dad's London flat now the band had finally split. He was also spending more time with Pippa and Gil in Hartfell, and according to Rory, the Norfolk cottage where he went alone to write songs had been empty for a few weeks.

'It's in your case, in the car,' she replied. 'I washed it last night so you could bring it.'

'Thanks, Mum.' Rory grinned as he came over and Cassie wrapped her arms around her son, some of her tension slipping away as she held him. He let go and, at the door, turned to look at her again.

'Did you get Raf's message? He said he'd rung you twice but hadn't heard back.'

'I did, yes.' She caught sight of her phone on the bed and turned it over. She'd had enough of looking at that selfie, the four of them beaming into the camera, arms around one another. She wondered what could be so urgent that Raf had involved Rory. 'I've been busy getting ready for our time away and just forgot to ring him back.' It was mostly true. She had been distracted.

'Seriously?' Rory pursed his lips in the way she was so familiar with. 'Maybe he wants to come to Granny and

Grandpa's with us? It would be pointless to take two cars if we only need one. He might bring his bike so we can go out.' Diagnosed as dyslexic when he was seven, he'd always been a problem solver and able to see the bigger picture.

Rory's explanation was perfectly reasonable, and six months ago she would have said yes to Raf and been grateful for the offer to share a long drive. 'I don't think so, darling. I'm sure Raf will have other plans, and he won't want to hang around to bring us back.'

'You always say that now. I know he'd take us home if we wanted. Why are you being so weird about him?' Rory frowned and Cassie couldn't look at him lest the truth about that night in Australia and her guilt was splattered all over her face. 'How do you know what he's planning if you haven't asked him? I think he'd love to come with us to Galloway, and I bet Granny and Grandpa would appreciate the extra help. I'll message him now.' Rory reached for his phone in a pocket of his cargo shorts.

'No, Rory!' She smiled to soften the sharpness, seeing surprise flare in her son's face. 'And I'm not being weird. We don't want to put Raf under any pressure to help with the move. You know his plans often change, and he comes and goes as he pleases. He might be going to Norfolk, and that's hardly en route to London from Galloway.'

'He's not. I messaged him about my bike, and he told me he was at the flat.' Rory always seemed to know Raf's movements, and he checked in with her children regularly, took them out for pizza, to a movie or a gig. Anything he thought they might like and would make them happy. She totally appreciated it and was grateful for his support, even if some days she felt as though she was trying not to topple from a tightrope, balancing her children's happiness against the mistake she'd made in Australia.

Commitment, except to his music, had never been a concept Raf was familiar with, and she clung to his desire to roam as though her own life depended on it. He hadn't shown any inclination to make a permanent home with a partner, and his last girlfriend had been a stunning Swedish journalist from whom he'd split last summer. If he was seeing anyone else, Cassie knew nothing of it. But why should she? she reasoned, as Rory shuttered his disappointment and closed the door behind him. Raf had no reason to share his private life with her. They were friends, old ones, and he made a huge difference in her children's lives. There wasn't, and there never could be, anything more.

She crossed the landing to freshen up in the bathroom, a pale reflection staring back from the mirror above the sink. Some days it seemed she wore their bereavement on her face too, dark circles beneath her eyes evidence of disturbed sleep. Her brunette hair used to be longer, but now she wore it in a layered choppy bob skimming her jaw. The caramel- and honey-coloured highlights were different too, and occasionally she worried that she didn't now fully resemble the woman Ewan had known and loved.

Back downstairs she helped carry food and drinks into the garden. Pippa sent Gil to the stables in search of the girls while Rory played with the dogs on the lawn, dodging the huge tent set up for the teenagers as there wasn't enough room in the house for everyone. Cassie felt clumsy with nerves over meeting Jago, sloshing a jug of juice on the wooden table. She tried not to wonder what he would make of her. Not that it mattered, but perhaps the lunch might help her dust off some very rusty flirting skills.

Cassie was distracted by the view, a moment of calm following. A cool, damp few days had made way for glorious sunshine, and pretty white clumps of blossom were scattered across hawthorn trees like blobs of ice cream. Hay meadows were flourishing, speckled with bright yellow rattle and the soft pink of red campion. Purple foxgloves and nodding white cow parsley lined the meadow beyond the garden, and lambs in the field further on were already plump from milk enriched by lush spring grass, leaping in the air as their mothers grazed.

Soon the three adults were assembled around the old wooden table, a dark green parasol blotting out some of the heat. The teenagers had been excused from sitting with them and loaded their plates with flatbreads topped with mounds of creamy hummus and roasted vegetables. Jago was due any minute, and Cassie's eyes flickered occasionally to the gate across the garden. Chatting with Gil, she noticed Rory's face light up in welcome at the sound of car doors slamming. Her head whipped around, surprised by his reaction for a stranger.

The plate she held wobbled as she spotted Raf on the drive, and her stomach dropped in the way she had come to expect around him now. Her breath hitched as he stared back, the distance between them shrinking as a flush crept along her throat. Her shocked gaze leapt to the beautiful blonde woman at his side, and the tentative smile on Cassie's lips died. She hastily put down her plate, the food swimming in front of her.

Chapter Two

'Raf! What a wonderful surprise.' Pippa leapt up, but Rory had already taken off. He yanked open the gate and Cassie gulped when he flung himself on his godfather.

He stepped back once Pippa caught up and wrapped her brother in an embrace. Gil handed Cassie a glass of wine and she thanked him before taking a hasty mouthful, trying to force her expression to convey everything her racing mind was not. Once she would have welcomed Raf much like Pippa had, who was now leading him and the woman through the gate and towards the table. The dogs bounded across, he reached down to make a fuss of them, and Cassie heard him trying to refuse whatever it was Pippa had just suggested.

'Look, I didn't want to bother you. It was a last-minute change of plan, that's all. I got a lift up last night and stayed at the pub.'

'But you could have come with us,' Rory said earnestly, throwing Cassie a glance. She pursed her lips. At least the car had been too full for that. If necessary she'd have brought even more stuff to avoid making room for Raf.

'Thanks, buddy.' Raf dropped a hand on Rory's shoulder as his eyes caught hers. She wondered if she was imagining an unspoken apology, the realisation that he'd shocked her by turning up out of the blue, and not alone. 'Didn't think of that.'

Cassie had known him for most of her life, and until six months ago she'd never thought about him in the way she did now. How had she not noticed his eyes were the exact shade of melted milk chocolate? And had he always had those cheekbones, that square jaw and husky hint of tomorrow in his voice? The blond highlights from his band years were gone, his hair a textured crop with razored sides that made him appear leaner. His natural nut brown was shot through with grey, matching a beard barely more than stubble. When she was at university he'd modelled for a lark and some cash, turning it into a career, and age had brought a maturity that still occasionally earned him a place on the sexiest men alive lists. He wore a small gold ring in each ear, and she fixed her gaze on one to avoid staring at his mouth and those full bow-shaped lips as every reluctant step brought him closer to where she sat.

'But why didn't you let us know you were coming? And where's your car?' Pippa was used to her brother's changing plans, but this one appeared to have thrown her.

'I've swapped it for something different. I'm picking it up later.'

'Well, I insist you both stay for lunch,' she said firmly, giving the woman another smile. 'I'll fetch more plates.'

'Allegra's just dropping me off, Pippa, we're not stopping,' Raf said quickly. 'She gave me a lift to...'

'Don't be silly, we've got plenty of food. Jago's due any minute, then we can eat. Won't you introduce your friend, Raf?' She looked at him expectantly, but the woman was quicker.

'I'm Allegra Foxton, how wonderful to meet you all,' she said happily. 'I've heard so many amazing things, and it's so kind of you to invite us to stay for lunch.'

Cassie took a second generous swig of wine as Raf ran warily through the introductions. If she drank enough, hopefully everyone would assume the flush on her cheeks was alcohol-induced and not because of the man who dominated her thoughts way more than he should. The girls waved hello from the tent and Rory changed his mind about eating with them. Her heart cracked just a little more as he waited for Raf to choose a seat first in hopes of sitting beside him.

Gil got up to envelop Raf in a brotherly hug, and he shook hands with Allegra. Pippa looked as though Christmas had come early, and Cassie shuffled up to make room as Pippa shot back to the house for more plates and glasses. She stole another glance at Allegra as Raf pulled out a seat for her opposite Cassie, brushing away soft pink apple blossom from the cushion. Pale skin was flawless on a delicate, heart-shaped face, surrounded by tumbling blonde hair colour blocked in subtle tones of ash, enhancing a beauty that was enchanting. There was something both vulnerable and strong in such a face, and Allegra had the kind of tall, willowy figure Cassie would have once envied. She didn't miss the look Allegra threw him as she sat down, one she had seen so many times before. He turned to Rory on his other side, playfully ruffling Rory's hair and saying something which made him laugh.

It was time, and she needed to face the reality. The secret feelings she harboured for Raf had no place in her heart, and his friendship was too precious to lose because she had a crush on him after one incredible kiss.

She would make herself get over this; she had to. But why did he have to look so good? Those two gold rings glittering against suntanned skin, the muscled arms she remembered holding her that night. He'd pulled a pair of aviator sunglasses down from his hair, and she couldn't read his expression behind them.

'Raf's told me so much about you, Cassie.' Allegra leant forward, her bare arm brushing his.

'Oh?' Cassie forced out a quick laugh. So Allegra must be the reason why he had called her twice this week, and it was her own fault for not picking up. If she had, then at least she would have spared herself a new girlfriend being sprung on her like this. She rarely drank these days, and the alcohol was already hitting her bloodstream, making her head swim. 'I hope he said nice things.' He'd better not have referred to her as an 'old' friend.

'Oh, he was very kind.' Allegra had perfected the ability to stare coyly from beneath thick lashes. 'It's so sweet, how he takes care of his old friends.'

And there it was. Somehow that made her feel like an elderly dependant who could barely totter from A to B. Allegra probably hadn't meant it unkindly; it wasn't likely she perceived any threat around this table to whatever was going on between her and Raf. Cassie thought her face might crack if she smiled any harder as Pippa deposited extra plates on the table. The sound of another car had Pippa turning, and she hurried to welcome their latest guest. Cassie was only too thankful to shove her chair back and leap up, ready to be distracted by the new arrival. Pippa greeted him with kisses on both cheeks and tucked her arm through his as she led him to the table.

'Everyone, this is Jago Lynch. He's the most wonderful artist, and one who I'm beyond thrilled to be welcoming to the gallery in the summer.' Pippa made the introductions and Cassie wondered if she had imagined his gaze lingering on her as they shook hands. Her heart bumped. There had been no time to learn what Pippa had explained about her circumstances, and whether he knew she was a widow.

Jago had brought bottles of red and white wine, and Gil, whose eldest son ran a vineyard in Australia, was happily examining the red and searching for a corkscrew to open it. Pippa suggested that Jago take the seat next to Cassie, and for once she didn't mind her friend's collusions because he provided a welcome diversion from Raf and Allegra, who was busy checking her phone. Food was passed around and the girls were back, deciding to look in on Flo and her unborn foal in the stables. Cassie's appetite had vanished along with her composure, and she forced down some hummus and vegetables.

'So I hear your work is much influenced by the natural world and our place within it,' she said, turning a shoulder towards Jago. His eyes were a gorgeous shade of blue, she decided, like summer skies on a sunny day. So much nicer than brown. Less… *dangerous*.

'I am, yes.' His smile widened at her interest, crinkling laughter lines around his mouth. 'Should I be flattered by your knowledge of my work, or have you been speaking with Pippa?'

'Definitely Pippa,' Cassie confessed, and she liked him even more when he laughed. Hair tending to the sandy side of auburn was short on both sides, with the top swept back in a style which emphasised a narrow face and a neat beard more grey than auburn. He'd removed a brown leather jacket, sliding it across the back of his chair, and the white shirt with jeans was a classic look.

'So are you interested in sculpture?'

'In theory, but the reality is I've never collected any. Should I?' She tried not to cringe. That had definitely come out more flirtatiously than she'd intended. It must be the wine.

'Of course I'm going to say yes.' He raised a brow. 'I hope you'll come to my launch in July.'

'That sounds lovely,' she said. Was he speaking generally, hoping to entice a potential collector, or had he meant that to be a more personal invitation? She was so out of practice, she probably wouldn't even realise if Jago attempted to flirt with her. 'I'll have to check my calendar and our summer plans. Pippa did mention it.' Better not to commit either way. She wasn't a fan of making a fool of herself with strangers.

'Great.' One finger was circling the top of his glass. 'Pippa tells me you're a publicist for a very successful hotel group.'

'Yes, I'm based at The Bennington in London. Do you know it?'

'I do. I've had some very nice lunches there. Famous for their steak tartare, as I recall.'

Cassie began to relax as their conversation continued, comparing their parenting experiences and places they both knew in London. He liked to talk, and she didn't mind letting him. But eventually Pippa turned the discussion back to Raf, and Cassie recognised the gleam in her friend's eye.

'So what brings you here?' Pippa glanced at Raf as she cleared plates while Gil topped up glasses. Cassie refused more wine. She'd had quite enough, and the hit had passed now. 'We thought you weren't coming up for another couple of weeks.'

A simple enough question, but one she knew was loaded. Pippa was trying to find out who Allegra really was and if she was potentially welcoming someone significant to their inner circle. Raf brought so few girlfriends home, and Cassie didn't need Pippa to tell her how meaningful this apparently casual drop-in really was.

'Something came up, I'll explain later,' he replied smoothly. He leant back, implying a relaxation Cassie couldn't hope to achieve sitting opposite him.

'We've been to see a house.' Allegra charmingly thanked Gil for refilling her glass with water, seemingly unaware of the bomb she had just lobbed right into lunch.

'A house?' The stack of plates in Pippa's hands rattled. 'Seriously?'

We. Allegra had said *we*. Cassie's pulse was pounding, her mind caught on that single word. All these months she had been working, mothering, checking in with her friends and family, getting on with life and trying to forget what had happened in Australia, and Raf had been, what? Developing a relationship so meaningful that he and Allegra had already been to see a house together, and not a single person in his family appeared to know.

'An actual house?' Pippa couldn't seem to make sense of Allegra's explanation either. She sat down so hurriedly that Maud, underneath the table, shot out of the way with a yelp. 'But where? In Hartfell? For you? Or…?'

'Just outside the village.' Raf ran a hand across his jaw. 'Look, before you all get carried away, nothing's decided, yeah? I haven't made up my mind yet.'

Cassie sensed him looking at her, and she was not about to give him her eyes. She couldn't bear for him to read everything she was feeling in this moment. So this was the result of her self-imposed exile from his company.

She'd refused to connect, believing that she could only properly protect herself by avoiding him. So why wouldn't he exclude her, when it was the very thing she supposedly sought? She had no right to be hurt by his bringing someone else home six months after their stupid mistake.

'Oh, but there isn't much time to decide, Raf.' Allegra turned wide indigo eyes on him, a hand briefly on his arm. 'If you want to make an offer, you simply mustn't hang around. Loads of people will be after it once it goes online.'

'Is it the house I told you about, Raf?' Gil had returned from the house with pudding, and he paused dividing cheesecake into generous slices. 'The client whose wife passed away, and he wanted to move to be near his children?'

'Gil!' Pippa's new expression was one of nonplussed amazement. 'You knew about this?'

'There wasn't much to know.' He shrugged. 'Raf's been spending more time here and we all knew he was thinking he might like a base eventually. It just came up when we were out cycling one day and happened to pass the house.'

Raf wanting a base in Hartfell was certainly news to Cassie. It was at least a comfort to realise that Pippa hadn't known he had viewed a house either, and kept it from her.

'Allegra's the land agent who's handling the sale,' Raf said. 'I got in touch after Gil mentioned it, and we went back for a second viewing this morning.'

'Well, I think it's wonderful, and I'm so pleased Raf brought you to lunch, Allegra.' Pippa beamed at her. 'You must tell us everything about the house. I'd love to see it sometime.'

'Oh, it's absolutely stunning! Such a perfect family home, and it's so obvious they adored it.' Allegra leant past Raf to speak to Pippa. 'It's definitely in need of an upgrade, and if it were up to me…'

Cassie barely heard another word as Allegra continued to enthuse, touching Raf's arm occasionally, and once resting her hand on his. She turned back to Jago, happy to hear more about his work and inspiration. She liked that he was interested in her career too and she made a mental note to check the date of his launch in July. He was chatty and fun, and she could imagine worse first-date candidates, if she ever took the plunge.

'Muuuuum…'

Harriet and Isla were tearing across the lawn with Alfie, Harriet's boyfriend, behind them. A young farmer who lived locally, Alfie was often at Home Farm, helping Harriet with the ponies. Maud and Lola had already caught the new excitement, and Maud tumbled over as she raced towards them. Harriet stuttered to a halt and helped her up, catching Isla up on the terrace and thrusting her phone at Pippa.

'It's actually happening, Flo's about to give birth! Look!' Harriet rushed on to explain the pony had been showing signs of 'bagging up', when her udders began to fill with milk. Since feeding and mucking out earlier, they'd left her alone to give birth in peace, and from the camera Gil had set up in her stable, they could see Flo was restless and pacing.

'Oh, wow. That's so exciting!' Pippa and Cassie clustered around Harriet to stare at the images. The pony was pawing impatiently at the ground, a thick bed of shavings piled up to her hocks around the walls.

'Gil said her udder is waxed up, when colostrum starts to leak from her teats.' Harriet easily absorbed information, especially where animal science was concerned. 'She's been staring at her tummy and getting up and down, which is stage one of labour. Her waters have broken as well, which means the birth should happen soon, and she's having contractions. Oh look, she's lying down again,' she finished eagerly. 'This could be it, Mum! Flo's about to have her foal!'

'Doesn't someone need to be with her in case she needs help?' Pippa glanced worriedly at Gil, who shook his head.

'No, Gil said she'll be fine on her own. Mares often give birth overnight, but it's important to keep checking on them. Oh wow,' Harriet shrieked, waving the phone again, Isla squealing across her shoulder. 'Look, a foot! It's actually happening! The other foot comes next, and the foal's chin should be resting on top of it, like it's in a diving position.'

'That's amazing, and you've learnt so much already, Harriet. Come back and tell us the minute you have more news, okay?' Pippa watched as the girls, Rory and Alfie ran back towards the yard with Maud. 'I'd love to go too, but we'd better not crowd Flo.'

Pippa offered coffee, but Jago couldn't stay any longer, and he kissed both Pippa and Cassie goodbye, murmuring to Cassie that he hoped he'd see her again at the launch. Raf took the opportunity to leave as well, making his and Allegra's excuses. If Allegra was disappointed at the abrupt exit, she covered it well, and Cassie finally felt as though she could breathe again.

Lola settled beside Cassie, and her hand drifted down to stroke the Labrador's head, warm from the sun, and

Lola's tail thumped a lazy reply. Spring days like these made winter seem like a distant memory. The dogs often accompanied Gil on calls or spent time in the practice, and Pippa sometimes took Maud to the gallery, where she had her own cosy bed in the office. Cassie loved her long Galloway walks with her parents-in-law's two black Labradors, and she always missed the dogs' cheery and uncomplicated company when she returned home. Somehow their hectic lives in London had never quite seemed equal to having a dog of their own, even though she knew Isla and Rory would adore it too.

'Any plans for this afternoon?' Pippa glanced at Cassie. 'It's such a lovely day and I wondered if you fancied a wander to Dorothy's to pick up some eggs. Harriet was going to do it, but I think she'll want to stay with the ponies.'

'I'd love to. It would be good not to miss my walk, and catching up with Dorothy is always fun.'

'Did I tell you she's gone and got herself a horse?' Pippa shook her head and Gil chuckled as he stood up, excusing himself to head over to the stables and cast an eye over Flo.

'You're not serious? Isla will be thrilled! What's it like?'

'It's a ride-and-drive cob, a very sweet one, apparently. I know Dorothy's got loads of experience, but she is nearly eighty-four. I did ask what would happen if she came off and did a hip or something, but she wasn't having any of it. Gave me one of her looks and informed me she hasn't fallen off for over sixty years and has no plans to start now. Gil reminded her that she also hasn't ridden for forty of those years, but she ignored that as well. She got Erin to give the horse the once-over, and he was secretly hoping it wouldn't be fit enough to ride, but apparently it's in cracking form. Dorothy also said that in the unlikely event of her falling off, Harriet could manage the farm with her eyes closed, so there was nothing for us to worry about.'

'Gil's great aunt is certainly one of a kind.' The two women shared an understanding smile. 'So is Harriet still set on Cambridge and veterinary medicine?'

'Totally. She and Alfie have been over to Erin and Oli's cottage a few times, and now they've told her more about studying at Cambridge, she doesn't want to go anywhere else. I just hope she's not crushed if she doesn't get in. But volunteering with Dorothy should help if she gets great results, and she goes out with Erin to see practice whenever she can.'

'I'm sure Harriet will be fine. She's so like your dad, and that determination and work ethic will take her a long way.'

'Thanks, Cassie. I know you're right. But we never stop worrying about them, do we?'

'Nope. So is there anything else you need while I'm out?' Cassie stretched, allowing the sun to do its work. At least her conversation sounded breezy, even if her mind was still full of Raf showing up with Allegra. 'I can always pop down to the shop, you know how much I love that place. Every time I visit, I feel as though I really am on holiday and can treat myself to all their goodies.'

'Don't we all, it's an absolute treasure trove. I can't imagine the village without it, or Daphne and Violet at the helm. Edmund's been helping when he can, but he's over eighty as well.'

Edmund was a local historian who was fiercely intelligent, loved company and was as active as his knees would allow. Last year he'd helped Pippa unearth a family connection to Hartfell and they'd discovered a long-lost painting by her great-grandmother, for whom the new

27

gallery was named. Since its conversion from a youth hostel, the gallery had also become a busy community space where locals and visitors gathered to chat, share food and enjoy creative courses.

They stood up and set off for the kitchen, Pippa going to the dishwasher to begin loading it while Cassie returned leftovers to the fridge. The phone in her jeans pocket buzzed and she checked it, always alert to notifications. A new meeting invite had dropped into her calendar. She clicked on it to read the details and hadn't realised how loud she'd sighed until Pippa was beside her.

'What's the matter?'

'Oh, it's just work.' Cassie frowned. 'The managing director wants to meet when I'm back in the office on Wednesday.'

'And that's a bad thing?'

'I'm not sure. He hasn't included an agenda, which is unusual.' She left the phone on a worktop and resumed helping. 'Rumours have been circulating for a while, and I have a sneaking suspicion they're going to make me redundant.'

'Redundant?' Pippa spun around, an empty bowl in one hand. 'Oh, Cass. But why would they do that? You know the hotels better than anyone and you're brilliant at your job. You go above and beyond, they'd be crazy to let you go.'

'Thanks, Pippa, that's so kind of you, and very loyal. But even with Jas helping at home and the hours I do, I'm still not fully available, not like before.'

Jas had only come into her life four months ago, and Cassie couldn't believe she'd ever managed without the younger woman's practical efficiency and boundless energy. Without family of her own nearby, Cassie had finally given in to Pippa's pleas that she needed some backup at home, and had quickly found Jas. The daughter of a former colleague, Jas was taking a year out to decide on a career after dropping out of a law degree. In the meantime she'd moved into Cassie's spare room and helped with whatever needed doing. Cassie really appreciated having someone she trusted on hand to help care for Isla and Rory, who both adored her.

'I always try to put the children first, but working for a business that's twenty-four seven is getting harder, and I often seem to be saying no to someone.' She dropped her head into her hands, voice muffled. 'Oh, it's all such a mess. If only Ewan were here...'

'Darling.' Pippa pulled Cassie into her arms, holding her fiercely. 'I'm so sorry he's not. What can I do?'

'You already do so much,' she muttered into her shoulder. 'You're a constant support, and I lean on you and Raf too much.' She could mention his name while Pippa couldn't see the guilt on her face and suspect a reason for it.

'Please don't think that,' Pippa said gently. 'I'm here for you always; we both are. I know how much he loves all of you.'

'He actually said that?' Her question was a startled one. Surely he hadn't meant...

'Not in so many words, but you know what I mean. He's always cared about you.'

Of course he hadn't said he loved her. Why would he? 'And we care about him.' Cassie fumbled for a tissue as she eased free. 'As long as we're not holding him back.'

'Never think that, because I know he doesn't. So have you thought about what you'll do if they offer you redundancy? Maybe a change would be good, and you could take some time off to decide what's next.'

'I'm really not sure.' Cassie scrunched the tissue between her fingers. 'If they've already decided, then I doubt I'll even have a choice. I've always worked, even through university, and I can't imagine not having that routine or pulling those hours.'

'Try not to think about the meeting now, if you can.' Pippa rummaged in a cupboard and removed some empty cardboard egg boxes. 'You've still got a few days off to enjoy first.'

The back door flew open and the girls burst in, Lola and Maud bounding behind.

'It's a colt,' Harriet yelled, waving her phone wildly. 'Flo's had her foal, Mum, and it's a boy. He's so cute, a piebald, which is black and white, and Gil says he's beautifully marked.'

'Oh, that's wonderful.' Pippa dashed across to hug her, and Cassie followed suit, all huddled around the phone.

'He's gorgeous, Harriet, so sweet,' Pippa said wistfully.

'Gil said you can see him if you want, but just quickly, okay? They need time to bond.'

'Shall we?' Pippa looked at Cassie, who nodded eagerly.

'Absolutely, I'd love to.'

Rory and Alfie were outside the stables when they arrived. Posy, their resident Shetland pony, who loathed Gil as much as she adored Harriet, was banging her door impatiently, cross at being left out of the excitement. Pippa paused to make a fuss of her, and Posy flattened her ears the moment Gil left Flo's stable to stand nearby. He grinned as Pippa and Cassie crept nearer to peep over the door.

'Oh, he's adorable,' Cassie murmured. Flo was standing, and the foal was trying his best to get to his feet as well, staggering through the shavings on uncoordinated limbs before toppling back over. Flo began to lick him, and he shook his head, large ears flapping noisily. His black face was brightened by a white blaze, and on his left side, a white shoulder and tummy ran into black quarters splodged with more white, a fluffy tail short above black legs and four white socks.

Cassie gripped the stable door as the foal tried to stand again. This time he managed to stay upright for a few moments before skidding back onto the shavings as Flo nosed him gently. Cassie shot Isla a smile, and her daughter beamed back at sharing such a special moment.

'I'm keeping an eye to make sure he takes a drink,' Gil said. 'It's vital he gets that first feed of colostrum, but so far the signs are all good. And I don't think the stallion was another cob,' he added drily. 'The foal's finer boned than Flo, and a pretty big one for a thirteen-hand mare. Perfect size for riding when he's old enough, I reckon.' He smiled at Harriet, still recording these first few minutes in the foal's life on her phone.

Cassie swiped at a happy tear sliding down her face. 'So what are you going to call him?' she whispered to Harriet.

'I thought Hero, because Flo was starving when we brought her home, and the foal has survived even though she was so neglected.' She gave Gil a grin. 'And because I'm surrounded by them.'

Chapter Three

Following the excitement of Hero's birth and happy he was doing well after a first feed, Harriet and Isla decided to join Cassie for her walk to Dorothy's so the ponies could have some peace. Gil headed into the practice, and she wasn't expecting Raf to return after he and Allegra had left the lunch. He decided to join the walk, so Rory opted to come too, the girls still enthusing about the foal when the five of them set off.

A flicker of sorrow pricked at her burgeoning happiness as they strolled, reminding her that Ewan would never be a part of Hartfell as she and the children were. And with his parents' imminent move from Galloway, so much of the life she had known with him would vanish. Was this progress, she mused, forging a new life and experiencing new places without him? She supposed they had no choice. However bereft she still felt at times, it was her children's loss that pierced her most. But right now Rory was laughing at something Isla had said, a welcome break in their usual squabbles.

'I didn't think you'd want to come with us,' Cassie said to Raf idly. In a retro band T-shirt and a pair of jeans ripped across one knee, her stomach somersaulted unhelpfully when his eyes caught hers. She was determined to keep conversation casual and not stray towards questioning him about Allegra, or the house he had viewed.

'I'm not that scared of Dorothy.' He grinned as Harriet dropped back and tucked her arm through his. 'So this is nice. Am I still your favourite uncle?'

'Yeah, but don't tell Freddie.' Harriet bumped into him on purpose. Jonny's youngest son Freddie was only four years older than Harriet, and they were more like cousins than uncle and niece.

'So wait until you see Dorothy's horse, Raf. He's huge.' She'd dropped the 'uncle' a while ago. 'But he's so sweet, and he really looks after her. She's teaching me how to drive the trap.'

'Oh?' Raf raised a brow. 'And does your mother know?'

'Yeah, she's cool with it.' Harriet freed herself from him, and Cassie took the opportunity to slide an arm across her shoulders and tug her close, thankful her goddaughter still indulged such motherly gestures.

'I think you've had another growth spurt, my darling. You left me behind about three inches ago. So what's he called, this horse?'

'Bob the Cob. He's crossed with an Irish Draught, which is why he's so big. I'd love to have taken him, but Mum said we've got enough for now, with the foal and the kittens, plus everything else.' Harriet rolled her eyes and Cassie laughed. 'Gil said it really is like living at work now. He's taught me how to inject Posy with her meds so he doesn't have to do it.'

'I'm sure that's a relief all round.' Cassie had seen Posy's animosity towards Gil when his back was turned one day, and she'd given him a sharp nip on his thigh.

A couple of cyclists whizzed by, hands raised in greeting. Rory stared after them, before falling back to talk with Raf. Cassie was content to walk with the girls and listen to their chat. Eventually they turned onto a rough track and Harriet opened a sturdy five-barred wooden gate fastened with orange baling twine. As they approached the old house, set in the centre of a pair of stone barns, a pack of dogs was already rushing to greet them, and the teenagers hurried on to say hello as Cassie hung back.

'Cass?'

She jumped at Raf's hand on her arm and that urgent tone. 'What?'

'We need to talk,' he said quietly, dropping the words so close to her ear that she felt his breath skimming her skin. 'Please.'

'We don't. Everything's fine.'

A small rough-coated terrier growled, and Harriet fondly told it to shut up. She took hold of his collar just in case as a three-legged lurcher, a black-and-white collie stiff with age and a sleek red setter wagged their tails and nosed greedily in pockets for treats. Isla had come prepared, and she shared some with Rory so he could feed the dogs too. He'd spent less time at Dorothy's than her, and Cassie noticed his caution around the terrier as he gently stroked the setter leaning against his legs.

Harriet loosened the terrier, and he scampered away as Dorothy emerged from a barn, a black-and-white baby goat wedged securely under each arm. The nanny was trotting at her heels, bleating softly, and Isla abandoned the dogs to rush across with Harriet and exclaim over the kids' cuteness.

Glasses held together with tape rested halfway down Dorothy's nose, and grey hair spilled from a loose bun on the top of her head, a screwdriver stuck through it. The stiff waxed coat she wore all year round was open as a concession to spring, instead of tied around her middle with twine, her usual pair of men's suit trousers and an unravelling woollen jumper visible beneath it.

She peered down her nose at Raf, gaze level with his. Many people would be thrilled to have a rock star drummer dropping in for a visit, but Dorothy was famed for her disdain towards men. The only ones she respected were vets, feed merchants and farmers. Cassie realised it was perhaps one of the attractions of Hartfell for Raf, that not everyone knew or cared about his history.

'I take it you've come to see m'cob?' The dogs were swarming around Dorothy's legs, and the smile she gave Isla was kind. 'Thought we could take him out in the trap if you want?'

'I'd love that. Thank you.' Isla beamed back, and Cassie appreciated the flash of excitement in her daughter's face. 'That's okay, Mum, isn't it?'

'Of course it is.' Cassie didn't fancy her chances of saying no if Dorothy had made up her mind, and she did have years of experience even if it was ages ago. 'Just be careful, okay? Wear your hard hat.'

'I will.' Isla had brought her riding hat just in case and she rushed ahead with Harriet and the dogs.

Dorothy led the nanny to a small paddock and opened the gate, calmly ushering it in and putting the kids down. They took a couple of hesitant steps before scurrying back to their mother's side, and she bleated softly as she nudged them. Both kids nosed beneath her and began to drink, and Dorothy closed the gate with a grunt of satisfaction.

'Right, this way. Chap's in the barn, brought him in off the grass a couple of hours ago. Can't have him blowing up or getting laminitis.' She set off towards the furthest

35

barn, the girls already out of sight as Cassie, Raf and Rory followed more slowly.

Cassie glanced at Rory, wishing she could give him a shot of Isla's confidence and smooth away his anxiety. Both her children missed their dad immeasurably, but it was Rory that had been closest to Ewan. A rush of gratitude for Raf followed. She must make every effort to rebuild and maintain their friendship for Rory's sake, if not her own. Perhaps she ought to have listened to what he had been going to say.

Inside the cool shade of a barn divided into stables by wooden bars, at first Cassie thought she was seeing two horses, not one. But then she realised the smaller of the two was actually a very large dog. Harriet and Isla were already stroking the stocky dapple-grey horse next door. Rory went to the dog, which Cassie recognised as an Irish wolfhound. Even though they were familiar with her parents-in-law's two Labradors, she clutched at his arm when the dog placed both front paws on a wooden bar and stood on his back legs, taller now than Raf.

'Be careful,' she warned quietly as Rory stroked the dog's head, its tail wagging happily. 'He might seem friendly, but there's probably a good reason why he's not running loose with the others.'

'Can't let him out, that's why. He's a sighthound and he might take off after something.' Dorothy slid back the bolt on the door and went in to the dog, who got down. 'But he's a friendly chap, aren't you, laddy? Only been here a few days. Never had a wolfhound before.'

Cassie swiftly decided that Dorothy must have the hearing of a bat. She released Rory's arm as he followed Dorothy into the stable. A huge cosy bed sat on straw in one corner, and he bent to ruffle the dark grey coat. She longed to join him but didn't want to crowd the dog, who might feel upset or threatened by too many new people all at once.

'What's his name?' Rory looked at Dorothy, who was holding the dog's collar and muttering soothing words. Cassie had a sudden image of the dog taking off and Dorothy being towed along behind, like a cape flapping in the wind.

'Flynn. Came from someone who had to go into care and the family didn't want to know. Lovely old chap, bred wolfhounds for years, so he knew what he was doing. He'd kept this one from his last litter and didn't want to part with him. Had no choice in the end.'

'That's so sad,' Cassie murmured. It wasn't difficult to picture a life drastically changed by illness, and giving up a member of the family must have been an impossible choice. But she mustn't be swayed by the joy in Rory's face as he grinned at Raf, or the friendliness in Flynn's eyes and the way he nudged Rory's hand to continue stroking whenever it stopped moving.

'Hoping to rehome him eventually, but not everyone's capable of taking on a dog like this. They're not straight-forward, given their size.' Dorothy indicated that Cassie could enter too, and Rory stepped aside so she could stroke Flynn, his coat shaggy and wiry beneath her fingers. 'Cost quite a bit too, with food and vets and whatnot.'

He flashed her a look and Cassie knew exactly what it meant. *Can we, please*, his gaze was imploring her, but she shook her head firmly. They couldn't possibly take on this dog; he was enormous and would probably need his own bedroom. No doubt he would cost as much as another teenager to feed, and she had enough on her hands with two bereaved ones already. She made herself

37

step away, hating to see the swift hope and happiness in Rory's expression fade.

'He's well socialised, used to grandchildren popping in and out. They're a breed which like a lot of company, so he can't stay in the house all day on his own.' Dorothy gave Flynn a final pat and shut the stable door, bolting it firmly top and bottom. Cassie thought he could clear it with ease if he fancied a go.

'So he has to sleep in here as well?' Rory turned stricken eyes on Dorothy.

'No, he sleeps in the house with the rest of m'pack.'

Cassie glanced back as they moved on to the stable next door. Flynn's head was leaning on the bars as he watched them, and she looked away, unable to bear the disappointment in his gaze too.

Bob, the sturdy dapple-grey cob, was gorgeous, and she understood exactly why Dorothy had decided to take him on. Aged fifteen, he'd come to her via a friend who'd recently given up horses at ninety, and he was politely accepting polo mints from Harriet and Isla, curling a hairy top lip and revealing teeth beginning to slope and turn brown. Dapples were fading with age, and his mane and tail were thick, matched by white feathers, the long hair beneath his knees and hocks falling to his hooves. He obligingly lowered his head so Dorothy could slip on a halter, and she looped the lead rope across his neck.

'You're a marvellous chap, aren't you. Best sort when they've got four legs,' she told him fondly.

Cassie grinned as Raf muttered something behind her, hoping Dorothy hadn't caught it. Isla sent her a wistful smile, and she felt a pang of sorrow for her daughter. If they'd moved to Galloway before Isla had started high school, then she would probably have been able to have her own pony, and Rory wouldn't have to cycle the streets of London. But that dream had vanished, consigned to thoughts of what might have been if Ewan were still here.

'There's no rush to come home, girls,' Cassie told them quietly, trying to make amends for their lack of pets by giving Isla more time here. On the way she'd overheard Rory and Raf making plans to cycle tomorrow, as Raf was apparently staying over tonight. 'Just let us know what time to expect you back, okay?'

'We will,' Isla assured her. 'We've got to feed Posy, Flo and Hero as well.' She found a hoof pick hanging outside the door, and Cassie, Raf and Rory left them to it as they returned to the yard with Dorothy.

Cassie had brought the empty egg boxes to fill, and they spent fifteen minutes trying to locate fresh eggs, which the hens and ducks laid all over the place. Eventually they had a dozen brown eggs in the two boxes, and she thanked Dorothy, who said she'd call at Home Farm at some point to see the new foal.

Back at the house Cassie excused herself and set up her laptop in her room to host her work meeting. Thirty minutes later she was glad to finish, satisfied all was in place for the VIP influencer and their magazine shoot the following week. She picked up her phone, headed downstairs and found Pippa on the terrace. Lola and Maud were stretched out on the grass nearby, ever alert for sneaky treats coming their way. If it wasn't for her terrible secret, she might feel as close to content as possible in this moment, bathed in warm spring sunshine beneath a cornflower-blue sky.

She wouldn't ever tire of the view, even though the landscape was so different to Galloway, where she and Ewan had spent so much time. They'd met when, aged fourteen, Cassie had joined Pippa, Raf and their younger sister Tilly on holiday in the remote beachside cottage Jonny had bought, always striving to make his children happy after losing their mum when Pippa was fourteen and Raf thirteen. Ewan had lived next door, a few hundred yards along the lane, and he and Raf had been mates from the beginning. They both loved messing around in the water, sailing, hiking and cycling, and they were always together. Ewan went to school in the village, and his life couldn't have been more of a contrast to Raf's in London as the son of a rock legend.

Ewan was different to the boys Cassie had known then, and he'd been so sure of his future career as a surgeon. She'd found his confidence and certainty very reassuring and appealing amidst the turmoil between her parents at home, and she'd quickly been drawn into the heart of his loving family, one which bore little resemblance to her own. They managed to keep their relationship going for a year but eventually drifted apart as their lives expanded with college. When Ewan moved south a couple of years later to read Medicine at King's College London and discovered she was there too, reading Psychology, they reconnected and resumed their relationship, which soon became serious.

Cassie watched Pippa's hand straying to Maud when she wandered across, gently stroking the happy little spaniel. Between the gallery, the work underway extending the practice and Cassie's career alongside the demands of their families, they didn't see as much of one another as they used to. She doubted there would ever be a time when she didn't miss having Pippa in London, but it was clear life in Hartfell suited her and Harriet. Pippa and Gil had developed a rhythm and a togetherness as a couple that she recognised and missed very much. There was so much to learn as a single parent, so much to navigate alone.

Cassie jolted and it took her a few bleary moments to remember she was in bed in Pippa and Gil's guest room, not at home in London. She'd dozed off thinking about what to record in her journal. Sleep didn't come quite so easily since losing Ewan, and sometimes she woke in the early hours, gripped by fear for Isla and Rory. Would there ever come a day when she didn't miss him, both for herself and their children? Would she live without wanting to weep for the loss they'd suffered, and the new lives forced upon them? In daylight, she knew that she would. Those unsettling thoughts stole into her mind during the darkened hours, when the fight-or-flight sensation was at its worst, and she'd wait, heart clattering, for the adrenaline to subside. But then morning would arrive and she'd get up, ready to face the hours ahead and make them matter.

It was her counsellor who'd suggested writing down her thoughts to help make sense of the days, to understand that sometimes small steps amounted to huge wins. She had toyed with the idea for a while before buying a journal last year, and now she'd filled three. Without Ewan the world seemed bigger, scarier, lonelier, and the small details she recorded reminded her it wasn't always. That there was love and hope too, and health and times of happiness. Slowly, gradually, their family was healing.

One day she planned to read her journals again and understand how far they had come. But for now, it helped to remember how she, Isla and Rory were coping, to acknowledge the grief at the heart of their lives while finding ways to thrive. Life and the world had moved on, and it had taken months of counselling to help her realise that she and her children were steadily moving on with it.

Cassie switched on the bedside light and, checking her phone, saw it was only midnight. She decided to fetch a glass of water. The house was silent as she crept downstairs, and in the kitchen Lola and Maud greeted her sleepily without rising from their beds. She bent down to stroke them, quietly apologising for the disturbance, before finding a glass and filling it from the fridge.

'Cassie?'

She shrieked, the glass sliding from her hand to shatter into pieces, which skidded across the tiles in a puddle of water. She spun around to see Raf hovering in the doorway. Lola and Maud's tails were thumping in welcome again, and her breath quickened.

'Sorry, I didn't mean to make you jump.' He stepped forward as though he was about to help clear up, and she flung a hand in the air.

'Just leave it,' she rushed out, thankful her feet weren't bare as she lunged for kitchen roll. He switched on a light, making her blink. 'I'll sort it out.'

'You're going to need more than kitchen roll. There's glass everywhere.'

'You don't say,' she retorted, hunching down to mop up the water. 'Make sure the dogs stay in their beds.'

'I'll fetch the hoover.'

'Raf, there's no…' But he was already turning for the hall and the cupboard under the stairs. The dogs made to follow, and Cassie sharply told them to stay put in case they stepped on glass. They obeyed, unused to her stern command. She dropped sodden kitchen roll and chunks of glass in the bin, keeping out of the way as he ran the hoover over the rest.

'Thanks. I hope we haven't woken anyone.' She glanced up as though she could check on her sleeping friends from where she stood. Anything to avoid looking at Raf and acknowledging they were alone in the near dark for the first time since Australia.

'So how long are you staying?' She hoped to find conversation that wouldn't drag them straight back to that night six months ago.

'Not sure. I've got some stuff to sort out before I head back to the flat.'

'Ah yes, your new house.' She winced; that had been more scathing than she'd intended. 'I'm sorry I didn't reply to your voicemails. Work got in the way.'

'So Rory said.'

She flushed, sure he'd seen through her usual excuse. The filter he had worn at lunch to disguise his thoughts had gone, and her skin heated more as his eyes skimmed over her short pyjamas. Her stomach curled with longing, and she made to move past him.

'Well, good night. I need my bed after the drive up.' She pressed her arms into her body so there was little danger of brushing against him.

'What about your water?'

'I'm not that thirsty.' The scratch in her voice suggested a different story. But this was madness and she couldn't allow herself to linger in harm's way.

'Cass, there's nothing between me and Allegra, whatever Pippa thinks. I barely know her. And it was a mistake, bringing her here. I'm sorry. I didn't know about the lunch, and she was only supposed to be dropping me off until Pippa got carried away.'

'Oh, hey, whoever you see has nothing to do with me, Raf,' she told him casually. 'We both know that, and Allegra seems lovely.'

He ignored that, allowing the silence to bloom before he spoke again. 'I wanted to ask if you'd come with me to see the house tomorrow.'

'Me!' Cassie's quick laugh was astonished, her voice rising with every syllable. 'Why?'

'Because I'd really like your opinion before I make a final decision. I can't stay with Pippa and Gil forever, and especially not when the builders move in.'

'You don't need me to see it. It's your choice.' Six months ago, she'd have been glad to help him if she could. Now, all was different. He was always going to move on, so how could she have imagined otherwise? He ran a hand through his hair, outlining the curve of a tattooed bicep. She swallowed, her pulse reminding her exactly how it felt to have those elegant and skilful hands on her body. Would that night never go away? Would she be forever trapped, yearning for a man she couldn't have?

'But I'd like your thoughts all the same.'

'I don't think so,' she muttered. He was far too close, and nerve endings were alight with expectation, the spicy amber and leather scent of the cologne she would only ever associate with him filling her senses. 'We're leaving for Galloway after breakfast. It's another long drive, and there's lots to do there. Good luck, whatever you decide.'

'You say that like we're not going to see one another again for ages.' Raf raised an arm, as though he might be about to brush away the hair spilling over her face, and Cassie took a hasty step back, crashing into a cupboard.

She winced at the sharp pain in her hip, willing her body not to betray her again.

'It might be a while.' She raised a shoulder to suggest she didn't mind. It wasn't a thought she'd share with Rory, though, who would be disappointed not to see Raf soon. She went to step past him again, but his words, as firm as a hand on her arm, stilled her a second time.

'Don't you think we should talk?' he said, his voice low and soft and dangerous all at once. 'I know you're avoiding me, and the kids have noticed, in case you're wondering. Rory asked if I knew why you were being weird with me.'

'What did you tell him?' Her heart pounded even faster at the thought of Rory suspecting anything was amiss. That one foolish moment had affected their friendship to the extent her son had noticed that she was different around Raf now.

'That you were busy with work and not to worry, we're fine.'

She looked up, trapped by that intense stare which seemed to see straight to her soul.

'But we're not, are we? Not when I know you'd rather run than talk about what happened.'

'There's nothing to talk about,' she told him hotly, careful to keep her voice down. 'We were both emotional that night and it was just a hug that went too far. A mistake. Neither of us meant it to happen, and I've forgotten all about it.'

'You're a terrible liar, Cass.' Raf's voice followed as she hurried up the stairs to her room in search of safety. 'Because I don't think you can get it out of your head either, and pretending it never happened won't make it go away.'

Chapter Four

In the morning Cassie's journal was still beside her on the bed. She'd dreamt of Raf and Australia again, and she flung the duvet aside and got out of bed, crossing the landing to shower. Last night was the first time they'd slept in the same building since they'd taken the children to Lapland at Christmas, a trip she'd arranged before Australia. Despite the magic and Isla and Rory loving it, she had felt distant and unsettled around him after that moment of madness in Queensland.

Back in her room she dried her hair and sat on the bed, glancing through her journal to read what she'd recorded yesterday. She'd written about the happy anticipation of time away with friends and family, and being in Hartfell again. Nothing, as ever, about Raf, unless it included her children. Her thoughts about him were ones she could never consign to paper, because then they would exist beyond her own imagination. She closed the journal at a tap on the door, hoping it wasn't Raf looking for another opportunity to talk.

'Brought you a coffee,' Pippa called.

'Thank you, what a treat. Come in.' Cassie shuffled over, and Pippa left a mug on the bedside table and settled opposite her. 'I thought you might appreciate a few more peaceful minutes. The kitchen is full of bleary-eyed teenagers raiding the fridge. Alfie stayed over last night as well, and I'm not sure any of them got much sleep in that tent.'

'Let's hope they're not too grumpy later.' Cassie's gaze slid away from Pippa as she reached for the mug. 'Thank you for caring for and looking after us.'

The only benefit in living so far away from her closest friend was that she didn't have to constantly disguise her guilt over Raf. Pippa knew her so well; could she somehow tell that Cassie had cheated on her husband with his best friend? Was it written on her face as clearly as it was etched on her heart? She tried to force the thought away and focus on what Pippa was saying instead.

'Always, Cass, that's what I'm here for. Rory was so excited to go out with Gil and Raf, bless him. Heaven knows what time they were up.'

'They've gone out already?' Cassie quashed her usual concern for Rory. He wasn't allowed to ride his bike at home alone on those streets after what had happened to Ewan; that was still a step too far. She was dreading the day when she wouldn't have a choice other than to let him go. But right now she still made most of the rules, for both of her children. 'I thought Raf would still be in bed.'

'No, he was up at first light with Rory, and all three of them disappeared soon after.'

Despite her feelings about Raf, Cassie was very grateful he'd brought his own bike and had made good on his promise to ride with Rory whenever he could. Raf had only begun cycling again because Rory did, to help ease her son through the fear he carried after losing his dad the way he had. She knew Rory was afraid sometimes, and she was so proud of him for finding the determination to push through.

47

'Gil's enjoying getting back into cycling after Oli persuaded him to have a go, and he bought a bike.'

'How are Erin and Oli? Is her partnership with Gil sorted yet? I seem to remember you saying there was some final paperwork to sign. Sorry, things go in and out of my mind all the time.' Cassie was thankful to turn the conversation to Gil's veterinary practice instead.

Erin had joined the practice last September and had bought a cottage in the village. She'd met Oli when they were students at St Catharine's College, Cambridge, and they'd resumed their relationship at Christmas when he took a locum job for the holidays. He'd moved in with Erin, and between Oli, Erin and Gil and the rest of the team, they shared a busy rota of companion animals, rural farm visits and equine clients.

'Yes, it's all complete, and Gil's over the moon now he and Erin are officially business partners. He hasn't said, but I imagine one day that will probably include Oli, too. It's wonderful to see the practice growing, although he's sorry to be losing Elaine to retirement in the summer.'

'Erin and Oli were brilliant when we stayed here in February and Posy had colic. Poor Harriet was distraught at the thought of losing her and they looked after Posy so well.'

'Bless her, she absolutely adores that pony,' Pippa said fondly. 'The girls have already mucked out, and Harriet's introduced Isla to the new kittens we've somehow managed to acquire from Dorothy. They're farm cats, though, so they're living in the stables rather than the house, but we'll see how long that lasts. Harriet's already feeding them in the kitchen.'

The two women shared a smile. When Cassie had last been here in February, house and Harriet sitting so Pippa and Gil could have a few days away, Harriet had brought home five battery hens she was nursing back to health and hopefully laying. She'd named them after the members of her grandad's band, and it still amused Pippa and Cassie to hear Jonny and Raf being spoken of as Rhode Island Reds rather than the famed lead singer and drummer of one of the most successful bands in living memory.

'So how are you?' Pippa asked gently.

'I'm fine.' It was her standard response to most enquiries about her wellbeing. 'Thank you for asking.'

'Come on, Cass, this is me you're talking to.' Pippa leant forward and drew Cassie into her arms. 'I know you too well to be fobbed off by that. Tell me how you really are.'

Being held was one of the things Cassie missed the most. Her parents had never been huggers, both preoccupied with their own lives and equally emotionally distant from their only child. Her father had been an MP, and she'd never forgotten being paraded outside the house to face the press with her parents when his scandal had reached the newspapers, his affair with a younger member of his parliamentary staff a story as old as time. His blustering apology as the cameras flashed in their faces, her mother's silent and seething humiliation as she'd stood beside him, Cassie bewildered and scared by the attention.

He was forced to relinquish his position in the Cabinet after that, and her parents' marriage staggered on until he died suddenly at home when Cassie was twenty-one and in her final year at university. Between the political demands and the blazing rows, she had often escaped to Pippa's home across the street for a more normal and loving family life. Pippa and her family had gradually become Cassie's world, shielding her from the worst of the gossip about her parents and keeping her close.

'Really, I am fine.' Cassie relaxed into Pippa's hold, chin resting on her shoulder. For a wild moment she almost blurted out what had taken place between her and Raf. But she couldn't, because then there would be no going back. Pippa might feel torn between them, her loyalty to her friend and her brother divided as she tried to support both. And Pippa would know that Cassie had betrayed her husband with his best friend. Her stomach was churning with the usual fear of discovery and what those she loved would think of her then. So she couldn't allow herself to remember how it had felt when Raf held her that time, their startling new feelings and desire suddenly laid bare.

'You're sure?' Pippa's hands were firm on Cassie's back. 'Because you can tell me anything, you know you can, and I'll listen. I just get the sense you're a little distracted.'

'I'm sorry, I don't mean to be. And thank you, I really appreciate it. Work's on my mind, that's all.' Cassie eased free and they separated. That was always an excuse she could fall back on. 'I'd better head downstairs.'

'There's no rush. Enjoy your coffee, then come down when you're ready and I'll feed you a hearty breakfast on the terrace. It's a glorious morning; we should make the most of the sunshine.' Pippa's expression changed to one of casual curiosity. 'So what did you think of Allegra?'

Cassie, picking up her mug again, took a moment to reply. 'She seems very nice.' And beautiful, young and talented, with a brilliant career to boot. She'd heard Allegra chatting about the jewellery she designed in her free time, as she'd held out a slim arm for Pippa to admire a delicate silver bangle.

'But don't you think it's significant, Raf bringing her to lunch like that? You know as well as I do how difficult it is for people to see past the famous drummer to the man underneath. Apparently she was headhunted to manage a new office in Leeds. And viewing a house in Hartfell! I can't believe we didn't know. I thought I might invite her to dinner on the pretext of hearing more about it. They certainly looked good together, and she's clearly into him.'

'But did he actually say they were dating?' Cassie thought of last night in the kitchen with Raf, his assurance that there was nothing between him and Allegra. 'I'm sure he wouldn't thank you for interfering.'

'Don't care,' Pippa said breezily. 'My little brother has been roaming the world for ten years, and if there's even a chance of him settling down with someone, I'm going all out to encourage it. Did Allegra say she was vegan or am I imagining that?'

'She did, yes,' Cassie replied faintly. At least she would soon be back in London, far away from Raf, and Pippa's attempts to matchmake.

Pippa made for the door and looked back. 'That reminds me, I'm trying to pin Raf down about his birthday. It's only a couple of months away and he doesn't want a big fuss, but it is his fortieth. I thought you could have a word with him?'

'Me? Why?' She wasn't quick enough to tone down the alarm in her reply, and Pippa's brows drew together in surprise.

'Because he'll listen to you, Cass. He always has. Is that okay?'

'Sorry, yes. Of course I will if you think it'll help. I suppose I thought he wouldn't want to bother about his birthday. He doesn't usually.'

'He might not, but I want to find out. Maybe it'll include an extra guest.' Pippa winked and then she was gone, the door quietly closing behind her.

Cassie sank back and thumped a pillow. Perfect. Now it was down to her to find out how, *if*, Raf planned to celebrate his birthday in July, and with whom. She groaned, covering her face with her hands.

Once she'd dressed, she picked at granola and juice outside in the garden before coffee and croissants, a rare treat. It was already warm and the dogs were content to laze on the terrace with her and Pippa, swallows swooping by as they hunted for insects on the wing. Harriet and Isla were in the stables, and Pippa said they were preparing Flo and Hero for a first walk to the paddock. The girls didn't exclude Rory on purpose, but their love of netball, Billie Eilish and current brands simply didn't chime with his own interests in cycling and chess. He enjoyed occasional weekends with his grandparents when Isla was off doing something else, and Cassie tried never to say no, aware that Ewan's parents found their own solace in being with their grandchildren. They spent every summer holiday in Galloway, but this family tradition, which had continued without a break since the children were born, was now at an end with her parents-in-law's move.

Her attention snagged on voices across the garden, and she saw Raf follow Gil through the gate, propping their filthy bikes against the wall as the dogs rushed to greet them. Raf was laughing at something Gil was saying, and even covered in mud, with helmet hair and wearing Lycra, he still made the breath falter in her throat. He glanced across and she caught the quick incline of his head, the glimpse of a smile, and it was enough to bring a rush of heat to her cheeks. She watched surreptitiously as he ran a hand across his jaw, sharply reminded of those same fingers smoothing away her tears in Australia, and how they'd felt on her body as he'd pressed her against him.

Her gaze went past the two men in search of Rory, and she told herself she was being ridiculous as her heart bumped in alarm when there was no sign of him. Gil dropped down to cuddle Lola and Maud, laughing as they tried to clamber onto his lap. Satisfied he was once again within reach, the dogs ran back to the terrace as Raf strolled across. He dropped a kiss on top of Pippa's head, and it would have been strange had he not offered Cassie a similar greeting. She stilled as his hand went to her shoulder, his lips and the brush of his beard brief against her temple.

'Have you saved any for us?' He nodded at the remaining croissants on the table as Gil caught up, pulling out a chair to sit down before leaning across to kiss Pippa.

'Of course, you can have the last two.' Pippa pushed the plate of pastries towards her brother and Raf took one while Gil poured juice into two glasses.

Cassie spotted the girls leading the ponies slowly along the drive towards the paddock, Harriet gently guiding Hero, and she looked at Raf. 'Where's Rory?'

'He's not back yet?' Raf's hand holding a croissant was halfway to his mouth and he paused, eyes narrowed.

'What do you mean, not back yet? He went out with you!' Her pulse spiked as she shoved her chair back and leapt up.

'Yeah, but then we bumped into Alfie's cousin Jacob, and Rory asked if they could ride on their own.'

'I know who Jacob is! And you let him?'

A year older than Rory, Jacob lived in the village, and Cassie was grateful the boys stayed in touch when they were apart. Usually she loved that her son had a friend here too, someone who included Rory in much that went on.

'Seriously, Raf!' She glared at him, unable to hold back a stab of sharp, cold fear. It was impossible not to think of the terrible phone call from the police after Ewan's accident, the frantic dash to the hospital and arriving too late. Adrenaline was already flooding her limbs and making them tremble. 'And you didn't ask where they were planning to go, or how long they'd be? Rory knows he's not allowed out on the bike by himself.'

'Darling, he's not by himself.' Pippa stood too, and she came around the table to Cassie. 'Jacob knows the village like the back of his hand and I'm sure Rory's fine. Why don't you call him?'

Cassie nodded frantically, clumsy fingers trying to unlock her phone. It was another minute before her call went straight to voicemail. She couldn't allow herself to think about him sprawled in a heap somewhere after crashing from his bike, unable to summon help if his phone wasn't working.

'Probably just lack of signal. There's a route we were planning to take another time, so maybe they're trying it out.' Raf was on his feet and he caught Cassie's hand, halting her pacing. 'We'll find him, okay? He won't have gone far. Try not to worry.'

'It's just not like him to go off without saying where.' She stared up at him, biting her lip and not daring to let herself fall into the assurance in his gaze when she didn't know for sure that her son was safe. 'He's usually so careful.'

Rory liked certainty and knowing what was coming next, much as she did after growing up with parents who had often been absent and cared little about boundaries or routine. He took after Ewan in so many ways, but not this. Ewan had been a risk-taker, whereas Rory was cautious. He was quieter than Isla too, and Cassie watched them both carefully for signs of trauma. At school, his behaviour was much the same; he still excelled in maths and science, and sometimes she wondered if his hard work and diligence were in some way a tribute to his dad.

'Maybe Alfie would know where Jacob might go?' Pippa was crossing the garden with Maud as Gil hurried to his car, Lola at his heels. 'I'll get Harriet to call him.'

'What if…?' Cassie's gaze on Raf's was stricken, and he drew her into his arms, placing his lips against her temple.

'We'll find him, I promise,' he murmured gently. 'And I'm sorry, I just didn't think. At his age I was barely in school, and I never checked in with anyone.'

'But it's different now,' she whispered, struggling not to cry and lose it completely. She leant into his embrace, wanting him to hold her for just a little longer. To not always have to do this alone. 'The world's such a scary place.'

She hadn't used to be so afraid, and it was just one of the reasons why she made time for mindful exercises, to practise thinking clearly and not catastrophise everything. It had been so much easier when her children were small and she'd been able to keep them close, had known where they were every minute of the day. At least at home in London they had their usual routines, and everyone knew the rules. Out here, in this vast, unending landscape with fells stretching to the sky and acres to be explored, Rory could go anywhere, far from her reach and ability to keep him safe.

'Keep calling, okay, and let me know if you hear from him.' Raf let her go as Cassie nodded, watching as he sprinted to his bike. Her fear calmed a little as Gil took off down the drive in his Land Rover, and she could only assume he was planning to retrace their steps from earlier and check out the route Rory and Jacob might have taken. It helped to know how much they cared too, and she tried Rory's phone again, willing him to pick up.

Chapter Five

Cassie couldn't settle, and when Isla and Harriet returned, she didn't need to see her daughter's face to recognise the fear for her brother when she found out he hadn't come home yet. Cassie tried to be calm and positive as she rang Rory again and again. Each time the calls reverted to voicemail and nausea was turning her breakfast to ashes. Maud, so sensitive to the altered mood amongst her family, stuck close to Pippa as the four of them waited in the garden for news.

Thirty minutes later, Isla leapt to her feet. 'Mum, they're here!' She shoved her chair aside as she raced towards the yard. Cassie was only a stride behind, almost tearful with relief as a mud-spattered and grinning Rory propped his bike against the wall and Raf dismounted.

'Rory, where the hell have you been?' She forgot every attempt at calm and immediately realised her mistake as his face fell. But he was here and safe, and that mattered far more than her own fears. She stuffed her phone into a pocket as she caught Raf's eye and mouthed a distracted thank you.

'I went to Dorothy's with Jacob,' Rory muttered. He seemed to shrink as his face paled with worry.

'But why? What were you doing there?' Cassie simply couldn't imagine.

'We went to see Flynn.'

'Flynn?' It took her a second to place the name. 'The wolfhound? But Rory, we barely know him, or if he's safe around children! Please tell me you didn't go in the stable on your own and...'

'No, of course we didn't. Dorothy let me feed him.' Rory's chin rose. 'She doesn't think I'm stupid. And I'm not a child.'

'Rory, I don't think you're stupid!' And now wasn't the time to take issue over whether her teenage son was still a child or not. 'But why would you go and see Flynn without telling anyone? I could have gone with you.' A vision of the dog watching them yesterday, stood in his stable, dropped into her mind.

'Because he looked sad when we left him. I know what that's like and I didn't want him to be sad. I thought he might like some company.'

'Oh, darling.' Cassie rushed forward and wrapped Rory in her arms, trying to blink back tears. He already topped her by a few inches, this tall, gangly boy who still loved a hug. Sometimes when she was working at home he'd appear at her desk, and she'd pause, hold out her arms. And her boy, her lovely, sensitive and gifted boy hurtling towards adulthood, would step into her embrace. She'd hold him as she'd never been held by her own parents, and remind him how much she loved him, how proud of him she was and that they travelled this new road together. 'But as long as you're okay, then that's all that matters. Why didn't you pick up when I called you?'

'I forgot to charge my phone. Sorry, Mum.' Rory was never quite glued to it as much as the girls were to theirs.

Cassie always felt she wasn't enough for her children on her own, and much as she knew Rory loved her, he wanted his dad around too. There were times when he tried to step in and help, to be the man around the house, watching online videos to learn how to take care of some tasks together. She was careful to encourage and thank him, while trying to not make him feel responsible for more than he should be at his age.

She released him, scuffing her shoe on the ground as she glanced at Raf. Pippa was on her phone, presumably letting Gil know. 'I'm sorry for panicking and dragging you into this. And everyone else.'

'Hey, it's fine. It's what I'm here for.' He looked from Cassie to Rory. 'So how was Flynn? Happy to see you?'

'Yeah.' Rory's face lit up, and her heart lurched at the sight. 'After we fed him, he put his paws on the bars so I could stroke him, and he was wagging his tail the whole time. Dorothy said he's really gentle and it's not his fault he's clumsy because he doesn't actually know how big he is.'

'Right,' Cassie said faintly. She knew where this was going and needed to get the idea out of Rory's head before he ran away with it. They couldn't possibly have Flynn; it would be lunacy, and she hadn't ever looked after a dog full time. 'Rory...'

'Then we took him for a walk in the orchard, but Dorothy said not to let him off in case he tried to chase something. He's so big, Mum, his head is up to my waist. He was really good, though. We had to pass some sheep and he didn't do anything.'

She managed to refrain from pointing out that had Flynn wanted to run after the sheep, there wasn't a single thing either Rory or Dorothy could have done about it. 'He does seem very sweet, darling, but perhaps it's because he's not used to living at Dorothy's yet. He might be different in a few weeks when he's feeling more settled.'

'Dorothy thinks he'd be better in a new home. She said he's too young to stay with her forever, but it would need to be a very understanding one because of his size and that he can't be left alone for long.'

Cassie hated to extinguish Rory's hope, but there was simply no other choice. She had a sudden image of being towed around London streets by a dog as big as Posy, and that was enough to strengthen her resolve.

'Rory, Dorothy wouldn't let us have Flynn,' she said gently, steeling herself against his disappointment and resentment. 'Our house and the garden are way too small, and we couldn't give him the space or time he needs. Maybe after the summer, we can think again, about a dog.'

'You mean it?'

'We can definitely talk about it,' she promised. She'd always wanted one and her walks in town felt emptier without the company of her parents-in-law's two Labradors. Maybe there was a way they could manage, even with work, and the effort would surely be worth it if having their own dog brought more happiness to their home. 'You must be hungry after that early start. Let's get you some breakfast.'

'I'm okay for a bit, thanks. Dorothy made us some porridge. It was amazing, I've never had goat's milk before.'

'Dorothy did?' Cassie heard Raf's chuckle, and she smiled. 'Well, you're very fortunate. I don't think she makes breakfast for just anyone. We should get going soon; it's a long drive to Granny and Grandpa's and I don't want to be on the road all day. Go and pack your things, and please would you let Isla know to do the same?'

Rory nodded as he pulled his phone out of the back pocket of his cycling top, heading for the tent. Cassie was mentally running over what she had to do before they left, embarrassed by her overreaction.

'Maybe it is something to consider,' Raf remarked. He typed something on his phone before locking the screen.

'What is?'

'Getting a dog.'

'I will think about it, but it's complicated,' she said helplessly. 'And it definitely won't be Flynn.' She thought of the hope and happiness in Flynn's gaze when they'd stroked him yesterday and made a gentle fuss. 'And we all know what will happen. Isla and Rory will lose interest after a bit, and I'll be doing all the work. Maybe a kitten would be better.' Jas would help, and there were plenty of pet-sitting services in London for when they went away. The new tabby kittens living in the stables were very sweet-looking, if rather ferocious when approached.

'I wouldn't get a kitten.'

'Why not?' Raf's back was facing the sun, and she had to squint into the light to look up at him.

'I don't think it's worth saddling yourself with pets they don't want.'

'So you're suggesting that to keep Rory happy, I should take on a massive rescue dog who'd barely fit in our house and we hardly know anything about?'

'We know he had a lovely home and is used to family life.'

'That's not enough, Raf! Don't you start too; I've got enough on my plate without adding another problem to the mix. I'm sorry, but Flynn is not an option.' She tried not to picture the wolfhound at home, curled up in bed, the company he'd provide when the children weren't there. 'We'd be nuts to take him on, and what am I supposed to do with him when I'm at work? Get a babysitter? And besides, what would you know about committing to anything?'

'More than you probably think,' he replied with a shrug. 'And you always wanted a dog.'

'Yeah, but that was supposed to be when Ewan and I moved to Galloway, and that's never going to happen now.' Cassie gulped back a rush of sadness at the loss of her dream.

'I was just trying to help. Stop you making a mistake.'

'Well, that's not actually your job,' she retorted, still searching for calm after the worry of Rory disappearing and then his silent plea over Flynn. 'So thanks, but just leave it, yeah?'

Five hours and a hundred and fifty miles later, Cassie was approaching the tiny harbour village in the Scottish Borders that she'd known since she was fourteen. When the kids were little, she and Ewan had used to play Spot-the-Sea, when the first person to catch a glimpse was declared the winner and would receive a small treat. Isla and Rory had lost interest in the game with age and now it was only Cassie watching for that first sighting and the sense that she was nearly home, because in Galloway she was so at peace. She felt a pang for their younger days, when they'd played endless games of I Spy and chattered instead of going online with ear buds in. It still occasionally took her breath away to realise she was in sole charge of parenting these two wonderful young people into adulthood, and she was very thankful for the love and support of family and friends. At least her parents-in-law, Fiona and Gordon, would be waiting as usual to greet them.

'Nearly there, Mum.'

'We are.' She smiled at Rory beside her – he had swapped into the front when they'd stopped at the services – not wanting the gesture to be a sad one. These few days were going to be difficult for them all, and she didn't want to linger on the poignancy of their final journey here.

'Are you okay? How do you feel now about Granny and Grandpa's move?' They'd talked about this before, and she knew how much he'd miss his grandparents' home. How could he not, when she too would be leaving a part of her heart behind in this place?

'Sad, but happy too, 'cos I know they're pleased to be moving nearer to us. I'll be able to get the train up to stay with them.'

'Yes, and your new bedroom will be fab too, with a bathroom just for you and Isla once it's all ready. It certainly won't be draughty, with high ceilings and those rattling windows letting the wind in.'

'I don't mind the windows. I am going to miss it, though, Mum. Especially the cycling.' Rory sighed as he turned over the phone in his hand. 'This was where Dad taught me to ride a bike.'

'I know, sweetheart.' A splinter of sorrow pierced her heart at those quiet words. 'And Granny and Grandpa are really going to miss it too, even though it's the right decision for them. It's such a lot to look after since Granny took on the garden at the Big House as well, and they're not getting any younger.'

Fiona and Gordon had bought their farmhouse and the two small cottages which adjoined it a few years after they'd got married, part of an estate which had been divided up. The farmhouse sat beside a walled garden and an orchard, a narrow track running through woodland leading to a tiny horseshoe-shaped bay with clear waters and soft white sand. Since retiring from her nursing job, Fiona had taken on the management of the historic garden surrounding the Big House but was ready to hand it over to someone new.

'Do you think they feel as though they're leaving Dad behind?' Rory's question was a quiet one, and Cassie's hand found one of his. 'We have loads of memories here and I think Dad would agree with the move, but he'd be sad too.'

'Exactly that,' she murmured. 'But Dad would say that we take him with us wherever we go, and he loved London.'

'That was because you were there, too.'

Cassie was reminded of her university days, how much she'd loved her degree course and had planned to follow it with a master's before other events overtook them. 'Yes, but Dad was offered a great opportunity once he became a consultant, and it made sense to stay in London.'

How huge those decisions had seemed at the time. The simple reality was that she and Ewan had loved each other, and she'd wanted to make her home with him. And he'd wanted London. 'Granny and Grandpa are brilliant at making friends and taking care of people, so I don't think it matters where they live. There'll be new things you can do with them, like the cinema and stuff.' That wasn't a great sell to console Rory; they had cinemas and every other kind of entertainment in London.

'Yeah. I s'pose.'

Fiona and Gordon had fallen in love with the Dales when they'd joined Cassie and the children in Hartfell during February half term, staying in a nearby B&B. It had been a precious time filled with happiness and love, despite the ever-present sadness they all lived with. Towards the end of the week they'd tentatively broached the idea of leaving Galloway for good. Amidst the tears, she'd said they had to think of themselves first and she would support whatever decision they made, even though her heart had ached at losing another link to Ewan. But it did mean her parents-in-law would be nearer, and she'd be able to combine visits to them with ones to Pippa, Gil and Harriet as well.

Things had moved at pace since February, and the sale on the bungalow Fiona and Gordon had found was almost complete, the property set in a garden large enough without being too much. Fiona had made it clear they wanted their new house to be a home from home where Cassie could work if necessary, and the children could stay before the demands of college and university overtook them.

Cassie pulled up at a crossroads, the village and its harbour to her left, ahead the drive which would take them past the Big House. It really was like coming home, and for a few uneasy moments she wondered how she would bear the move, too. Never seeing this view or the farmhouse again, or the leafy track through the garden they'd walked and cycled to the village so many times.

'I love you, you know.' She gripped Rory's hand again and felt him squeeze back. Sometimes it was the only thing to say, and she reminded her children constantly. She wanted her love planted deep in their hearts in a way it had never been for her, to carry the certainty of it every moment of their lives. 'There's no reason why we couldn't come back and visit if we want to.'

'I know. It just wouldn't be the same.' He turned his clear gaze on her and she nodded. How could it be the same? Because for all the beauty and brightness, the sea and the sunshine, it was family that had truly made it home. Without Fiona and Gordon here and Ewan gone, the heart of this place would go with them.

'I really feel Dad when we're here, Mum. Sometimes more than at home, because we were always together, and he didn't have to go rushing off to the hospital the whole time.'

'Oh, baby. Come here.' Cassie's eyes were damp, and she put the car into park before easing Rory into a hug, Isla on her phone behind them. At least there was no traffic to trouble them, or angry drivers ranting about being held up. 'Are you worried about losing that feeling?'

'Yeah.' Rory sniffed into her shoulder and slowly eased free.

'Then maybe we should make a promise, whether it's just us three, or Granny and Grandpa as well, that we should come back and visit the beach every year.' She was thinking out loud and didn't know if her suggestion was a brilliant idea or one of those things they meant to do and never managed. 'Then we can talk about Dad, remember all the good times and make sure we share our memories and keep them alive. Do you think it would help, if we knew this wasn't the very last time?'

'I'd like that,' Rory said earnestly. 'I know Dad's not here, not really, but it could be on his birthday or something, couldn't it? I think if we celebrated it here, we might not feel so sad. And I know he wouldn't want us to be sad, and he'd want Granny and Grandpa to be happy too.'

'That's lovely, Rory. And just think how many wonderful memories they've given all those other people who came to stay, too.' Cassie let go and sent the car forward. 'Change always feels unsettling, especially when it's connected to someone or something we love so much. The new house will be brilliant, and they'll have more free time to come and stay with us, too.'

'Thanks, Mum.' His smile was brighter. 'I didn't know whether to tell you, because I know you're sad too, and I don't want to make you unhappy.'

'Oh, darling.' Cassie swallowed. 'The only thing that would make me sadder is you and Isla not telling me how you feel. I'm here for you both always, okay? Promise, no matter what.'

'I know.' Rory's phone pinged and his face lit up some more. 'Raf's messaged, Mum, he's coming too!'

'He is?' She nearly shot onto the grass verge and hastily righted the steering wheel. They'd barely spoken since disagreeing about pets earlier and their goodbye in Hartfell had been a stilted one in front of everyone else. 'When?'

'He thinks maybe tomorrow. He asked Granny if she could use any more help to pack up the house, and she said yes.'

'I see.' Given Raf's own history with Ewan and his parents, it shouldn't be a surprise that he, too, was planning to make this final journey north.

'Maybe he'll bring his bike and we can go out one last time, ride some of the routes Dad and I used to.' Rory was busy on his phone. 'I'll ask him.'

'I'm sure Raf would love that.' For Rory's sake, she *was* pleased, even though this week promised to be difficult enough, packing up the house and their memories along with it. She couldn't begin to imagine Fiona or Gordon's dismay if they suspected that something had occurred between her and Raf. How could she face them if they knew she'd betrayed their son with his best friend? Her palms were clammy and she took a steadying breath. It would be fine; she was perfectly capable of putting one stupid kiss behind her.

Sunlight was dazzling as they emerged from woodland and Cassie passed the Big House standing serenely to her left, divided now into holiday apartments behind railings. The bend in the drive where Rory had fallen off his bike when he was seven, then spent a night in hospital with a concussion, his neurosurgeon father sleeping in the chair beside him. Moments later the farmhouse and orchard came into view, the ancient apple trees peeking above the wall, their gnarled branches bright with creamy pink blossom.

She pulled up beside the grassy expanse where they'd played countless games of cricket and rounders, heard the familiar scrunch of gravel beneath the wheels. If she closed her eyes, she imagined she could almost hear Ewan roaring with laughter as he raced around with the kids, casually tossing balls in half-hearted attempts to bowl them out. He was everywhere here, her darling husband, and she missed him so much. Before she'd even turned off the engine, Isla and Rory were gone, finding a new burst of energy now they'd arrived and could escape the car.

Cassie got out too, the unmistakable smell of briny sea air hitting her senses. She stretched tired arms, spotting Fiona and Gordon hurrying from the house.

'Och, you've made great time. I wasn't expecting you for another half an hour after Isla's message.' Fiona's Borders Scots accent was gentle, a wonderfully familiar voice that had comforted Cassie through so much. She was wise in a way so few people were, and Cassie trusted her with everything. A dull thud of guilt prodded at her as she remembered Raf. Not, now, with everything.

'We got lucky with the traffic. Thankfully most people seemed to be heading in the opposite direction.'

The children threw themselves on their grandparents, who pulled them close, exclaiming about growth spurts and surely they must be hungry after all those miles in the car. Cassie dropped down to cuddle Bramble and Briar, the mother-and-daughter black Labradors who'd come to greet her excitedly. Isla and Rory hugged the dogs too, then shot indoors in search of the treats Fiona had promised, the dogs bounding behind them and in on the game. They knew what to expect.

Gordon wrapped Cassie in his arms. Tall and lean, his sandy hair now turned to salt and pepper, he'd passed on his square jaw, evenly spaced intelligent blue eyes and wide forehead to his only child. Then it was Fiona's turn, and she and Cassie held one another tightly, one loving mum to another. Every embrace felt sadder and more meaningful; Fiona was more of a mother to Cassie than her own had ever been. Fiona's short grey hair was tucked behind one ear, tending to curl if she left it too long. Pale hazel eyes were flecked with blue, and she was always ready to laugh, even now.

'We're just so happy you're here.' Fiona followed to help as Cassie turned back to the car. She popped the boot, and Gordon joined them to begin unloading. 'Swim first? Or something to eat? It's only sandwiches to keep you going until supper. I thought I'd do a risotto.'

'There's nothing "only" about your cooking, Fiona.' She tucked her arm through Fiona's as they made for the house carrying bags. 'I adore it, and I'm thankful for every meal you feed us. I think I'll eat first and swim later, if that's okay?'

69

'Of course it is.' Fiona shooed Briar out of the way as they walked into the hall. 'Swim whenever you're ready.'

It was family tradition when they arrived to dump their bags and head straight to the bay, whatever the weather. Warmed by the Gulf Stream, the water was reasonably mild, at least in summer. Isla and Rory had grown less keen, and eventually it was just Cassie and Ewan who had raced through the woodland and plunged into the sea. Afterwards they'd hurry back to the house and warm up with one of Gordon's hot toddies. But today, she didn't feel up to the tradition, on her own for this final time.

'How are you?' Cassie's question was a simple one, but it always meant so much more, especially this week. Boxes littered the hall, another sign that this really was it and the move was happening. Giving up the home in which Fiona and Gordon had brought up their only son had been a huge decision and one they hadn't taken lightly. Perhaps they simply couldn't bear to be here without him, she mused, living with the knowledge that Ewan would never again tear into the house, filling it with his energy and zest for a life lived at pace.

'Och, you know.' Fiona found a smile, laced with sorrow. 'I'm fine, really, we both are. Sad, of course, but here we are. I'm so glad you're here to help. Gordon's wonderful in many ways, but he does like to hang onto things, and this is the perfect opportunity to have a good clear-out. We're already on our third skip and I want it full before we leave. I wouldn't have said we were hoarders, but the attic and the wardrobes tell a different tale.'

'I wish we could've come sooner, then you wouldn't have had to do most of this on your own.'

'You couldn't do that, darling, not with work and school.' Fiona slipped her arm from Cassie's to enter the kitchen. 'And I'm so glad you're here now, which is what really counts. We love you for it, as well as everything else.'

The view of the kitchen hit Cassie like a punch straight to her heart. It was achingly familiar, and she could picture a teenage version of herself here with Ewan, sitting at the table the summer they'd first met, the butterflies she'd felt whenever she was around him. It hadn't been long before she'd known he'd liked her too, and she'd been giddy with the exhilaration of falling in love for the first time.

He'd asked her to marry him in this room, an unplanned and perfectly romantic moment she'd treasure for the rest of her life. They were just back from the beach the day before her twenty-first birthday, and he'd dropped down on one knee as she was about to stuff their towels in the washing machine, saying he couldn't wait a minute more. He'd already chosen a ring, and after he'd slipped it onto her finger, his ecstatic parents had been the first people with whom they'd shared the news.

Then Ewan still had another three years of his degree left, plus two more in foundation as a junior doctor, and Cassie planned to continue studying with a master's before exploring a career in counselling. But then her father had died suddenly and the home she had shared with Ewan had to be sold. She took a summer job with an events planning company so they could move into a first flat of their own, a dingy studio a mile from university. They married at Gretna Green two years later, her summer job progressing into a full-time role that eventually led her into public relations, her master's abandoned in the need to earn a living. The work had come naturally, and she loved working with people, despite the increasing demands of high-end events and the frantic pace of Ewan's burgeoning career.

Their long-term plan had been to move back to Galloway to be closer to Fiona and Gordon. But Isla and then Rory had come along, and the reality had always seemed just out of reach as the children settled into primary and then high school. Ewan always found a reason to remain in London, to delay their plans for another year. Eventually she had realised he saw the move more as a slide into retirement when the children were gone, rather than one in search of a less frenetic and demanding life. She accepted it, understanding that he made almost impossible choices every day, life-or-death decisions, and she put aside her dream so he could follow his.

Cassie shook those thoughts away, blinking back a tear at the sight of Isla and Rory plonked in their usual places as Gordon poured drinks and the dogs slumped in their baskets. The old pine table was exactly the same, and more meals, birthdays and Christmas celebrations had been shared around it than she could recall. Hogmanay too, seeing out the old year and welcoming in the new one with the best company and endless fun. Her dream to move to Galloway had never come off, and now it never would.

An hour after they'd shared Fiona's risotto for supper and Isla and Rory had helped clear up, Cassie decided to go for her final swim. The children chose not to join her, and although she was disappointed, she understood. Their memories and the tradition didn't reach back as far as her own did. Galloway for them was more about their grandparents and the fun and freedom they had, rather than the loving home she had found here all those years ago.

She slipped out of the house, following the familiar path to the beach. She would know it blindfolded, aware of the gentle hiss of waves growing louder. Woodland gave way to the sandy bay, curving neatly between two granite crags. She slid her flip-flops off, the soft crunch of sand scraping her feet. Across the water, the uneven shape of Lake District fells was visible in the distance, indigo against turquoise beneath the lowering sun and expanse of sky.

Cassie pondered Rory's suggestion of returning here on Ewan's birthday to celebrate his life. Perhaps they really would find a way. Make the pilgrimage north and remember him here, share what they loved best about him, and missed the most. They would laugh and cry, and somehow go on, one foot in front of the other, day after day. She reminded herself how far they'd come already, how well they were doing most of the time, as her journals could attest.

She took her sundress off and left it with her towel on a clump of rocks worn smooth by the tides. Her phone was back at the house; Isla and Rory were with their grandparents, and she had no need to worry for them while she was here. She took a deep breath, thinking of the swim ahead and preparing for the chill. The waves tickled her toes, the water cold around her thighs and waist as she waded deeper, ready for the drop when the sand fell away in a steep shelf. She began to swim across the bay, letting the sensation take possession of her mind and free it from all that troubled her.

She swam easily, with purpose and calm. Here, she could think clearly, and decisions seemed simpler. She would meet with her boss on Wednesday, resolve the situation at work and find a new way to cope at home when Jas left in the autumn. She would come to terms with Fiona and Gordon's move and support them in their new lives. And above all, she would take care of Isla and Rory.

She reached the opposite end of the bay and flipped over, swimming back to where she'd begun. It was too nice to leave the water yet and she turned a second time, the sun warm on her back. Further on there was a tiny and secluded natural cove where they all used to hang out. She would sit for a while and think, find a way to say goodbye to this place. She waded out of the water and rounded the rocks to the cove, hands sweeping the hair from her face before stuttering to a sharp halt.

'Raf!'

Chapter Six

The flight from Sydney to Brisbane had been a short one after the long haul from London, and Cassie, Isla and Rory had been exhausted and elated when they'd emerged from the plane into a dazzling Australian spring. Raf was there to meet them, and Cassie had held back tears when he'd hugged them tightly. He'd driven them to the band's hotel and, from the moment they'd arrived, they'd had an absolute blast. The band had one final appearance coming up in the Sunday legends slot at Glastonbury and then Blue at Midnight would be over, consigned to history and the memory of all who loved them.

In between gigs, Raf had surprised Cassie with a trip away, just the four of them. They'd flown north and picked up a Jeep, driving further up the coast and taking a ferry to Magnetic Island. Isla and Rory were ecstatic at this new adventure, and she had been happy too, grateful to relax. It was bliss not to have to plan every moment, and she'd given herself up to the experience, aware that such treats didn't come around very often.

Their secluded beachfront house had huge windows offering exceptional views of their swimming pool and the ocean beyond it. Isla and Rory had changed immediately and flung themselves into the water, exhilaration bringing a return of their more carefree selves. They messed around for hours as Cassie meandered around unpacking and settling in, marvelling at the views and the dazzling light after the gloom of a dreary London autumn.

She laughingly shooed Raf away to the pool when he tried to help prepare dinner. The tour was going brilliantly, but she saw how wired and yet exhausted he was when he came off stage and the band rolled on to the next date, another city, another stage. Giving him the space to kick back and escape was her way of thanking him for all he'd done to make this trip unforgettable.

The following morning she swam early and was relaxing on the steps of the pool when Raf appeared. He dropped a hand on her shoulder in greeting before stripping off his T-shirt and carving through the water with sharp, efficient strokes. Suddenly she found it impossible to tear her gaze away as a quiver raced across her skin, leaving her flushed and captivated by the width of his shoulders, and a body sculpted from years of drumming and working out. She was very aware of his public profile, especially here, but it didn't intrude much into her family's life. In private he was just Raf, her friend, not the world-famous rock star drummer. But now she was seeing him as countless other women must, and she made herself steady her breathing.

He'd got his first tattoo at sixteen: the image of a rose intertwined with Slash from Guns N' Roses on his left forearm. Pippa, a year older than Raf, had been shocked, but Jonny had laughed and asked him what he was planning to have next. He'd followed up the first with a tattoo of forget-me-not flowers encircling a woman holding her three children close, and Pippa had cried when she'd seen it. Now his left arm matched the full sleeve of tattoos on his right, and Cassie noticed a midnight-blue guitar held in the centre of a Celtic rose representing the band, with *Give Me Your Love*, the title of their most successful album, winding through the petals.

When Isla, Harriet and then Rory had been born, Raf had added tattoos for each of their birth flowers. For Isla this was violets for February, with April daisies for Harriet and snowdrops for Rory in January. These were inked on the inside of his right forearm, and Cassie loved that he was reminded of the children whenever he glimpsed the images. Across his sternum and the top half of his chest, Raf had a warrior kneeling before an angel and offering a sword, an image chosen to represent strength and humility, two things very close to his heart.

She was sitting, arms behind her back, when he swam over. She wondered if she was imagining the suggestion of awkwardness in his quick smile as she tried not to stare at the water glistening on his suntanned chest, the outline of a bicep as he ran a hand through soaking hair. They'd swum together countless times on holiday in Galloway, but now she was very conscious of her bikini, one she'd bought out here and hadn't even been sure she'd wear. Not on the beach at least, with the slight roundness of her stomach that had never gone away since giving birth. Cassie had tried to diet away the curves her mother had lamented until she'd learnt to appreciate them.

'Looking forward to our day out?' Raf joined her on the steps, and she was utterly conscious of his wet body beside hers as he propped himself on his elbows, the width of his thigh against her paler one. The braided leather bracelets around his left wrist never came off, and she didn't think she'd ever seen him without the silver chain and cross beneath it, a twenty-first birthday present from

Pippa and their younger sister Tilly. 'But just say if you'd rather hang out here.'

'No, I'd love to go, and the kids will too.' She glanced at his profile, struck by an electrifying bolt that she was horrified to realise was desire. She inched away, putting a little distance between them as she reminded herself sharply of her responsibilities and his loving role in her family's life. But those thoughts vanished as he stretched, raising both arms above his head. It was probably her hormones and would pass once she'd returned home. 'If you're sure you're not too tired?'

'Nope, I'm fine. Leave in an hour?' He stood up and their eyes caught as she nodded quickly, hoping her discomfort and the reason for it wasn't as visible to him as it felt to her.

After a hearty brunch at a beachside cafe later, she took the wheel to drive the Jeep around the island. They hiked through eucalyptus and acacia woodland to the ruins of a fort, and everyone was rapt to spot a koala. Afterwards Isla and Rory opted to return to the house for another chill night around the pool. Once they'd eaten, the teenagers headed indoors to watch a movie. They crashed into bed first, and when Cassie went to say good night, they were already asleep. She kissed them anyway, smoothing Isla's long chestnut hair from her face.

Tomorrow they would rejoin the band and the bus, but not before snorkelling and lunch at a nearby restaurant. Then they'd catch the ferry back to the mainland and drive north to Cairns. She couldn't bear to go to bed yet; she didn't want to miss a moment of this magical hideaway. She refilled glasses from the bottle of wine they'd opened over dinner and joined Raf on the deck, the pool and endless expanse of ocean shimmering before them.

'Raf, it's been perfect.' The smile she gave him was weighted with sadness. 'Well, almost. You know what I mean. Thank you for everything, we'll never forget it.'

'My pleasure.' He leant across so they could clink glasses. 'So here's to Ewan, and a life well lived. He made a difference every single day and that's a wonderful legacy.'

'It is. But I wish he was here with us.' Sorrow clutched at her throat and made those last words a gulp.

'I know.' Raf's free hand briefly found hers. 'Me too. It's a whole other world, this one without him.'

'Yeah.' Cassie sipped her wine, trying not to let her mind dart ahead to London and the new normal waiting there, forced on them by bereavement. She loved her job, and it had helped keep her going these past couple of years, even if there were moments when she was drained by the pressure and keeping all the balls in the air. But she was no different to anyone else in the same situation; she simply had to get on with it. She landed on another subject instead.

'So how do you feel, now you're actually here and it's almost over? Your Instagram's going crazy.'

'Sorry?' Raf seemed distracted as his troubled gaze found hers, and she wondered if he was thinking of how much his life was about to change, what he might do next.

'About the band, everything finally ending. I hope you don't mind me asking.'

'Of course I don't.' At once he was right back with her, and he raised a shoulder. 'I'm fine, or at least I think I am. I guess now I really do have to grow up and find something sensible to do.'

'Sensible, you?' She nudged his leg with her foot. 'This I'm looking forward to. The band has been ten years of your life; it'll take time to get used to being without it.'

'I think I'm ready, though. I never imagined it would last this long. I only planned to do one tour, and then we just kept going.'

Cassie didn't know the full story of why he'd suddenly abandoned his modelling career and joined his dad's band, the only non-original member after their first drummer passed away. Raf had shared most things with Ewan, and she guessed that Ewan had known the reason and had kept his confidence. Pippa had suggested it was something to do with the end of a serious relationship, but even she hadn't known all the details.

'I always thought my life would be different.' His smile was a reflective one, long fingers toying with his glass.

'Different how?'

'Not this.' He raised a hand to the pool, the beach, the ocean beyond it. 'A different view every week, another hotel room, another city. Don't get me wrong, it's been incredible and such a buzz, and I've been so lucky to be a part of it. But yeah, I'm going to kick back for a while, think about what's next.'

'I think that's a good idea,' she told him quietly. 'You know you're always welcome to come and stay with us.'

She almost went to refute her offer as soon as she'd made it. He had access to the London flat and the Norfolk beach cottage, which was his. He hardly needed to squash in her spare room.

'Thanks, Cass. I'd like that. It would be good to spend more time with Isla and Rory. And Pippa's asked me to stay with them.'

'And will you?'

'Probably. I quite like the idea of becoming a country gent.'

They shared a grin, and she was thinking how he was such easy and familiar company. There was a simplicity to their being together that didn't always need words. They'd sometimes squabbled as children, but he'd always been there for her. Her parents' marriage had been notorious, and her father had often been in the press. Cassie had never forgotten the day when a creepy photographer had followed her from home in search of more scandal. Raf had spotted him, came roaring across the street and tipped the bloke into a hedge. It was only some very fast talking by Jonny and a solicitor that had kept him out of serious trouble.

Even during those later teenage years, she'd been aware of Raf's girlfriends coming and going, the abundance of natural charm he'd possessed from an early age, so like Jonny's. But before then he had been chronically shy, and speech therapy had followed counselling. He'd gradually overcome a stammer by adopting a version of himself, a character everyone expected from a boy who looked as he did, with a rock star for a father. Cassie understood it was a means of hiding Raf's true self, a man who kept the grief of losing his mum so young close to his heart, and one who didn't often let strangers in. It had carried him through years of modelling and a decade of drumming for a world-famous band, and kept some of the adulation which came with it at bay.

On stage he was confident and exuberant, wild at times, and the fans, new and old, adored him. A self-taught musician, he was desperate not to be seen as riding on the coattails of his dad's success, or that his place in the band was purely down to nepotism. He spent time alone in Norfolk, finding the space to unwind and settle back into a more ordinary life, writing music he refused to share with anyone because he always said it wasn't good enough. And so those crazy thoughts she'd had about him in the pool this morning had no place here; he was her dear and trusted friend. And more than that, he was Ewan's friend.

'I'd like to see more of my niece too, if Harriet can make time for her aged uncle.'

She laughed; he was very far from the picture those two words had painted. Her nod was understanding; life was also like that for Isla and Rory. They went from one activity to the next, and sometimes Cassie wondered if it was too much. But those thoughts were soon followed by ones about having too much time to think, to dwell on their loss. Christmas would arrive in little more than a month, and they would be spending it as usual in Galloway with Ewan's parents.

'Pippa would love having you in Hartfell. Not that I envisage you tramping around the Dales in walking boots and taking up bird watching.'

'No?' Raf eased out long legs and rolled his shoulders. He'd disappeared for a workout when they'd returned from their hike, maintaining the fitness he needed to perform. 'Maybe I'll surprise you.'

'You always do.' She stood up, suddenly restless, and put her glass on the table. She crossed the deck to lean on the railings surrounding the pool, staring out over the ocean. She'd swum while he'd been working out and had slipped a short cotton dress over her bikini, a gentle spring breeze warm on her skin. The last rays of the sun glittered on the water, light bouncing from one to the other, and she let the beauty hold and soothe her.

'What are you thinking?' He joined her, resting his arms beside hers. Cassie caught sight of the flower tattoos representing the three children he loved, and something tugged at her heart.

'Oh, just the usual,' she replied lightly. 'Wishing I could hold this moment still and keep us here forever. Not go back to London and all the messy life stuff. I suppose holidays always make us feel like this because we never want them to end.' She paused. 'But it's not normal life and I know we have to go home.'

'We could come back, if you love it so much.'

'That's a wonderful thought, thank you,' she said wistfully. 'But right now I think I'd love anywhere that took me away from my own life for a bit. And it's never the same when you go back. I'm not sure you can ever recapture the magic of seeing a place for the first time.'

Unbidden, tears came, as they often still did. She hid her face, not wanting Raf to think she was unhappy here, because it was the most like happiness she'd felt in months.

'Hey, come here.' His hands went to her shoulders to turn her, and he opened his arms. Cassie hesitated before stepping into his embrace. He was so familiar and kind, and in bare feet, the top of her head fit snugly under his chin.

'Sorry.' She sniffed, the press of the silver cross on his chest cool against her cheek.

'Don't be.' His hands were smoothing a circle on her back. 'There's no timescale to tell you if you'll ever stop missing him and when it's supposed to get better. You're doing so great, and the kids are incredible, a total credit to you both.'

'Thank you. It's lovely of you to say so.' She tipped her head back and the tears almost began again at the understanding in his gaze. 'I can't tell you how much I appreciate everything you do for us. I don't just mean this house and the tour, but being there for us. Talking to Rory about missing his dad and helping him find a way through, taking him out on the bike. I don't think I could bear him riding it at all if it wasn't with you. Making us laugh, sharing stories and memories we'd forgotten, keeping Ewan present in our lives. It means so much, especially when I know you love and miss him too.'

'I'll always be there for you, Cass, no matter what. That's a promise.'

'What about when you finally meet someone you want to settle down with?' She meant it teasingly, trying to imagine that time, and the difference it might make to Isla and Rory when he was no longer quite so available. But she couldn't hold him back and keep him close in her family forever. What she and Ewan had shared, the life they had built together, had been solid and real, and she wanted the same for Raf. But this time a different ending, a longer life. So she would wish him well and cheer him on; there would be no other choice.

'Because one day it will happen and the three of us can't be tagging along like left luggage.'

'Hey.' He gripped her shoulders, his unwavering gaze fixed to hers. 'I'll always look out for you, and if anyone does come along, they'll have to accept you're part of my life.'

Her nod was a quick one. It occurred to her he hadn't mentioned the children, and it was as though she was seeing him for the very first time. How had she missed those golden flecks in his irises, perfectly framed by long, dark lashes. Had his chest against hers always felt like this when he'd held her before, or her skin heated in quite the way it was doing now?

An impulsive rush of desire landed like a punch in her stomach, and she went to step back. To free herself from his embrace and the way he was suddenly looking at her. As though he, too, was seeing straight through to her innermost thoughts and the new longing her body was betraying in the pink cheeks and the catch in her breath. His hands on her shoulders tightened almost imperceptibly, keeping her close as his gaze searched hers, and she gasped as she realised he felt it, too.

A moment and then another flew by as she fought to make herself walk away, free herself from this madness. Then his hand dropped to the small of her back and Cassie was lost when Raf pulled her hard into him. She tilted her head, poised, every single sense alive to his touch, his fingers splayed on her hot skin as she watched his eyes and then his mouth fall lower. Their kiss should have felt strange, and it didn't. It was like coming home, and she was kissing him back just as fiercely. Her lips parted beneath his as she gave herself up to the sensations he was igniting as his tongue continued the work his lips had begun.

Her hands found their way into his hair to hold him, her thin cotton dress as light a barrier as the T-shirt he wore. One hand was on her face, the other still pressing her against every hard outline of his body. She let go long enough to reach for his T-shirt, impatient to feel his bare skin against hers, to savour again the view she'd had this morning. He helped her drag it over his head, and when his hands reached for her dress, about to slip the straps from her shoulders, she froze.

She leapt back in horror, her mind at odds with her body still clamouring for more. Raf was staring at her with an intensity and a desire she'd never seen before, and he raked a hand through his hair. She was desperate to look at anything other than him, to think of anything but how he had made her feel for those few brief moments.

'Raf, this is crazy! We can't,' she blurted out. She spun around and gripped the railings with both hands to steady her trembling legs, pupils still wide with shock and desire. 'I'm sorry, I have no idea what just happened. I can't… Ewan… It's not right.'

She let go and turned to the house. She needed to escape, indoors, into the night, home, it didn't matter where as long as she could flee from Raf and what they had done. He scooped his T-shirt from the deck and gently caught her hand, stilling her.

'Cassie, please, don't go. I'm really sorry, I didn't see that coming, I swear.' His breathing was every bit as agitated as hers and she couldn't look at him, couldn't find his eyes and learn what was in them now. 'But all day, I sensed it. There was something, and that felt… You were… incredible.'

'Don't say that!' Cassie tugged her hand free, distraught at the thought of her children witnessing this, a cold horror dawning at her betrayal of their dad. 'Forget it. It never happened.'

'We have to sort this out,' he said helplessly. 'Where we go from here.'

At the door she faced him, still trembling, with lips swollen by their kiss, and skin pink and tender from his beard. She ran her fingers across her mouth, as though she could swipe away the kiss along with her guilt. She saw him watching and heat pooled in her body again, betraying her a second time in the scratch of her hollow voice.

'There is nowhere for us to go,' she whispered tearfully. 'I should never have let it happen. It's madness. You're my friend, and my children need you. I can't let anything get in the way of that. And you're Ewan's best friend. How do you think I feel about cheating on him with you?'

'It's not cheating,' Raf said roughly, the T-shirt still dangling from one hand. 'You're not…'

'Don't say it.' She flung an arm in the air, hand flat in front of him. 'In my heart I'm still married, and that won't ever change.'

Chapter Seven

Galloway, Present Day

Raf's arms were around his bent knees, and Cassie's eyes were automatically pulled to his. She saw it at once, the memory of their kiss as his hungry stare drank her in, desire flooding her body. He'd seen her like this so many times before. But not since that night. Not since he'd taken her in his arms to comfort her and they'd felt something so different in those few moments, had ignited something which refused to burn out.

'When did you arrive?' She crossed her arms. She couldn't think what else to do with them, facing him like this just a metre apart.

'Ten minutes ago. Traffic wasn't great.' He looked past her, shuttering the recollection from his gaze.

'And you came straight down here?' Of course he had; they always did.

'Yeah. One last time. I haven't been to the house yet. I'm sorry, I didn't mean to disturb you. You were already in the water, and I thought you'd leave without seeing me.'

She always noticed him now; she simply couldn't not. Since their stilted goodbye in Hartfell earlier, he'd changed into ripped jeans and a white T-shirt, emphasising suntanned skin and the short, newly grey and brown hair that looked so good on him.

'Are you planning to swim?' Her pulse flared some more at the thought of him undressing and wading into the water.

'Maybe.' Raf stood in one fluid movement and removed his T-shirt. He held it out, the deep timbre of his voice skating across her skin, so different when they were alone. 'Take it. Don't want you to get cold.'

There was absolutely no danger of that. Cassie felt almost branded after the intensity of that stare a few moments ago.

'There's no need, Raf, really...' He tossed the T-shirt, and she automatically caught it, tugging it awkwardly over her head. It was impossible now to avoid his bare chest and the tattoo she loved, the kneeling warrior offering his sword before an angel. 'I should probably head back anyway.'

'Don't leave because of me. Please.' He sat down again, and she hesitated before inching towards him, his still-warm T-shirt brushing her thighs. He shuffled up to make room and she settled nearby, desperate not to touch him.

Sunlight was bouncing off the water and she rested a cheek on her knee, trying to cling onto the peace and clarity she'd felt in the sea. If only she could let it carry her family's burden of grief far away, to a place it could trouble them no more. When Raf wasn't with her, everything was simpler. But when he was this near, the heat of his body so close, she wanted only one thing. A wave of guilt swiftly followed at the wish to lose herself in the pleasure she'd found in their kiss, to allow a repeat.

'I'm sorry about this morning, snapping at you about getting a dog.' It had bothered Cassie on the drive up, parting on a bad note when she hadn't expected to see him again so soon. 'I know you were only trying to help.'

'Hey, it's okay. I get it. And it's your decision, whatever you want to do.' His low voice was every bit as disturbing as his touch, and she rushed on.

'I was still uptight after launching straight into panic mode when I realised Rory was missing.' It was impossible not to recall the fear and that she'd automatically assumed the worst. 'I will think about getting a dog. I don't want to get their hopes up yet, though, not until I've worked out how we'll manage.'

'That sounds great. They'd love it.' Raf sighed and she sensed him shifting, stretching out long legs, pale grey suede Nikes dusted with sand. 'We go back so far here, don't we? You, me and Ewan.'

'More than half of our lives. Sometimes I feel as though mine has been divided in two. The one with Ewan and the one after him.'

'Cass, I'm sorry,' he said quietly. 'If there's anything…'

'You already do so much for us. I know you love and miss him too.' She swallowed, holding on to tears. 'I'm sorry sometimes I forget that. Until we lost Ewan, I didn't really think about what he meant to everyone else. We all have different memories, a different story.'

'Yeah. Exactly that. It was the same with my mum. To us she was just our mum and we loved her, but she was so much more. She was the calm in my dad's storm.'

Cassie tilted her head and stole a glance. 'Do you think about her a lot?'

'Every day.' He raised a shoulder. 'That's one of the reasons I want to stay close to Isla and Rory. I know what they're going through.'

'Thank you. It means the world, and I so appreciate it,' she said softly. 'Even if it doesn't seem that way sometimes. I'm sorry you went through it too.'

'I know. Thanks.'

She stilled as he reached across, gentle fingers smoothing wet hair from her face. He removed his hand just as quickly, leaving her longing for more. 'I don't know how I'm going to say goodbye to this place.' She sniffed. 'Sorry, I have so much to be thankful for and I don't mean to be ungrateful.'

'It's fine. Me neither, and you're not. I hate hearing you apologise for stuff that's not your fault. You think that leaving here feels like we're leaving Ewan behind?'

'Yes. Rory said the same. It sort of gets easier and harder all at once. Every day we get a bit better at finding a way to live without him.'

'I don't think that's a bad thing. We all need to find a way through grief when it comes, and trying to cling on to life as it was before won't change where you are now.'

'It's just this is where he grew up, where we all did, really.' She rested her chin on bent knees, arms wrapped around her legs as she stared at the water. 'And it feels like the end of my dream because we'll never live here now Fiona and Gordon are leaving too.'

'I'm sorry.' Raf's hand was gentle, brief, on her shoulder. 'Whenever it came up, Ewan always said it was never the right time. That he wasn't ready to give up everything he'd achieved to move back here.'

'I suppose he did see it as giving up,' she said sadly. 'Whereas I imagined it being a better life. One where he wasn't so busy and we had more time for the kids, and each other.'

Anxiety flared in her mind as Cassie wondered if she dared ask Raf a question. Maybe there was no harm in sharing something so secret now. But admitting her marriage hadn't been perfect wasn't easy, and she'd clung to the best parts of their life together as a means of keeping Ewan close. There was so much that had been wonderful, and those who loved him best didn't need to know how fraught her marriage had been at times. She took a deep breath.

'Did Ewan ever tell you about America, and the job offer he'd had? I thought he might have done.'

'He never said anything to me.' Raf's exhale was a rapid one and she felt the weight of his stare. 'Are you saying he planned to move to the States? Seriously?'

'We never managed to resolve it, but he wanted to go.' Cassie thought back. 'Two weeks before the accident, he was approached about an opportunity at the Massachusetts Institute of Technology in Boston. It was only supposed to be for a year, but I was struggling to see how we could make it work, with school and my job, plus his parents. Ewan was so excited, and he kept saying how it might lead to other opportunities and we could go anywhere. Anywhere except here, it seemed. I thought Galloway was our dream, and I finally realised then it was just mine. He said he couldn't practise here, that it would be too stifling and he'd get bored. For me it was the first place I truly felt I was home after London and how my parents were.'

'Cassie, were the two of you having problems?' Raf ground out the question, his voice hollow with shock.

'No, not really.' She covered her face with her hands, the sigh slipping free. 'Nothing we wouldn't have worked out. We loved each other. You know how I feel about Fiona and Gordon, and the thought of being close to them was so comforting. Ewan didn't really get it; he said they were perfectly fine and I'm not sure he ever envisaged a day when they'd need more from us. Looking back, I can see that whenever we were here, Ewan was always ready to leave, while I wanted to stay forever. I felt safe here, that I could keep Isla and Rory safe too.'

'Oh, Cass.'

She tensed as Raf shifted to slide an arm around her, pulling her gently into his side until her head rested on his shoulder. Perhaps it would be okay, and they could relearn what they had been before. She hated the stiltedness between them since their kiss, that she needed a barrier to keep her feelings buried. Now every hug or shared smile seemed layered with something different, something that felt dangerous and desirable. Cassie let him hold her, leaning into his comfort and friendship.

'Please don't ever mention this to the kids, or Fiona and Gordon,' she told him fiercely. 'I don't want to upset them or have their memories of Ewan blurred by suspecting he and I weren't always on the same page.' At times she'd felt like a buffer between him and the children, fending off their pleas for a dog because Ewan always said no, the time never quite right.

'Promise.' Raf's cheek was against her hair, a hand idly stroking her arm. His soaked T-shirt clung to her body, and the tremble in her limbs had nothing to do with the cold. 'Does Pippa know?'

'No one does. It's not something I was ready to share until we'd found a solution.'

'I'm glad you told me because now you don't have to carry it alone,' he offered quietly. 'And it's absolutely okay to mourn the life you thought you'd have here. But you would've found a way to work things out, right?'

'Of course. And I would've gone with him to Boston; we all would. I suppose in a way we kind of orbited around his career, and he was so brilliant, so well thought of.'

93

'What about your career? What would you have done in Boston?'

'I don't know,' she murmured. 'We never got that far. He just always said there would be something out there for me. I've always been cautious, I suppose. Always needed to know I'd find a way to cope, and having Isla and Rory really brought that home to me.'

'You're amazing, and so are they,' Raf muttered. 'Never doubt it, and Ewan was so lucky to have you.'

'Thank you,' she whispered. She tried to make herself believe it, when mostly she felt so much less. She raised her head as he removed his arm, restoring the distance between them, one bare foot tracing a pattern in the sand. 'Before the band, I used to think you wanted to make a home like we did.'

'Once, maybe, but then I thought that kind of life wasn't meant for me.' He slid lower and Cassie was aware that sitting here was altering them again, shifting the ground beneath their feet. But she couldn't leave now and risk losing the chance to restore their friendship. He hadn't often shared much of his private life with her. Pippa sometimes brought it up, usually when she was worried about him. But even she hadn't been certain why he'd suddenly stepped away from modelling.

'So Ewan never told you why I joined the band?'

'No. He just said it came at the right time, and you were ready to give music a go. That you'd had enough of modelling.'

'Right.' Raf exhaled, his breath a whisper brushing her skin. 'So in the spirit of sharing the truth, I'm guessing you didn't know I was supposed to be getting married and that there was a baby on the way?'

'Seriously?' Cassie gasped. 'Are you talking about Mia?' She could think of only one person about whom he could have been so serious. The only woman he'd ever brought home more than once.

Mia had been a model too, and she and Raf had been a gift for tabloids and online gossip. Her life had felt as far away from Cassie's as the stars were from the sea, and she'd seemed like the perfect fit for Raf, her cool blonde beauty a match for his own looks. They'd been madly in love, and so the break-up had come out of the blue.

Afterwards he'd crashed with her and Ewan, refusing all offers of work beyond those he was already committed to. Cassie had been preoccupied with her family and her own career as Ewan's star continued to rise. She'd looked after Raf as much as he'd allowed, slotting him into her home as Ewan helped take care of him too.

'Yeah. I found out that the baby wasn't mine a couple of weeks after we got engaged,' Raf said bluntly. 'We hadn't told anyone else at that point. Mia wanted to wait.'

'Oh, Raf,' Cassie whispered. She shuffled onto her knees to face him, pulling him close. She felt him tense in her embrace before he relaxed, his forehead resting on her shoulder. His arms went around her too, and despite the comfort she meant to offer, she was utterly aware of his chest pressed against her breasts. She closed her eyes to hold this moment close before slowly drawing back, letting him go before she let herself go. 'I'm so sorry. I had no idea.'

'I didn't tell anyone except Ewan and my dad. Not even Pippa.' He leant back, arms propped behind him as she settled beside him. 'She was busy with her family too, and I didn't want her worrying about me again. Everyone bought it when I said we'd broken up because we were too busy to make it work.'

Cassie drank in his profile as he stared ahead. There was such strength and beauty in his face, and it was obvious why he'd been so successful as a model. She was shocked by the longing to comfort him still, to hold him in every way possible. His T-shirt was all that was warming her now they had separated, and she never wanted to take it off.

'I don't think even Ewan knew how scared I was about the band.' Raf tilted his head, a thoughtful smile tugging at his lips.

'Scared?' The word was a whisper. 'I never think of you that way. You've always been so strong and taken care of everyone you love.'

'That was the easy part.' His troubled gaze found hers, and she understood they were on the edge of a conversation they'd never had before. At least she could be his friend and try to help him. Whatever else had occurred between them, he deserved this from her.

'Scared of what, Raf?'

'All of it. Letting Dad down, messing up playing, my voice not being good enough. The attention, the commitment. The stammer coming back.'

'I'm sorry you felt that way. I didn't know. The fans adore you, and your dad loves you no matter what.' She was falling into that bottomless brown gaze again, sadness gripping her at the uncertainty in it. 'Have you found a way to acknowledge your success and how brilliant you are?' Sometimes even the truth staring you straight in the face wasn't always easy to accept.

'Yeah, a bit.'

She'd seen him on stage often enough to recognise he was a superb musician. Raf played with a raw passion and boundless energy that the fans idolised. He'd gone viral after posting a video of himself rehearsing topless, sweat glistening on his body, lost in the music as he drummed. Cassie understood *that* Raf was a stage persona he'd created, and she realised now it had been necessary to him, a means of keeping his private, wounded self hidden in plain sight.

'If I can help at all...' She instinctively laid a hand on his shoulder. The tide was slipping away from the shore, the sun a fading orange glow reflected in the sea above the outline of distant mountains bruising the sky.

'I know. Thanks. Before I knew the truth about Mia, I thought the baby was my chance to have a family of my own. And then...' He eased out a breath as she removed her hand. 'It wasn't. So I walked away from almost everyone and took off with the band.'

'You did what you had to do to protect yourself, Raf,' she told him gently. 'Everyone deserves that when they've been let down by someone they love.'

'I guess. I haven't been big on committing to a relationship since then. It wasn't easy with the travelling, and the band was the perfect excuse. I was scared of getting caught out again. Scared of giving my heart away and having it smashed up again.' He stared at her, tears glittering. 'I wanted kids, and maybe it's too late for me now. So that's the price I pay for keeping my distance, never getting in too deep. Isla, Rory and Harriet, they mean the world to me, and I won't stand by and let anything happen to them.'

Cassie's heart ached and she understood him in a way she never had before. She recognised the strength he'd had to draw on to perform, when as a teenager his stammer had sometimes left him struggling to communicate. She found his hand, winding her fingers between his. The moments moved on, and she wanted to hold on to this one forever.

'Thanks for listening.'

'Anytime.' And she meant it; she couldn't avoid him if he needed her.

'I wanted to tell you about the house in Hartfell, and I'm sorry you found out the way you did.' Raf was staring at their entwined fingers on the sand. 'I heard today that Allegra's managed to get the vendor to agree to my renting it for six months while I make up my mind about buying it.' He paused. 'And now you're not going to be here for the summer, I thought that maybe you might like to spend it in Hartfell instead? The house is big enough for all of us.'

'I'm sorry?' Cassie laughed, because what other reply was there? 'Spend the summer in your new house? With you?'

'Is that such a terrible idea?' He smiled and she was searching for a way to refuse without revealing the truth. That she simply couldn't put herself in his way for weeks on end and constantly disguise feelings that were growing day by day.

'Isla can see Harriet, help with the horses. And I'd be around to ride with Rory, and we could do some stuff together, the four of us.'

'That's so generous of you, Raf,' she exclaimed. 'But I can't let them think they can come and go from your house whenever they want.'

'So you don't think Isla and Rory would like it?'

Her children *would* utterly love it; that was the problem. And Cassie wasn't sure how she would get through another London winter without the space and calm she relied on each summer in Galloway.

'Jas is taking them to my mother's for a few days in August,' she said quickly. For one week every year, her mother was the perfect and attentive grandmother, and the children adored staying at her glorious villa high above the Amalfi Coast. This would be the first time they went without Cassie, and the plan still filled her with trepidation. Her mother – who couldn't bear to think of herself as a granny and would only answer to 'Gigi' – insisted they were perfectly old enough to manage without her, and it was only because Jas was travelling with them that Cassie had even agreed in the first place. Jas she trusted with her children, her mother not so much.

'I do appreciate the thought and it's so kind of you, as ever.' She bit her lip. Surely she was imagining that his eyes were telling her more, that he wanted to please her too. 'I'll only be taking a couple of weeks off work, and I was thinking of camping in France for a change. I can't impose on Fiona and Gordon with the move; they'll have enough to do. And I don't want to be in your way.'

'You won't be. And I'll be spending more time in Hartfell anyway,' Raf replied casually. 'Kenny and Vince from the pub have asked me to invest in a distillery they're taking on, so we're going to be business partners. They thought I might be interested, and I plan to be involved in the day-to-day.'

'Okay, and wow!' Cassie hoped she had hidden the hurt that he hadn't shared this with her before now. Perhaps he had tried, and she'd fended him off as usual, making some excuse about being too busy to see him. But he needed something else after the band, and she'd simply have to get used to it.

'Congratulations, how exciting. You really are setting down roots. A new business *and* a new home.' Her eyes were shimmering, and she blinked. He wouldn't be in London as much as before. 'Does Rory know?'

'No. I was going to tell him once I'd spoken to you. I thought maybe we could do that together?'

'I think that would be good.' She tried to balance her relief over Raf being out of reach against Rory's disappointment.

'Cassie, this doesn't mean I won't see him or Isla.' He squeezed her fingers before letting go, and she was glad. It was difficult enough to think straight when he was close, much less if he was touching her. 'Or you.'

'What about Norfolk? Won't you miss being by the sea? You always loved it there.'

She thought of the open expanse of beach merging into unending skies backed by sandy dunes, a place he'd often escaped in between travelling. But he always returned to London. Always. The city was a part of him, its vibes and the hustle, the music scene and the clubs he used to frequent, and Cassie couldn't imagine him leaving it fully behind.

'Yeah, probably. But I'm selling the cottage.'

'Seriously? But what about your writing? I thought Norfolk was your inspiration, your muse?'

'Those songs are just for me, no one else.' He shrugged. 'If I carry on, I can write wherever I am.'

'If? But you love writing music.' Something she had known for a long time.

'Yeah, but Dad doesn't use the cottage now and I haven't spent much time there recently. I thought maybe I should let it go and try somewhere new.'

'Raf?' Cassie laid a hand on his arm, her voice barely more than a breath. Her fingers were pale against the tattoos, telling the story of his life and those he loved. 'I hope one day you'll share your music. I hope you know how wonderful a musician you really are. That you earned your place in the band and you're brilliant.'

'Thank you.' He shifted, so her hand fell away, his eyes somewhere else entirely. 'I wanted to say that we've always been friends, and I hope that will never change. We've both apologised for what happened in Australia, and I think you're right. We should move on and put it behind us.'

'You do?' The relief wasn't as overwhelming as the disappointment, but it was absolutely the right course of action. 'But what you said last night, that you couldn't get it…'

'Forget what I said. It doesn't matter.'

Chapter Eight

Raf walked with Cassie to gather her things after she'd taken his T-shirt off. His eyes never left hers as she replaced it with her dress and he pulled it back on, the damp fabric clinging to his chest. They strolled back through the woodland as the last of the light slipped into darkness, and feeling thankful for his friendship, her hand found his. He threaded his fingers between hers, holding them tightly before they separated at the house. She wasn't quite sure what that gesture meant, but she wasn't ready for her family to notice and have to attempt to explain it.

Fiona and Gordon leapt up and hugged Raf in turn, exclaiming their pleasure that he'd made the journey. Cassie pleaded tiredness with a busy and emotional day ahead, and escaped, her thoughts caught on Raf's revelation about his life on the beach. Her bedroom had been Ewan's growing up, and tomorrow she and Fiona would be emptying it. How much of a life to save when someone has gone, she pondered, and how much to send away? What more should she keep from this treasured home and carry with her into the future? Where did she even begin to decide?

But she wasn't alone on this journey. So many people loved and understood her, and her family would be okay. In bed after saying good night to Isla and Rory, she picked up her journal. It was difficult to pin down her feelings, and she settled on a mix of gratitude and love for her family and friends, and hope for the future while acknowledging the sadness of the move. Of Raf, she made no mention, other than he was here to share in the coming goodbye. She had no need to write more about him; those words were fixed in her heart and belonged only to her.

In the morning Gordon was at his usual spot at the Aga, Isla and Rory already tucking into a full Scottish breakfast. Fiona arrived back with the dogs, who bounded up to Cassie, and she laughingly apologised for not joining their usual early-morning walk. Raf appeared, and they shared a greeting which she hoped didn't reveal anything of their conversation last night. She thanked Gordon for the plateful he set before her, half listening to Rory making plans with Raf to ride later. Raf thanked Gordon for his own breakfast, and her father-in-law disappeared to speak with the solicitor about the completion of the sale tomorrow, which was when the removal company was due. When he'd finished eating, Rory got up and stuck his phone under Fiona's nose as she wiped the dogs' bowls clean.

'Look how massive he is, Granny! Dorothy said he's a gentle giant who doesn't know how big he actually is.'

Cassie realised he was talking about Flynn, the endearing Irish wolfhound they'd met at Dorothy's over the weekend. She'd thought of him herself since then, recalling his quiet calm and the friendly way he'd greeted them. She'd deliberately not said anything more to Rory, not wanting any mention to raise her son's hopes about having a dog at home, especially one that size. One day she'd find a way, just as soon as she learnt what was going on at work and how it might impact her family. Perhaps she shouldn't wait too long to have their own dog; the perfect time might never arrive, and she didn't want to miss the chance and add it to her regrets. She smiled at Rory when he came to sit next to her, smoothing a hand over his hair.

'Can I ride down to the village?' He turned a hopeful face on hers. 'But it's okay if not. I can go with you or Raf later.'

Cassie felt the heaviness of regret like a shudder running through her. How much of her own fear was she planting into his mind? That was the last thing her children needed to carry as well as everything else, and he was thirteen now, officially a teenager. 'That's fine,' she said gently, loving the pleasure rushing into his expression. 'Two rules, okay? Always wear your helmet and don't leave home until your phone's fully charged. Actually, three rules. Always let someone know where you're going and when you'll be back.'

'Okay!' He shot out of his chair and the dogs leapt from their baskets to follow. 'Thanks, Mum, love you.'

'Love you too,' she called after his retreating back. 'Rule number four, don't ride on a full stomach, yeah? That's more of an advisory, Rory, but trust me, it makes sense.'

Isla was excused from helping pack because their rooms were almost done. She disappeared upstairs to revise for her upcoming exams online with Harriet, and Cassie loaded the dishwasher while Fiona put the kettle on.

'Let's have another cup of tea before we get started,' she said brightly. Cassie caught her swiping away a tear and crossed the room. 'Och, don't mind me.' Fiona tried to laugh as they embraced. 'It's just the last time Gordon will ever stand at that old Aga, cooking breakfast. Thousands, he must've made over the years.'

The two women separated, and Cassie saw that Raf had got up to make the tea instead. Everyone teased him for his lack of domestic skills and the everyday tasks he hadn't needed to bother with, travelling to festivals and stadiums all over the world with others taking care of the details. His hand found its way to Fiona's shoulder as he fetched milk from the fridge.

'So tell me about this dating app you've signed up for, Cassie.' Fiona's tone was bright as they settled around the table with mugs. 'I've been looking forward to hearing how you're getting on.'

A scarlet heat filled Cassie's face so swiftly it felt as though her scalp was blushing too. She was aware of Raf casually waking up his phone, flicking a finger to scroll. The only reason she'd even mentioned the bloody app to Fiona was because she couldn't bear to keep a secret from her when it came to potentially dating someone new. She didn't need Fiona or Gordon's approval to move on with her life, but she wasn't about to do anything that might upset them or have them believe she'd left Ewan behind entirely.

'I've been desperate to ask if you've found a match yet.' Fiona lowered her voice as she leant in. 'I didn't want to say anything in front of Isla and Rory.'

'Nothing yet.' Cassie almost didn't recognise the high pitch of her reply and hastily cleared her throat. 'I haven't really been looking, I've only set up a profile so far. And I might not even carry on. I was just...' What? How to end that sentence with the truth, when she'd only joined to place a barrier between her and Raf. A sign that he wasn't anything more than a friend in her life. 'I'm not really sure I'm ready to date again. I suppose I was just seeing what was out there.' Like furniture perhaps, or a new car. Not a potential life partner who could even begin to understand her circumstances.

'Well, there's no rush, and I think it's a good idea. Don't you agree, Raf?' Fiona said blithely.

He looked up and nodded shortly, turning a blank gaze on Cassie. 'Sure, why not? If that's what you want.'

'I'm sure the right person will come along eventually, and we wish you well, darling, of course we do.' Fiona placed a hand over Cassie's. 'We want to see you happy again with someone, and you deserve the best.'

'Thank you,' she said faintly. 'I'm so grateful for your support. And if I ever do find a match, you'll be the first to know.' Pippa's new artist Jago Lynch hadn't wasted any time in looking her up, and yesterday she'd accepted the follow request she'd received through her professional networking platform.

Rory reappeared, ready for his ride, and Cassie was relieved to escape any more questions as she went out to wave him off. Indoors again, she trudged upstairs to begin the process of dismantling her bedroom. A knock came a few minutes later, and she opened it to Fiona. They'd agreed to clear it together, and she was thankful not to have to confront the memories it contained by herself.

'Right, well, we'd better get on,' Fiona said briskly, the tightness around her lips suggesting the smile was a slightly forced one. 'There's a box of Ewan's belongings in the dining room for you to look over. School reports, medals from athletic meets, that sort of thing. I wasn't sure you'd want to keep any.'

'Maybe I could take some home with us,' Cassie suggested. 'It would be nice for Isla and Rory to remember his achievements later on.'

His kilt already had pride of place in Rory's wardrobe at home. Gordon wore the shabby waxed jacket Ewan had left here to walk the dogs, and it would be making the move with them. It took two hours to go through everything, and Cassie sank on the bed when it was done, staring at the results. One small box for Fiona and Gordon, and a bigger one for Isla and Rory, packed with memories of their dad as a boy.

When she headed downstairs, Rory had returned from his ride to the village and she learnt from Gordon he had gone out again, this time with Raf. Isla appeared, revision finished for now, and the rest of the day vanished in a constant motion of shifting boxes, filling the skip and packing. Later they all strolled down to the village for a fish-and-chip supper on the harbour. Raf seemed distant and distracted, and Cassie longed for a return of the closeness they had shared last night, even while reminding herself more than that was impossible. Fiona and Gordon were still trying their best to lift everyone else, their stoicism and strength unaltered by their ongoing grief. If they could say goodbye to their beloved home and all the memories it contained, then so could Cassie. It was people that were important, not buildings. Her own memories wouldn't be sealed behind the front door once the keys were handed over to new owners.

–

They still lived in the compact mid-terraced Victorian house she and Ewan had stretched themselves to buy when he'd qualified as a consultant. London always felt frantic when Cassie returned after the expanse of sea and sky in Galloway, and the hay meadows and moorland fells around Hartfell, the roads heaving with traffic as she crawled through the city the following day. The move had been draining for everyone, and after the farmhouse, a bungalow was going to take some getting used to. The dogs had been baffled by the change in routine and the new environment they, too, would call home. Even her own house looked different as she pulled up outside, as though it had somehow altered in the time she had been gone.

Rory had lapsed into silence, and Cassie knew he was missing Hartfell and Galloway, and Raf. She and Raf had explained about his new house and the distillery to the children before they'd left Galloway. Rory had pleaded to see the house before they came home, but she'd said no. It was likely to be a temporary move, and although she hated disappointing him, she didn't want him getting used Raf having a base in Hartfell and Rory thinking he could stay whenever he liked. Friends again she and Raf might be, but she hadn't forgotten Pippa's hopes of encouraging a burgeoning connection with Allegra. So the last thing Raf needed was a couple of teenagers hanging around. Or her.

Thank goodness for Jas, Cassie thought wearily, as the young woman opened the front door and dashed out to help. It was like coming home to a ray of sunshine, and she was only too happy to catch up on Jas's news and thank her for the lasagne she'd put in the oven. Cassie wondered again how she would manage when Jas finally left.

After they'd eaten around the table – a rule she still insisted on – Isla and Rory disappeared to their rooms, and Jas went to meet her new girlfriend in town. Cassie loaded the dishwasher, remembering how patient Ewan had been with Rory, helping him with reading and homework. From a distance of nearly three years since their loss, she realised she loved Ewan for being a wonderful father and the strength and joy he brought to their children's lives as much as everything else.

Thoughts of the move to Boston still troubled her at times, and how they would have resolved their differences. She doubted she'd have been brave enough to stand her ground and say no, when he'd wanted to grasp the opportunity and had brushed away her concerns. She wasn't sure she'd ever get used to being a widow, not a wife. No longer married, except in her heart. That brought Raf to mind again, and the kiss they had shared, his assurance that she hadn't betrayed the husband she'd lost. How long would it take to feel like the single person she actually was? Would the dating app help? Should she swipe and find a match, someone who might understand because they'd been bereaved too? Just give it a go and not overthink it.

For all that Isla and Rory would love and miss their dad forever, their own lives would move on. They would become adults and begin careers, find partners and create homes of their own. Ewan would be a part of their past, someone bound up in memories rather than reality. It was her life that was in limbo, suspended between the past and an uncertain future, and even her career might well be on the line after the meeting tomorrow. She stuffed another plate into the dishwasher with a sigh. She could only wait and see.

Back in her office the next day, Cassie turned her mind firmly to work as she made her way to the board room for the meeting with her new boss. She'd got on well with James since the start. An elegant, handsome man whose grandparents had been part of the Windrush generation, he worked hard and expected the same from his staff. But he was adaptable too, and understood the line between home and work could occasionally be a blurred one.

James pulled out a chair for her, and she thanked him as she brought coffees across. Perhaps that was old fashioned of him, but it was mannerly, and she liked it. He waited until she had sat down before moving his seat, so they were facing one another. He began by explaining that this was more of an informal chat than a meeting which would go on record, and that eased a smidgeon of the tension in her shoulders. Informal or not, the next few minutes felt as though they could be seminal ones in the career she had grown over nearly twenty years. Was she too old now? Too sad, too burdened and distracted?

He enquired about her and the children, and she gave him an honest reply. Most people asked her this, but not everyone listened. She worked hard not to wear her bereavement like a badge everyone had to acknowledge before they could move on. Was he asking because he was genuinely concerned, or was her emotional health a means of managing her out of her job if change was on the way? If they wanted her gone, she wasn't sure she had the strength to try and fight it.

Fifteen minutes later Cassie stumbled from the board room in a daze. As it was lunchtime, something she normally spent at her desk so as to make most effective use of her time, she escaped into Grosvenor Square to think, longing to call Pippa or Raf. But she couldn't break a confidence, and gradually her usual sharp focus returned, her mind running over practicalities, the day-to-day at home and how to balance it against the news she'd just received.

She was still on tenterhooks when she arrived home later. Jas cooked supper, and afterwards Cassie asked Isla and Rory to hang around instead of going to their rooms. She was used to working unbalanced hours she fitted in around her family. Holidays interrupted, occasional school events missed, and she and Ewan had pulled together to support their children. But this new role would require another level of commitment, and with Pippa and Harriet, and now Fiona and Gordon in Yorkshire, Cassie wanted to spend more time with those she loved, not less. She took Isla and Rory through the proposed changes after swearing them to absolute secrecy and only needed to see the fear and uncertainty filling Rory's gaze to know she was doing the right thing.

'Global head of public relations?' Isla exclaimed, leaping up to hug Cassie. 'Mum, that's awesome and you totally deserve it.'

'Thank you, sweetheart, that's so kind of you. It's because we're merging with a European group, one that has hotels in Amsterdam, Paris and Prague.' Cassie paused. 'So it would mean quite a bit of travel, especially at the start.'

'Are you going to say yes, Mum?' Rory rubbed a finger with his thumb, the same thing she always did when she was stressed, and she took his hand. 'I mean, I know it's brilliant for you, and Isla's right, you totally deserve it. It's just…'

Cassie's other hand found Isla's, and she looked at her fingers entwined around her children's. If only she could keep them this close always. A moment of regret for her career passed through her mind, but she firmly shook it away.

'No, darling, I'm not. I think it's too much for us right now, and I want to be at home for both of you. I know you're growing up and becoming more independent, and that's wonderful and perfectly natural. But I think you still need me around for a while yet.'

Happiness clutched at her throat as she saw the relief rushing into Rory's face, and finally the burden of responsibility on her shoulders began to lift. She looked at Isla, searching for her daughter's response. Would Isla feel Cassie was letting her down somehow, failing in her example as a working mother? Cassie's future was stretching before her, strangely blank without the routine of work, running on adrenaline and coffee alongside the brilliant team she had built.

'Oh, Mum.' Suddenly Isla's arms were around her neck, and Cassie reached an arm around Rory too, so he could join in the embrace.

'I don't want you to miss out on something you love because of us,' Isla muttered. 'If you want to go for it, you should.'

'I don't want it, Isla, I promise,' Cassie assured her. 'The thought of promotion is a flattering one, and I can't deny I was tempted. But the reality would be more people to lead, more problems to solve, sitting in airports on my laptop and missing out at home. That isn't what I want, not now. Maybe one day I can go back.' But by then the world would have moved on again and she would be out of the loop, trying to step back through a door she'd always managed to push open. Returning twice after maternity leave and juggling everything else had been difficult enough.

'I'll miss the wonderful people I work with, but I know in my heart I'm doing the right thing, for all of us.' She gripped Isla's hand. 'You're not disappointed in me for not taking the job?'

'No!' Isla's eyes were shimmering with tears. 'Dad was always really busy, and I know he loved us. But I don't think a promotion would make you happy, and you always say, especially now, that we should go after what makes us happy. We love you loads, and I think it's totally the right thing to do. You can get another job.'

Doing what, Cassie really wasn't sure. But an idea had dropped into her mind earlier, and she planned to explore it as soon as she could.

'But we don't want to hold you back if you really want it.'

'Hold me back?' She gulped, swiping at her eyes. 'Darling, please don't ever think that, because you're absolutely not. I've always loved my job, but it's not the same since we lost Dad.' She paused, smiling through the sadness. 'And here's the bit I hope you're really going to like. I'm going to ask if I can give a month's notice instead of three so I can leave before you break up in July. I will need a job eventually, but we can manage if I take the summer off.'

'Seriously?' Exhilaration flew across Rory's face. 'You mean, no work at all? All summer? No emails or meetings when we're away?'

'I do. You'll be bored silly of me after six weeks.'

'We won't,' he told her seriously. 'Granny always says that family time is precious, and I think she's right.'

'So do I.' Cassie nodded. 'She's very wise, your granny.'

'So does that mean we can spend the summer with them in Hartfell?'

'I don't think so, Rory, I'm sorry.' She hated to disappoint him so soon. 'They have quite a lot of work to do on the new house, and the builders will be there for weeks. I spoke to Granny earlier, and she and Grandpa are thinking they'll take a holiday of their own, something they've not been able to do in summer for years because of running the cottages.'

'Okay.' Some of the hope fizzled out of Rory, and Isla was at the door, heading to her room to revise. 'It doesn't matter. It'll be nice for them to have a proper holiday, they deserve it.'

'Absolutely.' Cassie smoothed his hair. How typical of him to understand, to appreciate the bigger picture in play. 'And you two are going to Italy with Jas for some sunshine too, with Gigi.'

'Yeah.' Rory picked up his phone. However much her children would love the Italian adventure, for them nothing compared to weeks in a Scottish farmhouse with a beach at the bottom of the garden, and seemingly never-ending daylight.

Raf's offer, about spending time at his new house in Hartfell, fell into her mind. Could she ask him? Dare she? Cassie had been the one, after all, who'd said it wasn't a good idea, and Isla and Rory couldn't come and go in case they got used to it. But that was before another chasm had opened up in her life. If he did say yes, they'd be able to spend time with Fiona and Gordon too, help get their new home straight. She was sure Raf would ride with Rory, and Isla would adore helping out with the ponies at Home Farm, and maybe even Dorothy's cob. Cassie would be free from work for a while, and it might give her the space to consider what would come next.

She was reminded of Raf's words on the beach in Galloway, when he'd spoken of the three children he loved, his promise not to stand by and let anything happen to them. And Isla and Rory knew they'd have to return to London as usual once the summer was over. She understood Raf better now and she shouldn't be afraid of what she felt for him. They had restored their friendship, deepened it to a point where it was too precious to risk for another moment of madness. He wanted to forget what had happened in Queensland and so did she.

So maybe a summer in Hartfell could just work. And why wouldn't she try and indulge the pleasure it would bring her children for those few weeks? She had learnt the hard way that life was often short, and she'd told Pippa last year she ought to grab at happiness when it came around.

'I'll have a look at camping holidays in France again.' Cassie wanted a backup just in case. 'It would be fun, and we could pretty much guarantee the sun for a change.'

'Yeah, sounds great, Mum.' Rory stood up too, phone in hand. 'We love you millions and millions, always and forever.'

'Love you millions more,' she replied softly. It was their family mantra, one she'd instilled in her children from the beginning. September would come soon enough, but in a few weeks she would be free, to be a mum and a friend, a useful daughter-in-law. For the first time in years, she felt as though she'd slipped back behind the wheel of her own life.

Once the announcement of the sale of the hotels was made public the following day, Cassie rang Pippa and Fiona, hoping to sound them out about a possible summer in Hartfell. Both women offered wise counsel and assured Cassie she had made the right decision. Later, she took a deep breath and called Raf, her pulse hurrying as she waited for him to pick up.

'Hey, Cass. How are you?'

'Hi, Raf.' Her stomach flipped as she heard his familiar voice, the low, husky note in it, sensing his smile without needing to see it. Why did her own voice always rise when she spoke to him, even at a distance of nearly three hundred miles? She cleared her throat. 'I'm fine. How are you?' She wanted to tell him she'd missed him, even though it had only been a few days, and they were just friends.

'Yeah, good. Let me put you on speaker.'

'Are you alone?' A ripple of alarm followed, she hadn't considered that. Allegra and her cool blonde beauty flashed into Cassie's mind.

'Yep, at Pippa's. They've gone out for dinner and Harriet's off somewhere with Alfie. I had some things to sort with the distillery, so I stayed on.'

'Okay.' Cassie breathed out again. 'So is that Maud I can hear barking?'

'Sure is. I'm dog-sitting too, and working my way through the first stage of my course on distilling. I've even got to sit an exam.'

'Aren't you the professional now? I'm impressed.'

'So you should be. I'll be buying ties next, and chinos.'

'That I would like to see.'

Raf chuckled, and Cassie hugged the sound to her. They didn't often speak on the phone and there was an intimacy to their conversation she hadn't expected.

'Hold on, I think the dogs want out. On my way to the kitchen.'

She heard him open the door and she pictured the scene: Lola and Maud rushing across the terrace to the garden, the hens tucked up in the shed for the night.

'So what can I do for you?'

'I wondered if you were serious, about inviting us up to stay in the summer?'

'Totally. Why would you think I wasn't?'

'I didn't, I just wasn't sure how it might work.' She was smiling again, the load already lighter. 'I'm leaving my job in four weeks and that means I have the whole summer to make plans for something else.'

He gave a low whistle. 'Seriously? Wow, Cass, what's changed?'

'I was offered a promotion to global head of public relations. It would involve travelling, so I turned it down.'

'And you're happy with that? No regrets? This is huge.' There was a softness to his reply she loved, and she was imagining him propped against the door frame, waiting for Lola and Maud to return.

'No regrets,' she said firmly. She only had to recall Rory's relief to be certain. 'So what do you think?'

'I think you should pack and get in the car as soon as. I'm getting the keys to the house on Monday.'

'If only.' She had to laugh. 'There are still six weeks of term left, and Isla has exams.'

'Oh yeah.' Raf whistled and Cassie heard the dogs come bounding back, their paws skittering on the kitchen floor. The clunk of a tin being opened, treats offered, Lola grunting as she settled into her bed. 'Sorry, back now.'

'It's fine.' She hesitated. 'Are you quite sure, before I say anything to Isla and Rory, about having two sometimes grumpy and always hungry teenagers in the house, plus me, for a couple of weeks?'

'Sure enough to say come for the whole summer.'

'Raf…'

'What? Why not?'

'You're not serious?' But the idea did sound tempting. A summer in Hartfell, weeks without work, Fiona, Gordon, Harriet, Pippa and Gil nearby. All those she loved best. And Raf, in the same house, even nearer.

It would be fine, she told herself firmly. There was no option other than to be normal around him.

'Totally. So you'll come?'

'If Isla and Rory say yes.' But that was as good as a done deal, and she knew the kids would love it. 'We won't get in your way, I promise. I need to talk with Jas and see how it might affect her plans. And when you've had enough of us and want the house back, you must say so.'

'It definitely won't come to that. I'll be around too, I have a proper job now. Kenny and Vince only took on the distillery on the understanding that I'm part of it.' Raf paused. 'Look, I'm sorry I wasn't very supportive about your dating profile the other day. I think it's a good idea if you're sure you're ready.'

'You do?' If only Cassie believed it herself, and her shoulders slumped. Had she imagined the faint sigh she thought he'd uttered?

'Just promise me you'll be careful?'

'Of course I will,' she said, rattled by his easy acquiescence of her half-baked decision to join the dating app. 'So is there anything you want to tell me?'

'Such as?'

'Oh, I don't know. Anything you think I should know before we arrive. Who might be coming and going, birthday plans, that sort of thing.'

'Nope, nothing to tell. But there is another reason why I'm sticking around, and if you want to find out why, you're gonna have to come up and see for yourself.'

Oh, hell. So maybe there was something between him and Allegra, and Cassie's anxiety flared. Perhaps she was making a dreadful mistake after all. But everything except her own feelings for Raf made sense, and she'd be silly to turn down a summer in Hartfell and disappoint Isla and

Rory because she was finding it difficult to friendzone him. They were friends again, and she needed to nurture it. He would never know how she really felt.

She could do this, especially for her children, and Fiona and Gordon, who needed the help. Jas wouldn't mind; she had coping with change hardwired into her, and she'd simply shift gears to accommodate Cassie's new plan. Some of the ease of their conversation had vanished and she was ready to end it, her mind caught on what Raf wasn't saying.

'Well, thank you. It's so kind, and Isla and Rory will be ecstatic.'

'You're very welcome,' he said softly. 'Speak soon, yeah?'

Chapter Nine

The few weeks before the end of the school term passed in a blur of exams, packing for the summer and, for Cassie, the strangeness of leaving her career. Bar maternity leave, she'd worked since university, and she found it both sad and scarily exciting to have a free summer and a new future beckoning. Since her decision not to accept the promotion, she'd quickly fallen out of the loop as her colleagues moved on, and after two weeks her boss had quietly suggested she take the rest of her notice period as gardening leave, and she understood. She was surplus to requirements now.

Saying goodbye to her team had been difficult and profoundly poignant, and despite her relief at an escape from the pressure, it felt as though she'd shed a layer of her own self after that final day. Her mind was used to working at pace, and it had been odd, seeing Isla and Rory off to school without settling straight down to work afterwards.

Jonny and the rest of Blue at Midnight had reformed for their final performance at Glastonbury in June, playing the legends slot to a rapturous and adoring crowd. Raf had arranged passes for Cassie, Isla and Rory, and the whole weekend was unforgettable, as mesmerising as it was exhausting and exhilarating. The band had taken over a hotel and Jonny's entire family flew in, along with Gil's two sons plus Fiona and Gordon. When Raf and the band eventually left the stage after their set, triumphant and pumped, Cassie was the first person he sought out to hug.

Jas, madly in love, had decided to stay on in London as she and her girlfriend didn't want to spend the summer apart. She would travel up later on to meet Isla and Rory, and fly with them to Italy for the week with Cassie's mother in August. Cassie and Pippa spoke regularly, and although Pippa was busy with the family, with Gil's two sons at home, the house renovations underway and her work at the gallery, she and Cassie would at least be nearby and able to catch up whenever time allowed.

When school finally broke for the summer, Cassie loaded the car, and she, Isla and Rory headed north to the Dales. When they eventually arrived, she saw that July had brought a dryness to the landscape that was missing in spring, those vivid May greens faded to muted shades dried by wind and sun. The wildflowers in the meadows had gone too, the fields shorn of their crop for winter feed. Some farmers were still at work bringing in the hay as she drove along sunlit lanes, the buzz of tractors noisy as they scurried from farm to field before the weather broke.

She was a knot of nerves and anticipation when they reached Raf's house at the end of a quiet lane, one they had only glimpsed online. She hadn't seen him since Glastonbury, when they'd been permanently surrounded by people, his public self very much on show. Although they'd messaged regularly since, sharing information about her family's stay here, they hadn't spoken more than a couple of times. The sleek BMW coupe he'd adored had gone, replaced by a Land Rover, and she smiled at the mud-spattered vehicle and its practical, solid size. Country gent, indeed.

Rory was first out of the car to open the gate onto the drive, one which curved towards the house set further down, half hidden from the road. Isla hurried after him, both already snapping photographs on their phones, ones which they knew not to share. Respecting Raf's privacy was something they'd long understood, and Pippa had let Cassie know that while some locals were agog at having him move in, most were unconcerned and happy to let him be. She drove through the gate and parked, rolling her shoulders to loosen the tension as she got out of the car. She raised her arms, extending the stretch, aware of her children's exclamations over the house, and that it was theirs for the whole summer.

The house was built of the same local stone she recognised from Home Farm, chimney pots perched at either end of a wide slate roof, the gable wall facing her white with a half-glazed door set into it. A high stone wall surrounded what she assumed must be the garden, a narrow wooden door decorated with a lion's head knocker closed to whatever lay on the other side.

Birdsong was cheerful and welcome after the din of London traffic, and a tranquil happiness began to replace the nerves as she went to the boot in search of a cool bag with food that needed to go in the fridge. Finally they were here, and for now at least, there were no more difficult decisions to come. Packing for three over six weeks didn't come lightly, and it had taken her and Rory a good thirty minutes to stuff everything in. The quiet peace was shattered when he shrieked, and she yanked the bag free and hurried around the car. What now?

Cassie's mouth fell into a gape as Raf emerged from the house, and then she too was running, the cool bag forgotten. She stuttered to a halt and grabbed Rory's arm, his rucksack abandoned nearby. 'Rory, don't crowd him, okay? Three new people is a lot for Flynn to take in.'

He shook her free and dropped to his knees to hug the huge wolfhound, who didn't seem in the least concerned and was already thumping his tail as Isla watched. Cassie's gaze met Raf's, and she was laughing through happy tears as she raised both hands to her face.

'What have you done! Are you absolutely mad?'

'Yes, probably, but hey.' Raf let go of Flynn's collar now Rory had stood, and he grinned as Flynn ambled over to her. 'We were just two guys in search of a home, and we decided to make one together.'

'How has Pippa kept this quiet? And Harriet!'

'They were sworn to absolute secrecy. I can't believe we got away with it.'

But Cassie didn't care. She barely even had to bend to embrace Flynn, his thick grey coat rough and warm and perfect. He nudged her with a massive head, and she laughed as she wobbled. The last time she'd seen him had been in the stable at Dorothy's and he seemed even bigger close up. Did he remember her or was he just gently nudging her again because he wanted another cuddle? Either way, he was here, and a new thought had her looking over to Raf again. 'Is he really yours? Please tell me you haven't just borrowed him or something. Fostering?'

'I didn't think it was fair to bring him home if he wasn't allowed to stay.'

Isla rushed up and flung her arms around Raf, and he laughed as Rory did the same, before they bolted into the house. Apparently even teenagers could still whoop with excitement, and Flynn turned his head to stare after them.

'So you've actually gone and got a dog? But you've never had a pet before! Not even a rabbit or a hamster, something simple to start you off.'

'Gil put in a good word for me with Dorothy and I'm still on trial,' Raf said airily. 'She said, and I quote, that she'll have my balls for target practice and won't be responsible for her actions if I let anything happen to him. So I'm on my very best behaviour, and actually, so is Flynn. He's settled really well.'

'How long have you had him?' Cassie was still stroking Flynn, staring into an expression that seemed brighter, more hopeful. Her smile was a wry one; it was probably just her emotions running away with her again, and she was imagining it.

'Four weeks. He's great company and we seem to understand each other.'

'But I thought wolfhounds didn't like to be left alone?' Flynn dropped his head to investigate the cool bag, and she picked it up. Not that it made much difference, she couldn't reach high enough to keep it out of his way. Five minutes in and Raf had already thrown her another curve-ball, a very tall one with four legs and a gently wagging tail. First a house and now a dog? And the distillery, with Kenny and Vince. It was clear he was making a life in Hartfell.

'Well, we're working on that. I take him out first thing and leave him in the kitchen while I go do some work. Then we meet again for lunch, and after that he usually stays with me. He seems okay as long as he knows I'm in the house, even if I'm not in sight. I have done my homework, I promise.

'Harriet and I went to meet a couple who breed Irish wolfhounds, and I learnt a lot. I know they need loads of space, comfy, supportive beds, regular grooming and a good walk every day. This place is pretty secure, but I can't let him off the lead away from home in case he takes off after something.'

'But what about when you go away?' Cassie couldn't quite get her head around it. Practicalities and Ewan's reluctance were the reasons why they didn't have their own dog, and suddenly Raf had gone and done it without spending weeks and months pondering the decision.

'Pippa and Gil have him if he can't come with me, and he's getting used to it. We have Sunday lunch together most weeks at the pub or Home Farm, or here sometimes.'

'But you don't cook!'

'Well, I do now.' Raf's amused gaze caught hers and that tremor passed between them again. She hadn't allowed herself to think too much about staying here with him, and he looked so good. How was she going to manage, seeing him every day and denying what she wanted, what her body was betraying whenever he was near? She would simply have to find a way.

'Come on, Cass, I'm not completely useless. I've lived on my own quite a lot and I get by. Anyway, you'll find out how good I am because you are not spending the next six weeks cooking.'

'What else am I meant to do?' She laughed, because teenagers needed feeding constantly. She was always opening the fridge door and despairing at the empty shelves she'd seemingly only just filled.

'Walk, sleep, eat, read, see friends, make new ones. What else?' He reached for the cool bag, and she let him take it. 'Oh yeah, sleep and read and eat some more.'

'Raf, I'm not ill. I'm fine.'

'I know that, but you have just left your career, and then there's…'

She nodded, they didn't need the words. It was always present, their shared loss. 'But I am getting better; I can feel it. More hopeful, happier.'

'That's great,' he said softly. 'So welcome to your new home for the summer.'

'Thank you.' She caught his eye and her stomach dropped. Almost a month on from Glastonbury and this was the private Raf again, the man she knew best. Standing before her in a pair of cargo shorts and a green T-shirt, hair still damp from a shower. His suntan had deepened since she'd seen him last, accentuating the grey in his hair, the gold rings in his ears sparkling against his skin.

Before Australia she hadn't known what it was like to be held by him as he might a lover, to press herself against him and feel his immediate response as they'd kissed. She steeled herself to greet a friend she cared about and not a man who felt like so much more, even though she saw the memory of that night so clearly in his gaze as it roamed over her face. They were supposed to be moving forwards, and all she wanted was to drag them straight back to that night and feel his hands on her body once again.

'So, er, are friends allowed to hug one another?' He cleared his throat, the shutters dropping over those impassive brown eyes she knew so well.

'I think they are, yes.' She closed her own as she stepped into his embrace. His hands went to her back, drawing her close. Her face rested against his chest, and she was utterly aware of Raf's heart beating rapidly beneath her cheek, his mouth against her temple. Desire was a sharp kick in her stomach, her hands pressing him closer still.

'Raf, which room am I sleeping in? This house is amazing, Mum! Wait until you see the TV, it's massive!'

Cassie sprang back at Rory's exclamation, plastering a hasty and distracted smile on her face. Was she imagining Raf's reluctance as they eased apart, his hands sliding slowly down her arms before he squeezed her fingers?

'How fab, you can show me when we've emptied the car.'

'I thought you and Isla might like to choose your own rooms,' Raf said to Rory, Flynn standing patiently between them. 'The one next to the music studio is mine and I thought your mum would like the bedroom at the far end, with the big window. So you and Isla can pick from the other three, yeah? No falling out. Otherwise I'll have to decide for you.'

'Got it.' Rory turned his exuberant look on Cassie. 'Mum, it's so cool we're going to be here for the whole summer. I think it's going to be amazing.'

'It really is, Rory. We're so lucky, and it's very kind of Raf to allow it.'

He was gone before she had time to remind him to thank his godfather, the back door rattling behind him.

'Rory, the car!'

'Let's do it later,' Raf suggested. He quirked a brow and she was reminded of how careful she needed to be around him; she needed no more playful or intense looks. 'I can't wait for you to see the house.'

He held the door open so Cassie could enter first, finding herself in a boot room, its walls lined with cupboards, and the waxed jacket he wore in Norfolk hanging from a hook, a pair of green wellies beneath. Two dog leads were alongside it, a box of craft ale sitting on a worktop next to a white Belfast sink, and he dropped the cool bag beside it. They continued through a cool pantry, thick wooden shelves laden with food, most of which she recognised from the village shop, and into the kitchen.

Oak cupboards sat beneath dark beams, and two windows offered a view of woodland and rough crags behind the house. An Aga with six doors was set into a former fireplace, a thick mantel above it lined with miniature China teapots. Creamy white walls made the best of light Raf explained was north-facing, and seating for six was comfortable around an oak table. The décor was dated but pleasant, and it wasn't difficult to picture a family in here, the life and laughter the house must have known. A basket lined with a cosy mattress sat in front of the Aga and a warm glow followed as Cassie thought of Flynn sleeping there, snug and cared for in his new home. She quashed a moment of worry. She mustn't forget that she and the children would be leaving him at the end of the summer.

The kitchen led onto a passageway that ran the width of the house, separating the rooms facing the garden from those at the back. Opposite was a door into Raf's office, a staircase opening directly from there onto his music room above. At the end of the passageway he showed her the dining room with its green carpet, grand oak table and burgundy-backed chairs. They turned left, emerging in another hall with the staircase soaring above them. White-panelled walls were blotchy with faded outlines where once paintings or pictures had hung, and he opened the door to her right.

'This is the sitting room.'

She passed him to enter, glancing at an oak-beamed ceiling framing primrose panelling. The carpet was burgundy, matching the armchairs clustered around a pair of cream sofas pale amongst cabinets and a coffee table in front of an empty fireplace, rose-coloured cushions in the window seat faded with age and sunlight. The window framed a spectacular view, the garden an expanse of lawn enclosed by formal rectangular borders on either side, filled with mature shrubs underplanted with perennials, beneath a cornflower-blue sky uncluttered by clouds. A gap in the border at the far end led to a narrow hump-backed bridge crossing a busy little beck, tugging her gaze to a wildflower meadow and a fell rising in the distance.

A stone terrace ran the width of the house, beyond a border beneath the windows stuffed with old roses and lilac geraniums, enclosed by evergreen box hedging. Deep purple lavender in tall planters swarmed with bees below a long-established wisteria clambering out of sight towards the first floor, its thick stems heavy with green leaves and bright new shoots. She assumed he must have some assistance to keep everything in order, and she was determined to get stuck in, to help wherever she could.

'Raf, it's stunning. Truly beautiful. I don't know what else to say!' Cassie couldn't miss the pleasure in his gaze, the pull of his presence dragging her straight back into his orbit.

'I'm happy you think so,' he said softly, sliding one hand into a pocket. 'I hoped you'd like it.'

'I love it. The owner must have been so sad to leave,' she murmured. She thought of the family gathering in this room at Christmas, presents piled beneath a giant tree, the burgundy curtains open onto a starry and snowy night. 'They've left so much behind. It feels as though they could walk back at any minute.'

'For sure, it's been in the same family for thirty years. I like that it's not far from the village, but it's quite private and the last property on the lane, which doesn't lead anywhere except to a footpath onto the fell. That sense of family is one of the things I like best, because it already feels like a home. It reminds me of yours.'

'Mine!' She laughed, thinking of her busy London street lined with cars, the narrow house wedged between their neighbours. 'In case you've forgotten, it doesn't look anything like this.'

'It feels the same, though.' He was doing it again, holding her still with just a look in a way she'd never noticed before Australia, and her pulse quickened. 'Comfortable, welcoming. Like it's loved.'

'That's very sweet, thank you,' she muttered. 'This is so grand, though. I'm not sure I ever imagined you living in a house with stairs made of stone. I love how they curve past the arched window. Not sure about the flowery pelmet, but it's a gorgeous view of the wood at the back.'

'It's not that big,' he said drily. 'It's just spacious.'

'Says the rock star used to every luxury,' she retorted. It felt good to laugh together, to remember how precious their friendship was. But grand wasn't Raf, not really. He availed himself of drivers and the occasional lift in a mate's helicopter from time to time, but for the most part he avoided that life.

'At least I can rely on you to make sure I don't get too big for my boots.'

'Someone has to.' She made herself turn away from that look. 'Everyone else adores you.'

Across the hall the second reception room was more compact, the television Rory had admired on one wall, and Cassie was aware of thudding footsteps as Isla and Rory continued exploring. A climbing rose peeked through a pair of windows edged with shutters, an enormous sofa and two wing-backed chairs forming a square with the fireplace.

Raf was alongside her as they climbed the staircase to the first floor, feet tapping on the stone. On the landing, primrose wallpaper was cheerful above a gold carpet, and through doors open right and left, she spotted bedrooms and a large, old-fashioned bathroom. Isla and Rory were sprawled across a double bed in one room, and they looked up from their phones with merry grins. She smiled back as she spotted Rory's rucksack in the room next door; it appeared they had chosen where they would sleep. The landing followed the path of the passageway on the ground floor, and Raf pointed ahead.

'My room's down there.' He nodded towards the far end before opening another door. 'You're in here.'

'Raf, this is the master!' She whirled around, wondering if he had placed them at opposite ends of the house on purpose. 'You can't give me this room. It should be yours.'

'I want you to have it. I like the other one.'

The largest of the bedrooms she had seen so far, it faced the garden and the same magnificent view as the sitting room below. A pretty cushion crammed into a window seat was faded, and although she wouldn't have chosen such pink wallpaper and the chintz furnishings, it lent the room an old-fashioned charm she found endearing. Matching armchairs either side of the window softened oak furniture and a brass-framed bed, a fireplace already laid with logs. A desk fitted into an alcove, with a tall chest of drawers in the opposite one. The mantelpiece was empty bar a pair of brass candlesticks, and another two sat on the desk. A sturdy coffee table was nestled between the armchairs, a double wardrobe to the right of the bed.

Beside it was an open door leading to her own bathroom, a luxury she wasn't used to.

'What do you think? Like it?' Raf was lounging against the door frame, and she laughed as she turned away from one distraction to face another more dangerous one.

'Are you kidding me? I love it! But I would be perfectly fine in one of the smaller rooms.'

'Decision made. It's yours for as long as you want it.'

'Are you quite sure? Because I might never want to leave.'

'I could get used to that,' he murmured. His phone rang and he pulled it from a pocket. 'Sorry, I need to take this. Come down when you're ready, I'll make us a drink.'

Cassie settled on the window seat once he'd closed the door, tucking her legs beneath her and reaching for her phone. She was gradually weaning herself away from social media and doom scrolling. She put the phone down again; it was too easy to fall back into bad habits. Social channels had been essential for work, and she used her personal ones much less, sometimes keeping up with family and friends by calling instead. She valued those conversations; they felt more real and alive. Her eyes were heavy after the long drive, and she closed them. She could take five minutes.

When she woke again it was to silence, and she blinked, surprised to have fallen asleep so easily. She messaged Fiona to let her know they'd arrived. She had meant to do it earlier and forgot in her distraction over Flynn. Jago Lynch had emailed with an invite to his launch next week. They'd been in touch occasionally, and she replied to thank him and let him know she would be there. Mostly for Pippa's sake than his, but she was intrigued about seeing him again. She went to the bathroom and freshened up before returning downstairs.

A glance in the television room revealed Isla and Rory making themselves at home. Both nodded automatically when she asked if they were hungry. Here they had no usual routine or access to everything London had to offer, another disconnect from normal life. Cassie retraced her steps to the kitchen, planning to produce a simple meal from the food she'd brought with them. She'd tackle the car later.

'Oh!'

Raf was dicing something on a chopping board near the sink, and she smiled as Flynn got up. She ran a hand along his back and the shaggy coat, wiry between her fingers. 'What are you doing?'

'I think it's known as cooking.' He threw her a wicked grin and she swallowed. Why did he have to look delectable even while doing something so simple? 'Although I will admit that Aga takes some getting used to. You ready to eat?'

'Yes, but it might depend on what you're making,' she replied suspiciously. 'I still haven't forgotten the paella disaster at mine that time. I had to chuck my favourite pan away.'

'Yeah, but I got you an even better one.' He went to the fridge, and she didn't need to see his face to know he was smiling. 'Isla and Rory still like pasta, don't they?'

'Love it. It's a permanent fixture in our house, couldn't get by without it.'

'Then I thought I'd make spaghetti carbonara.'

'Wow. Please don't burn it, I am very hungry.'

'You really do have no faith in me, do you?' His glance was more amused than hurt, and she shrugged. She had too much; that was part of the problem.

'So what can I do? I feel a bit useless, watching you work.'

'You can stay put, is what. You're not doing a thing, at least not yet.'

'I'll set the table.' Cassie wasn't used to doing nothing, but she didn't feel quite enough at home here yet to be opening drawers and poking around. 'Where is everything?'

'Most of the cutlery and stuff is in the drawer near the sink. Glasses on your left.'

'Are we eating in here or in that grand dining room?'

'In here for sure. I think we can save the dining room for state occasions.'

Already there was a sense of his presence in the house: a hoodie slung over the back of the sofa in the television room; a book on distilling gin on the kitchen table; his keys on the windowsill, phone charging nearby. He diced pancetta as Cassie found place mats and cutlery, and it didn't feel as awkward as she expected as they worked around one another. Raf added ingredients to a frying pan on the Aga, and Flynn got to his feet, head just above the table as he looked on with interest.

'Sorry, buddy,' Raf told him gently. 'If we start that, then who knows where it'll lead? And Dorothy will be after me if she thinks I'm teaching you bad habits.'

'Maybe put some in his bowl,' Cassie suggested, feeling sorry for the wolfhound. 'It seems a shame for him to miss out. It's only a little treat.'

'Fine. Then you tell Pippa it was your idea when Flynn helps himself to the Sunday roast. He won't even need a seat at the table.'

'Deal.' She pinched a couple of pieces of pancetta and dropped them into Flynn's bowl on the floor, watching him gobble them up. 'Just remember who your friends are, Flynn, that's all I'm saying.'

She loved how the dog nudged Raf's thigh, and something clenched in her heart. Flynn might not have been here very long, but already he seemed to understand that Raf represented home. She hoped no disasters would befall them; she didn't want Flynn to be returned to that stable. 'So what else can I do?'

'Sit down and let me make you a gin and tonic. I can promise you it's the best, I know the brand.' Raf winked as he found a highball glass and Cassie pulled out a chair. He added ice, a measured shot of gin and followed up with tonic and a slice of lime, watching as she took her first few sips. 'Well? What do you think?'

'Gorgeous. I haven't had this one before when I've been to the pub. It tastes…' She paused, thinking. 'Spicier, and warming, like ginger.'

'Good, that's exactly what you're supposed to get.' He pulled out a seat opposite her. 'There's orange in there too, and all of the botanicals are foraged locally. Kenny's looking to innovate, and we're planning a pink peppercorn gin and a lavender one. Very few brands can afford to rest on their past achievements.'

'Listen to you and all this corporate speak.' She savoured another mouthful. She probably shouldn't knock it back on an empty stomach, even if it had been a very long drive. Soon the alcohol began to hit her bloodstream, making her feel lightheaded. Lunch had been distinctly below average sandwiches in the services on the way up. 'Who are you, and what have you done with the Raf Jones I know and love?'

'Love?' Suddenly the word was stuck in the space between them, and Cassie hurried to clarify as her face flamed.

'Figure of speech,' she blurted out. 'Old friends, that kind of thing. You know what I mean. So does the house feel like home yet?' She hastily redirected the conversation from such talk and the loaded look he'd given her. 'Even though you've not been here that long?'

'Weirdly, it kind of does. It feels welcoming and I like the history. You know me and London, but I haven't spent much time there in a while, other than to see you.'

She remembered how he would turn up during a gap in tours and crash for a couple of days, entertaining the children, taking them out, making their lives just that little bit brighter, especially now, and a wave of gratitude for his kindness followed.

'What you're doing for us, Raf,' she said quietly. 'It's so generous, and I can't tell you how much I appreciate it. Rory and Isla were ecstatic at the thought of a summer in Hartfell.'

'I want you to feel at home here, Cassie,' he said, effortlessly holding her gaze. 'It's important to me that you do. All of you.'

Chapter Ten

Once Isla and Rory had loaded the dishwasher and finished the clearing up, they disappeared to their rooms, still energised by the change in surroundings. Harriet was coming over tomorrow, and Rory was seeing Jacob in the afternoon. Raf had unloaded the car while Cassie had been dozing in her room, and she thanked him, grateful she didn't have to unpack the puzzle on her own. Their stuff seemed to be spilling everywhere already, and he waved away her apology as she hung coats in the boot room and stood wellies upside down on their pegs outside the back door.

The sitting room beckoned, but she didn't want to be indoors on their first evening, not with the sun slowly sliding west across the sky, the sweet scent of mown hay drifting in through the open door. Tractors were still scuttling to and fro, gathering bales onto trailers and carting them away. She stepped onto the terrace, and the roses, in full and glorious bloom, hit her senses at once. Her eyes misted over with a pang of sorrow amongst the happiness, and she found a smile.

'We miss you, Ewan,' she whispered. 'But we're doing okay now. You'd be so proud of our children and how amazing they are.'

It felt like hello and goodbye all at once. Wishing he were here, knowing he never could be. Grief still shadowed their days sometimes, but it didn't dominate in quite the way it once had. They were all finding ways to live with the loss, and slowly, little by little, they were healing. Cassie's heart lifted as she watched swallows swoop and dive in the meadow, the bright flash of white against red throats and dark feathers. Birdsong was cheery, the solidity of this house and its history at her back comforting as she touched a pink rose, its petals soft against her fingertips. Moments like these were the reason she had begun her journals; she could hold on to this feeling, and she understood it would come again. Contentment and joy were allowed, and the sensation settled inside her.

'It's a perfect evening. Fancy a drink out here?'

'Oh, hi!' She whirled around to see Raf leaning against the door. Flynn wandered outside and she slid an arm across his back.

'You look...' His gaze searched her face. 'Happy.'

'I feel it, like a bubble finally bursting free. I think it's being here, this view, Flynn finding a perfect home.' Their smile was an understanding one, and she felt something loosen inside of her. She hadn't dared include Raf in her pleasure, even though she'd wanted to. 'But let me fetch the drinks, you've done enough.'

'Tonight, you rest. I won't be long.'

She wasn't sure if Flynn would stay when Raf disappeared, but he followed her to the garden sofas clustered around a table and eased himself onto the grass with a grunt. Raf was back a few minutes later, with a tray he set on the table. She thanked him as she accepted another gin and tonic. A dry one this time, he explained, served with lemon and Indian tonic water.

'I could get used to this,' Cassie said wistfully. 'Drinks on the terrace in the sunshine, a friendly dog at my feet.'

'So get used to it, at least for the next six weeks. Give yourself permission to enjoy it.' He leant back, one ankle crossed over the opposite knee, arm lying across the top of the sofa facing hers.

She'd loved him for a long time as a dear friend, and she was glad their boundaries were back in place because she couldn't allow herself to think of him in any other way. She didn't want to lose him in her life, or her children's. He was a part of their family, and she wanted that role to remain the same, to keep him as close as any old friend could be. For Isla and Rory's sake she needed things to be easy between them again.

'Tomorrow it's my turn to cook.' She intended to focus on practical subjects. It was safer than allowing herself to fall into the way he was looking at her.

'Well, we can talk about that,' he replied, a smile playing around his beautiful mouth. She knew now what he could do with it; that was the problem. The thought had a wretched blush starting up on her cheeks.

'Any plans?'

'What?' She quickly tried to recall his question.

'Plans? For tomorrow?'

'Oh! To see Fiona and Gordon and find out if they're settling in as well as she says they are. You know what she's like, she hates to trouble anyone.'

'Yeah,' he said drily. 'Reminds me of someone else I know.'

'Ha, ha. I'd love to explore the village again and visit the shop, too. I love a village shop; they're the best. People have time for each other, and they aren't usually trying to elbow past everyone else. Plus they sell all the goodies I never eat at home.' She paused. 'Do you think it would be okay if I took Flynn with me when I walk? I'm used to walking Bramble and Briar, and I'll be very careful with him, I promise.'

'I think he'd love that.' Raf glanced at the snoozing dog, limbs extended on the grass. 'He's very good on the lead, and any extra walks are welcome, hey, Flynn?' Flynn opened an eye and raised his head.

Now Cassie was looking forward to the morning even more, thankful she hadn't booked the French camping trip. 'So how does Hartfell compare to Norfolk? You're closer to the village here.'

'It just feels right. I love London and always will, but Norfolk taught me that I don't want to live in the city twenty-four seven, especially now.' He watched Flynn's legs twitching as he chased something in his dreams. 'I've seen a lot of airports and cities in my time, and eventually they all start to feel the same. I need space and room to breathe. I thought this house would be good for all of us because I believe we can be happy here, now Galloway has gone. And we really need that, don't you think?'

'But what about when... If...' She didn't want to put into words her fear of him falling in love with someone else, despite the happiness she hoped for him to find. But one day he would, and she'd wish him well and step away – there could be no other choice. 'You meet someone you want to be with.'

'I'm not looking for that, Cass.' His gaze was open on hers and she wondered if she was imagining that it was telling her so much more.

'Yeah, well, those things usually happen exactly when we're not looking for them.' She wanted him, longed for him. Would that feeling never go away? Was one kiss really going to define the rest of her life, because it simply wasn't enough?

'You believe that?' He leant forward and put his glass down, hands loose between his thighs. 'Because I do.'

'I believe in doing the right thing,' she said shakily. She knew from Pippa's messages that his sister despaired of Raf's refusal to take advantage of the occasions when she had tried to bring him and Allegra together. Pippa had railed to Cassie that her brother was a lost cause where commitment was concerned, and she doubted he would ever make a success of a stable, long-term partnership. How would Pippa or Ewan's parents ever accept such a man in Cassie's life, when an eventual break-up would fracture the closeness they all depended on, especially Isla and Rory? Desire and longing for someone she couldn't have were temporary; her children's happiness was not.

'Define "right".'

'Not making the same mistake twice,' she replied quickly. How was it that their words and their eyes could be holding two separate conversations?

'And you think that what happened, what we did...?' He tailed off as her hand shot in the air between them.

'The only way I can deal with that is to never speak of it,' she muttered. 'Please, Raf, it's over. Let's not go there again. We agreed to forget.'

'We did. I'm sorry.' The shutters came down once again as he looked out across the gardens, before he turned back to her. 'I wanted to run something by you. Nothing too personal.'

'Oh?' That was a relief.

'Pippa's friends with someone who helps run a local youth programme and they've asked me if I'd be interested in speaking with the group. Share my experience about life at their age. They're similar to Isla and Rory.'

141

'And what do you think?' Cassie didn't want to apply pressure if Raf felt it wasn't for him and would expose parts of his life he preferred to keep private.

'I'd like to do it, and I wondered what you thought?'

'Truthfully, I think you would be amazing. You're so good with our three, and they really respect what you say.'

'For an old guy.' They shared a grin, more natural this time.

'Yes, even for an old guy.'

'It's not about the band and how I got into music.' He rested a hand on his thigh, one finger tapping a beat. 'I'm well aware I had a lucky break because of my dad. It's more about... growing up when life doesn't look how you hoped it would.'

'And you're okay with that?'

'I think so.' He nodded. 'No, I am. What use is my experience if I keep it to myself? I guess it would be an extension of what I already do with Isla and Rory, but that's easy, because I love them.'

'Please don't forget you worked very hard for your success and you're an incredible musician,' Cassie told him softly. 'You earned it, no matter how it started. They wouldn't have kept you on otherwise, and you brought the band a lot of new fans. And if I can help...'

'Thanks, Cass, I appreciate you saying that. Just being here to hold my hand will help. Metaphorically speaking.' Their eyes met before he smiled at Flynn gently snoring. 'So tell me how you are now you've walked away from your career?'

'Walked away?' Her laugh was a brittle one. 'You make it sound as though I've just given up.' Had she? Guilt was beginning to prod, reminding her that millions of other working mums succeeded where she had apparently failed. 'I couldn't leave Isla and Rory to take off wherever the group wanted to send me. Jas is wonderful, but she's not staying forever, and they need me. Are you saying you think I made the wrong choice?'

'Of course I'm not. I'm sorry, that was clumsily worded.' Raf stretched his arm out again as he leant back. 'You put your family before your career, and that's a nearly impossible choice given what you're all going through. My dad made a different choice to carry on working when we lost my mum, and who knows what our lives would've been like if Pippa hadn't stepped in when she did? But I don't blame him for that. He carried his own grief over my mum, and he made our lives secure in other ways.'

Cassie had seen firsthand that Pippa had done everything she could to fill the space her mum had left behind, loving her brother and sister fiercely and providing stability at home when their dad had been touring with the band.

'I get why your career doesn't just come down to what you want, especially now. It's tough, having to choose between a promotion and your kids, and they might never really understand what you gave up for them. But I see it.' Ice rattled in the glass as he picked up his drink. 'It was different for Ewan. He was the one racing to the top, and I don't think he knew quite how lucky he was, having you at his side.'

'Lucky?' Cassie's throat felt scratched, but she couldn't look away from the understanding and honesty in Raf's gaze. 'Why do you say that?'

'Because I think it's true. You were the one backing him up, taking care of your home and looking after Isla and Rory, keeping everything together. Whenever Ewan took another step up the ladder, I don't think he ever doubted it was the right thing to do. He was aware of the impact of his hours on you, and I know he tried to be around as much as he could. But he didn't ever stop and think, hey, maybe this time it's a no, because my family isn't all about me. He achieved his dream, Cassie, and that's incredible. But some of it was down to you, because you helped make it possible.'

Raf emptied his glass and put it down, before getting up to sit alongside her. 'So when you ask me if I think you made the wrong choice, no, I don't. You put your family first, and that's every bit as brave as saying yes to a promotion. Maybe even braver. One day Isla and Rory will realise you did it because you love them more than anything.'

He cupped Cassie's face, smoothing a tear away with his thumb. 'So when you work out what you want to do next, I'll be there to help you however I can.'

'Do you mean it?' She wanted to laugh away his promise; it wasn't something she could hold him to. She'd done everything she could to avoid touching him these past few months, bar the friendly hugs in greeting, and already she was leaning into his instinctive gesture, the kindness behind it. She was no longer married to his best friend, even if she still found it difficult to grasp the reality. Would she ever be able to allow herself the freedom to love someone else, when her heart still sometimes felt fastened to the past?

'Of course I do.' Slowly he eased away, and relief allowed her to breathe more easily. 'You need time to let everything settle.'

'I know what I want to do next, Raf.' The idea had been with her for months – in truth, years – and she felt the familiar mix of excitement and nerves at the thought of her new plan.

He raised a brow, lips quirked. 'Are you gonna tell me?'

'Before Rory started high school I was thinking of retraining as a counsellor, but I never quite managed to put everything in place.' She took a deep breath, ready to confess her long-held dream. To have Raf tell her it was still possible, and she hadn't let her own ambition slip away in the routine of family life and marriage to a brilliant man.

'You probably won't remember he fell off his bike and broke his arm just before the end of the summer holiday. He was already worried about changing schools, and I didn't think it was fair to take on something else when he really needed me. And then life kept taking over, Ewan was under pressure, and the timing never seemed quite right.'

'That's a long road, Cass.' Raf slid an arm along the seat behind her.

'I know that,' she told him hotly. 'And Ewan had enough doubts for the both of us without you pointing it out as well.'

'I'm sorry.' He held up a hand. 'It's not because I doubt you, but because it won't…' He paused. 'It won't be easy, after everything you've been through. I don't want to see you hurt again, that's all.'

'Isn't that my decision, if I want to do it?' Cassie's heart was clattering. She hadn't meant to express Ewan's doubts out loud. 'Being bereaved doesn't make me useless, just still very sad sometimes. My psychology degree is a first-class one, and the only reason I didn't go on to a master's was because I needed a job after Dad died.

'I know retraining will take years, and I'll have to learn how to separate my own experience and emotions from the people I'll meet. I also understand the training will be challenging and maybe highly emotional for someone in my situation. It could be draining and difficult, and perhaps I won't be right for it after all. But I feel that I am, Raf. I know that I can do it.' She thumped a hand to her chest, surprised by the wobble and fierce determination in her voice.

'By the time I'm qualified, Isla will be at university, or very nearly, and Rory will be in college. I know they'll still need me, but their lives will be different again, and I want to do this before it's too late. I've already signed up to an in-person level two course which starts in London in September. It's one day a week, which will leave me time to work around it, and I'll move on to level three once I finish in January.'

'Wow. You really have thought about it.'

She nodded as silence bloomed between them, pressing her finger against her thumb the way she always did when she was worried, just like Rory. 'Forget what I said, about Ewan.' She bit her lip. 'He was just concerned about me, that's all. Taking too much on.'

'Was he? Because sometimes it seemed to me there wasn't room for two ambitious people in his world.' Raf's voice was very low.

She and Ewan had rowed about her plan to retrain several times that summer, before Rory broke his arm and she'd abandoned the idea. Cassie had even wondered if Ewan had been relieved about the accident once they knew Rory was fine and had seen it as a means to halt her ambition so he could pursue his own.

'I'm sorry if I'm speaking out of turn. It was an observation, that's all. You were always happy with your family around you.'

'I was,' she said quickly. 'I am. But you're right, about Ewan's ambition. He didn't see why anything should hinder it. Not marriage, home, children, family. He was the most driven person I've ever met. It was exhausting, sometimes, trying to keep up. But we did love each other.'

She glanced into the house, checking her children weren't in sight. Their bedrooms were at the back, so she was safe to explore these thoughts out loud as long as they couldn't overhear, thoughts she hadn't even shared with Pippa. Life was just too much sometimes, to question it and wonder about a different one had she made different choices.

'I'm really sorry, Cass. I didn't know.'

'It's fine, and you weren't meant to. It was between me and Ewan,' she replied evenly. 'There was nothing you could have done. And so this time I am going to retrain while I have the chance.'

'So tell me how I can help?'

'You mean it?' Cassie allowed a smile at his show of support. Pippa had encouraged her then, but she had backed down in the face of Ewan's opposition when Cassie had said it didn't matter.

'This is me, and you and I are friends.' Raf nudged her foot with his. 'Of course I'm going to help you.'

'Thank you,' she replied softly. 'For not trying to talk me out of it or tell me I'm crazy, or too old. I have enough doubts of my own sometimes, so I don't think I could bear any more from you.'

'You could do anything you turn your mind too.' Raf took her hand, and she thought of that final night in

147

Galloway, when they'd talked on the beach and walked back hand in hand. How right it had felt, and how much she appreciated his strength and encouragement, even as she found more reserves of her own.

'I've got lots to learn, and coping with the situations I'll be faced with is just one of them. Thank you for listening.' Slowly, Cassie freed herself. However kindly he had meant it, she didn't want to see his fingers wrapped around hers, longing for a touch on her body she couldn't have. 'And I have a suggestion for you, something I could help with while I'm here.'

'I already have a gardener. Can't you tell? This lot isn't down to me.' He grinned as he swept a hand over the view.

'Not that, I'd probably chop down all the wrong plants. I thought I could put my experience to good use and help you with the distillery. I've already had a few ideas about contacts I could reach out to, and we could maybe explore a brand partnership if you're interested. If Kenny and Vince agree too, of course.'

'Cass…'

'Don't say it,' she replied firmly. 'Give me one good reason why not, and my lazing around all summer is not one of them. Let me do this, please. It's my way of thanking you for giving us a home for the summer. What do you think?'

'I think yes, if you're sure,' he said slowly. 'Kenny and Vince would snap your hand off and there's no one I'd trust more or rather work with.' He quirked a brow. 'Does that mean we'd have to have meetings and stuff? Get all official?'

Don't look at me like that, she wanted to say. But that would be admitting how much of an effect he had on her, although surely he knew? He was far too experienced to miss the catch in her breath, the dilated pupils, whenever they were alone.

'Yes, meetings and stuff,' she told him sternly, her smile belying the serious tone. 'And we'd track media metrics, digital engagement and qualitative outcomes to get a clear picture of what works.'

'Seriously? Now you're sucking all the fun out of it.' Raf groaned as he covered his face with both hands. 'So where would we have our meetings?' He parted his fingers to give her a mischievous look, and she shoved his foot with hers.

'You're the one who's turned corporate. I've just escaped that world.'

'Exactly, so why would you want to dive straight back in?'

'For you,' she told him softly, raising a shoulder. For once she didn't care what her expression might be revealing, if it was telling him exactly how she felt. 'Because of all this.'

Flynn stirred on the grass and clambered to his feet, wandering over and plonking his head on the seat beside Cassie, who yawned.

'I'm going to head up,' she said apologetically. 'It's been a long day.'

'Okay. Night, Cass, sleep well.' Raf's words drifted across as she made her way inside before she did something crazy, like leaning over to kiss him. He was just being kind, she reminded herself firmly. As any friend would.

She wasn't expecting Flynn to follow, and she tried to make him return to Raf in the garden. But he was still at her heels as she walked through the house, and at the foot of the stairs, she gave him a cuddle.

'I can't take you up with me, because it wouldn't be fair on either of us,' she told him sadly. She kissed his face, feeling the press of his solid body against hers, his head heavy in her hands. 'But I'll take you out tomorrow. That's a promise.'

—

Several hours later Cassie woke to a tap on her door, and she yanked the duvet to her chin in case it was Raf. But when she called 'come in', it was Rory's head which appeared around the door, and she rearranged the pillows to sit up.

'Hey, you.' She smiled, blinking drowsily. It had been a surprisingly peaceful night, and she felt rested, the almost empty day stretching before her. 'What time is it?'

'Almost eight.' He grinned as he came over and put a mug on her bedside table. 'Raf said you might like coffee, but not to wake you if you were still asleep.'

'Thank you,' she murmured. 'That's very thoughtful of you both. Coffee in bed is definitely a luxury.' She leant over to pick up the mug, wrapping her fingers around its warmth. Already the sun was bright behind her cream curtains, and she asked Rory to open them so she could appreciate the view. The landscape extended before her, lit by green and gold, tractors and trailers still out collecting bales of hay.

'How did you sleep, Rory?'

'Good, thanks. Raf helped me set up my Xbox and I was online with Jacob until eleven.'

'That sounds fun. Is Isla up yet?'

'Yeah, she's gone to Harriet's. She said she'd messaged you and that she'd be back tonight. They're going to Alfie's after they've been to Dorothy's.'

'Your sister certainly doesn't waste much time.' Cassie quashed a moment of alarm at Isla making her way through the village alone.

But Isla was used to London transport; Hartfell was a breeze in comparison, and Cassie loved that the two girls were once again within reach, just like her and Pippa. Their friendship hadn't faltered since Harriet had moved north; they'd simply switched it online. Rory looked cheerful too, and she patted the space beside her, absurdly grateful when he settled on it. It still caught her breath sometimes, to see Ewan's smile reflected in their son and that same clear-eyed, problem-solving gaze.

She missed the days when she'd cuddled her small children in bed, snuggling together and making up stories. When had her babies become so big, so independent? How would she bear letting them go when the time came for them to move on and make more of their own choices? She pushed such thoughts away. She wanted them to fly, and for that they needed wings. And roots; she hoped they were planted deep.

'Gigi's messaged me to check when we're coming to stay.' Rory's brow furrowed. 'She said she hadn't heard from you.'

Cassie held back a sigh. Her mother had never been big on family details, and with an assistant to run the mundane aspects of her life, Lois was free to do more or less as she pleased. She glanced at her phone and saw the message she hadn't yet opened. Her mother always began her days with an early morning swim and preferred communicating first thing.

After her father had died and they'd discovered he'd left them nothing but debts, defaulting on the mortgage her mother didn't know he'd taken out on their London house, Lois had bolted to Italy to stay with friends while Cassie finished university. Six months later, a book about her mother's life with a notoriously difficult and unfaithful husband was announced to the world with great fanfare. When it was published the following year, it topped the bestseller lists for months in multiple territories and had never been out of print. Lois had gone on to become a notable biographer of historical figures and remained on the Amalfi Coast, where she lived with a much younger DJ, and spent half of each summer in Ibizan clubs.

Cassie had had her share of tabloid attention when she was young. She'd loathed it and hated the scorn from other children at school, which made her desperate to protect her own family from any lingering gossip. She'd long recognised she had come a poor third to her parents' marriage and their individual problems. Counselling had helped her accept and understand, as well as cope. She and Lois had a cordial relationship now, and they had lunch whenever her mother came to London to meet with her agent and publishers. Lois would send the children all her best love along with a gift, then hop on the next flight home without seeing them. She was a bright star who glittered from afar in their world, and Cassie knew she would never change.

'I'll message Gigi and remind her about the date. So what time are you meeting Jacob? Don't forget we're having lunch at the pub tomorrow, and Granny and Grandpa are coming too.'

'I won't. Jacob said they're bringing the sheep down from the fell today.' Rory's look was earnest, and Cassie's heart clenched with love for her beautiful boy. 'Please can I go with them? Raf said there'll be plenty of adults there, and Jacob's done it loads of times. He knows the fells and what to do.'

'I think that sounds great.' She bit back her concern. She'd never been a risk-taker like Ewan, and together they'd found a way to allow their children to experiment. It was much harder, doing this alone. 'Just stay with Jacob, and make sure your phone is fully charged before you go. And let me know when you're back at the farm.'

'I will. Thanks, Mum.' Rory leapt up, already on his way to the door, and she called after him.

'Take water. And sunscreen, and…'

'Yeah, got it. Will do.' The door closed behind him, and she leant back to enjoy her coffee for a few minutes more, setting aside her anxiety as she read Isla's message. Almost everyone she loved was in Hartfell now, and her family's life in London seemed very far away from fells and sheep gathers and long lunches at the pub.

Chapter Eleven

When Cassie ventured downstairs she found Raf in the kitchen cooking bacon on the Aga, and she watched for a moment, unseen.

'I hope I can expect this level of service every morning. That smells amazing.'

'Morning.' They shared a smile as she bent to greet Flynn in his basket and the wolfhound's tail thumped. 'I thought it might be nice. Gordon always cooked on our first day.'

'That's a lovely thought. Thank you for remembering.' A tradition they'd all loved, waking up in Galloway and coming down to a hearty breakfast.

'How did you sleep?'

'Really well, thanks. The bed was very comfortable.' She went to the fridge and found the orange juice she'd brought, holding up the bottle as he flipped eggs. 'Would you like one?'

'Please. Isla and Rory have already eaten and disappeared with their friends.'

'So I heard. No wonder it's quiet in here.' Flynn came over and she gave him a cuddle, smiling at his inquisitive head level with the table. 'Sorry, you have to go back to bed when we eat,' she told him gently. 'It's not fair to torment you with food under your nose.' Raf had mentioned he was teaching Flynn to stay in his bed with a treat at mealtimes, a habit she had to follow too.

'So is this how you like to spend your Saturday mornings now? You'll be reading the papers next and buying slippers. At least it's something new for your Instagram, domesticated Raf.' She caught the sardonic glance he threw her. 'Your followers must be lapping it up.'

'Not anymore, they're not.' He pointed to a fresh sourdough loaf on the table, crumbs scattered around it. 'Help yourself. I got some of that butter you like from the shop as well.'

'You really are going to ruin me,' she said helplessly, picking up a breadknife anyway. 'So why won't your followers like this?'

'Because I've deleted my Instagram.'

'Seriously?' Cassie paused slicing as her gaze snapped up. She tried hard not to look at Raf's Insta now, and the algorithm had obliged by showing her fewer posts. 'I thought you liked it?'

'I do. I did.' He shrugged as he slid bacon and eggs onto plates already half full of mushrooms, tomatoes and baked beans. 'I decided I was done. It takes up too much bandwidth, I guess. It was fun when I was in the band, but now that's over I want a more private life.'

'Who are you and what have you done with Raf Jones?' She wondered if he'd always had those laughter lines around his mouth, or had she simply never noticed them before? And had he always looked at her that way? As though he could read her mind and understood her every thought before she'd even had it.

He brought their food over and she sliced more sourdough, dropping some onto his plate. He'd already set out brown sauce and ketchup, and she squirted a blob of brown onto her own, pulling a face when he added brown sauce and ketchup to his bacon butty, a habit he'd taught her children.

He explained more about the local youth group he planned to meet as they ate, which gathered weekly in the village hall. Afterwards, once Cassie had finished unpacking and exploring the garden with Flynn, she was ready for a stroll into the village. She offered to fetch shopping so she could cook this evening, and Raf accepted on the understanding that it wasn't her job to feed everyone every day, suggesting all four of them shared the kitchen duties.

He stayed behind to work, keeping up with his online distilling course. She changed her boots and found Flynn's lead, actually a harness that went over his head and fastened around his chest. Once she was satisfied he was comfortable, they set off. It really was like walking with a small pony at her side, and although he was interested in his surroundings, he didn't pull or try to tow her along. He attracted a few curious glances from people they met, and one or two stopped to admire him. He was very polite and well behaved, and she made sure to tell him so.

The church and school next door were in sight as she approached the village, dappled sunlight glinting between a row of chestnut trees. In places, cow parsley was still flowering gamely, flattened flower heads drifting in a light breeze. Occasionally Flynn raised his head in sight of something, and she clutched the lead a bit tighter as he stilled. But each time he relaxed again and settled at her side.

She paused at the church noticeboard and read about the community corner every Wednesday afternoon and the adult and toddler group which met in term time. A couple was sat on a bench on the village green, sharing drinks from a flask and tucking into chunks of what appeared to be crumbly fruit cake. She wasn't hungry after the breakfast Raf had cooked, but cake always sounded good. Especially on holiday. Perhaps Hartfell had always been this lovely, or more likely she hadn't been looking properly before.

Kenny was deadheading perennials in planters outside the pub, and when she went over, he cheerfully reminded her that he'd booked the family a table for lunch tomorrow. Pippa's gallery was opposite the pub and Cassie had arranged to meet her there later, after seeing Fiona and Gordon.

She said goodbye to Kenny and carried on, spotting Edmund down the lane outside his cottage, and raised a hand. He waved back as the door to the cottage beside his opened, and a young woman hurried out. Cassie recognised Erin, Gil's business partner at the practice, as she leapt into her pickup and took off, presumably on call and heading to an emergency. Her partner Oli emerged from the house, and he came over the moment he spotted Flynn, admiring the wolfhound and asking how he was settling in.

They talked about the ponies at the farm, and once they'd parted, she continued to her parents-in-law's new home a mile from the village. Work was very much underway when she arrived, with two vans and a huge skip parked in the driveway, a pair of builders in discussion with Fiona and Gordon outside the front door. Gordon waved and Fiona escaped to greet Cassie and Flynn, their two Labradors racing over to inspect this new arrival. Cassie tightened her grip on Flynn's lead, but Bramble and Briar sniffed him curiously and wandered off as Fiona made a quiet fuss of him. She had met Flynn before, when she and Gordon had gone to see Raf's house. Much as she loved it, she told Cassie ruefully, she worried about him having only rented it for six months and moving on again at the end of the summer.

Cassie filed those comments away as Gordon took her on a tour of the bungalow and the latest developments while Fiona made coffee. They sat outside to enjoy it away from the dust, with a fresh batch of Fiona's melt-in-the-mouth shortbread. It wasn't a surprise to learn that the builders were keen to be on site when Cassie discovered that Fiona was serving them brunch and afternoon tea every day. She thought the move was genius, especially as Fiona had promised to cook them a full Christmas dinner with all the trimmings if they finished on time. Her parents-in-law were exploring the possibility of a short holiday in Bath, somewhere Fiona had always wanted to visit in honour of her love for Jane Austen and *Persuasion* in particular.

Cassie brushed a few crumbs onto the grass, and Bramble and Briar leapt to hoover them up. Flynn hadn't budged and she reminded him what a good boy he was. Thank goodness she still had six weeks of his company left. It was way too early to think of the sadness when she'd have to leave him behind and return to London. Last night she'd watched as Rory took a photo of the instructions on the hefty bag of dog food in the boot room so he could enlarge the print to make it easier to read and feed Flynn himself.

They chatted for a while, and once she'd said goodbye, Cassie set off back to the village. Lunchtime was approaching and she wanted to stock up before the shop closed. Hartfell's only shop was run by Violet, who had lived in the village her entire life, and her younger sister Daphne. Inside the white-painted building, once the front room of a cottage, Cassie found the usual array of goods. Much of the local community depended on the shop for groceries, parcels, home baking and news. She shared a greeting with Daphne and enquired after Violet, who lived with dementia and with Daphne's help, still managed to bake something most days.

Cassie picked up ingredients for a simple chicken curry this evening. Another fresh sourdough loaf made its way into her basket – Rory went through toast like some children ate sweets. She couldn't resist an apple pie and a pot of cream from a local dairy as well, Raf loved it. Being sensible could wait for next week; she was on holiday. Bags heavier than she'd planned, she said goodbye and crossed the lane with Flynn to the gallery.

Once a coaching inn and then a youth hostel, the rooms upstairs had been converted into a community space with a kitchen and a new cafe opening out onto a terrace overlooking a compact walled garden, borders filled with evergreen shrubs and pastel-coloured perennials. She recognised Pippa's touch everywhere, from the subtle lighting to the personally chosen range of greetings cards and gift wrap. Pippa made sure to offer art appealing to a range of budgets, and much of her new ceramicist's work sold almost as fast as it arrived.

The main gallery was hung with paintings by a local Dales artist, a woman who had retired from nursing and was a keen hiker and wild swimmer. Pippa had fallen in love with her work inspired by the landscape, reflected in acrylic and oils on canvas. After the opening night preview six weeks ago, half of the paintings had been sold, and Cassie had her eye on one to welcome her parents-in-law to their new home. A carpet of bluebells framed by woodland backed by the sharp grey ridges of a fell, she was sure they'd love it. She wandered through the rooms and found Pippa at a table on the terrace. Maud leapt up with a madly wagging tail as she bounded across, an enthusiastic welcome Flynn returned more cautiously as the two dogs exchanged sniffs.

'I'm so glad you're here.' Pippa stood to hug Cassie, holding her close. 'Now I feel like summer can really begin. How's everyone?'

'We're all good, thanks. Grateful to be here.' They separated and Cassie pulled out a seat. She looped Flynn's lead around her chair leg, hoping he wouldn't take off after something and tip her up.

'Isn't he a sweetheart?' Pippa looked fondly at the grey wolfhound. 'He's been so good for Raf, even though I never imagined him actually having a dog.'

'You really are, Flynn.' He looked up at the sound of his name and Cassie patted him. Already she loved having him within reach, his presence a comfort. 'Size notwithstanding, you'd hardly know he was there, and we've all fallen in love with him.'

'I take it Rory's gone on the gather with the girls?' Pippa flipped open the cover of an iPad on the table. 'Alfie appeared at first light for Harriet, and they were waiting for Isla to arrive before they set off.'

'I didn't hear a thing when she left, I was well away.' Cassie scanned the menu, wondering whether to have the fishfinger butty or a healthy salad. 'The gallery looks wonderful, Pippa. You must be so thrilled at how it's all come together.'

'I am, and it's partly down to you we're so busy. You've been amazing at getting the word around.'

'It's my pleasure and the least I can do. I've offered to help Raf with the distillery, too,' she said casually. Just mentioning his name had a quiver darting across her skin. She was thinking of his hand on her face last night, the support he'd offered when he'd learnt she was planning to retrain. Did everything lead back to him? Even her own heart?

'But I thought you were supposed to be taking the summer off?'

'I am, but I can't sit around doing nothing for weeks on end. Isla and Rory are busy making their own plans, and using my skills to help you and Raf is my way of thanking you for all you've done.'

A young waitress arrived and Cassie made a snap decision in favour of the salad; breakfast had been much larger than usual. Every seat in the garden and on the terrace was taken, and she noticed a queue forming at the door for tables.

'I hope my brother is taking good care of you.'

'Oh, you know Raf.' She pulled down sunglasses from her hair to hide a quick flush. Would she ever get used to keeping their secret from his sister? How was she meant to forget, when every look, every touch, seemed to drag them straight back to that night? 'He's been very kind and typically generous.'

'I don't suppose you've managed to pin him down about his birthday yet?' Pippa lowered her voice, elbows on the table as she pushed the iPad aside. 'It's only two weeks away and he counters every suggestion I make with a reminder that none of the family were here for my fortieth last year, so why should he be any different.'

'No joy, I'm afraid, he told me the same. Maybe we should surprise him if it's not too late?'

Pippa nodded enthusiastically, grabbing Maud's collar before the spaniel could wander off and say hello to a pair of border terriers at the next table. 'That sounds great. I've been preoccupied with Jago's launch on Friday, so I must confess Raf's birthday had mostly slipped my mind.'

'He definitely doesn't want a fuss, so it shouldn't be a big party,' Cassie said firmly. Pippa was wonderful, but she had been known to run away with an idea before. 'Maybe a nice dinner with the family, at home?'

'That sounds good. Shall we put our heads together and come up with something? If I mention it, he'll only tell me to shove off again.'

Their lunch arrived, and as they chatted, Pippa was thrilled to hear of Cassie's plan to become a counsellor. She told Cassie firmly that she must go for it and grab every opportunity.

'I'm so happy you're planning to follow something you really want to do. And look at Raf.' Pippa thanked the waitress when she arrived to clear their plates. 'I never imagined I'd see the day when he took on a house here, invested in a business and decided to study.'

'He's becoming quite the grown-up,' Cassie replied lightly. She spotted lemon meringue pie being carried to a nearby table and decided to indulge this once, catching the waitress's attention to order. Maud had shifted to follow the sun, Flynn sprawled beside her, little and large.

'Not so grown up that he's making any headway with Allegra, though. She's lovely, so different to his previous girlfriends, and I really do think they'd be good together.' Pippa pulled a face as a sigh escaped. 'Not that I'm sure I'm doing her a favour by encouraging it.'

'What do you mean?' Alarm had Cassie's pulse spiking. Raf had barely mentioned the land agent she'd met back in May at Home Farm, other than to assure her they were not dating.

'I love my brother to bits, Cass, you know I do, but heaven help the woman who eventually takes him on. He's not exactly known for his ability to commit beyond a few months, and I think she'd need to be someone with very little baggage who has a complete life of her own, separate to his. The house is precisely a case in point. He couldn't make up his mind whether to buy it, so he got Allegra to persuade the vendor to rent it instead, giving him the perfect exit strategy. Who knows where he'll be for Christmas? Probably on some faraway beach while the rest of us are stomping through snow and a freezing winter.'

Their desserts arrived along with flat whites, and suddenly Cassie's bowl filled with pastry and lemon topped with waves of whipped meringue didn't look quite so appealing. She picked at it, flicking crumbs from the table for Maud while Flynn dozed.

But this was exactly what she needed to hear to remind herself that her crush on Raf was exactly that. A silly feeling which would pass. She lifted a nonchalant hand to cover the new blush staining her cheeks.

'Ah well, never mind, I certainly won't be able to change him. So you are coming to Jago's launch on Friday night, yes?' Pippa raised a brow.

'That's the plan. I'm looking forward to it,' she said casually. It would be a good distraction from Raf, too. Dipping a tentative toe in the dating pool, as it were.

'I'm sure Jago will be delighted. He made sure to let me know you'd been in touch.' Pippa dropped her voice. 'So is there anything you want to tell me?'

'About what?'

'Dating? Jago? Anyone else?'

'Nope, nothing to share.' Cassie was keen to keep things simple, as well as truthful. 'Jago and I have emailed and messaged a few times, but that's it, Pippa.' But given both Pippa and Fiona's misgivings about Raf, and her own determination to put their kiss behind them, there was no harm in seeing Jago at the gallery and celebrating his launch.

'Please don't get carried away,' she warned. 'He'll probably wonder why he bothered sending me an invite the moment he sees me again.'

'He won't, Cass, I promise you. And let's not forget the obvious, either.' Pippa's smile spread. 'He's hot, right?'

'I suppose. For an older guy.' Cassie would probably have swiped right had she been looking.

'He's forty-nine. Not that old.'

'Yeah, well, like I said…'

'I know, I heard you. You're not really looking. But maybe it's time to go with the flow and see where it takes you.'

Cassie had done that once before, and now she couldn't get that damn kiss out of her mind. She had zero intention of doing anything like that again, and definitely not with a middle-aged sculptor she barely knew.

Chapter Twelve

On Sunday Cassie and Raf gathered with Isla, Rory and Flynn for the walk into the village and lunch at the Pilkington Arms. She'd taken Flynn around the meadow earlier and had been astonished by his speed and strength when he took off, thankful the garden was securely enclosed. Raf had cycled with Rory first thing, and Rory was teasing his godfather about struggling to keep up, taunts that Raf took in good humour as he dropped in a few of his own. When they set off, Rory led Flynn, padding politely at his side, and Isla linked arms with Raf and Cassie. She was full of excitement about the ponies at Home Farm and how much Hero the foal had grown since their last visit in the spring. For Cassie that illusive sense of contentment arrived again, and she held the feeling close so she could record it in her journal later.

When they arrived at the pub, Pippa, Gil, Harriet and Alfie were already seated at their table, and Kenny came around the bar to greet everyone. Having taken early retirement from a previous career in marketing, he seemed to get more attractive with age, cropped gunmetal-grey hair suiting a sharp beard and a merry gaze. He and his partner, Vince, had bought the pub a few years ago and transformed its dreary 1970s décor into a comfortable and contemporary space popular with locals and visitors alike. Dark blue walls were hung with well-placed paintings, and Cassie detected Pippa's influence in the choice of art, which had altered since she'd last been here. Kenny kissed her on both cheeks, wanting to know what she thought of their gin, and she promised him she loved it and would definitely be trying more. He thanked her for stepping in to help with their distillery brand, something she knew Raf had already shared with his two business partners.

Typically on a Sunday lunchtime, every table was taken as staff bustled between them, and she noticed a few guests staring when they spotted Raf. He was usually obliging when approached for selfies or impromptu chats, and Pippa had mentioned the village was getting used to him now, generally leaving him alone. Flynn was drawing attention too, and given his size, it took a moment to settle him beside their table with Lola and Maud nearby. Raf joked with Kenny that he'd pay for an extra meal given the space Flynn needed, and Kenny waved that away as he took their drinks order and gave each dog a treat from the jar he kept on the bar for four-legged visitors.

'Menus for everyone.' Kenny passed them around. 'But as it's Sunday I can definitely recommend the roast beef, served nice and pink. Sorry, Pippa darling, but Vince *has* made your favourite mushroom and squash filo pie.' He winked and she laughed. She and Harriet hadn't eaten meat for years, although she sometimes cooked it for Gil, who loved a steak.

'And I've got the perfect wine to go with the beef, a super Grenache that's not too heavy for a tender cut.'

'That's me sorted.' Gil grinned and Kenny returned to the bar while everyone else opened the menus.

In the end most decided on roast beef while Cassie opted for the filo pie with Pippa and Harriet. The four teenagers were huddled over Harriet's phone, and Cassie took in the glow of sun-kissed skin on their faces, the easy banter between them. Last night, once they'd arrived back from the gather, they'd piled round to Raf's to watch movies on the big screen. Cassie, always prepared for more mouths to feed, had bought pizzas. She'd loved having them around the kitchen table, bringing yet more life and laughter to the house, and it had been late when she'd run them home. Kenny was soon back with their drinks, teasing Raf about opting for a low-alcohol beer instead of their own brand of gin.

'So you are coming to Jago's launch on Friday?' Pippa leant across to speak to him. 'Allegra's going to be there too. It turns out her parents are collectors and they're staying with her for the weekend. I wondered if you knew?'

'And why would I know?' Raf's eyes narrowed and Cassie didn't miss the irritated look he shot his sister. 'I haven't been in touch with her for weeks.'

'I'm sure she'd love to hear from you.' Pippa arched a brow as Gil chatted with Isla and Harriet on his left. 'Cassie's going to be there, aren't you? Jago made sure to invite her and she said yes.'

'Mostly to support you,' she said quickly. She'd dodged sitting beside Raf on purpose, but perhaps that might have been better than constantly trying to avoid his gaze. 'Not really for any other reason.'

'Have you told Jago that? I know he's looking forward to seeing you again.'

'Just leave it, Pippa, yeah?' Raf told her shortly. 'It's blatantly obvious what you're doing, and both Cassie and I are perfectly capable of arranging our own dates. Should we choose to.'

Lunch was superb and they lingered over coffee as people drifted away, soon replaced by more. The teenagers took off first, heading to Alfie's house. His mum had already promised to run everyone home afterwards, and Cassie watched Rory as he followed Alfie out, reading the change in his confidence, the scattering of freckles increasing now he was spending more time outdoors. Isla was tolerant of her younger brother tagging along to some things, but since their loss, they'd developed a closeness that meant she was fiercely protective of him, despite the usual sibling fallouts. When the adults were ready to leave they thanked Kenny and made their way outside, sharing hugs before Pippa and Gill crossed to the gallery, and Cassie set off with Raf and Flynn.

She was glad to have Flynn as a distraction from her thoughts as they strolled along, occasionally stepping aside to let cyclists pass by. 'So don't mention to Pippa that I've told you, but I'm supposed to be getting you to agree to a birthday dinner.' She gave Raf a sidelong glance as Flynn paused to investigate an old burrow dug into a grassy verge. 'Seeing as it's a week on Saturday and we're running out of time.'

'And it's your job to persuade me, is that it?'

'Apparently. She seemed to think I stood the best chance.'

'So what's your plan? How are you going to persuade me?' He quirked a brow with a lazy smile, and a bolt of electricity shot down her spine.

'I haven't got a plan,' she muttered, gently tugging Flynn's lead and encouraging him to carry on. 'And I couldn't. Persuade you, I mean. Not if you've made your mind up.'

'Oh, I think you could,' he murmured. 'We don't have to do anything. Forty's not that special.'

'That's not what you said when it was my turn last year.' Twelve months on from losing Ewan, she hadn't wanted to celebrate a thing, and especially not her birthday as it fell on Valentine's Day. Raf had arrived with Japanese takeout and funny little Valentine's gifts for her and the children, and they'd sat up long into the night talking through their sadness. In the days before Australia and their kiss, still blinded by grief, such things had been possible.

'So what would you like to do? We can't let it pass without some kind of celebration to mark you finally becoming a grown-up.' Cassie wasn't prepared to give up quite yet.

'Wow, thanks.' He clutched his heart. 'It just took me forty years, huh?'

'Yep. Welcome to the real world.'

'So as a concession to my great age, I have made a list of forty movies I plan to watch now I've got more time on my hands.'

'That's a nice idea. So what have you chosen?'

'A few classics I've seen before, like *Goodfellas* and *The Godfather*, some I haven't. Black and white, contemporary, all kinds really. I thought it would be a nice way to catch the ones I always meant to watch and never did.'

'I hope you've got some romcoms in there.' While Ewan had indulged her love of romantic comedies, Raf shared it. They both loved a happy ending, and some evenings Ewan had left them to it and gone to bed while Cassie and Raf stayed up to finish a film.

'Of course I have. Want to help me kick off the list and watch one tonight?'

'On our own?' She wasn't expecting the squeak in her voice. 'Maybe we should wait for Isla and Rory and watch it with them.'

'Okay. I'll let them choose, as long as there's no falling out. Cassie?'

'What?' Flynn raised his head to stare at something across the field, and whatever it was, she couldn't make it out. She gently shook his lead and he plodded on beside her.

'Me and Allegra, there's nothing going on, whatever Pippa might have said. My sister wants to marry me off like some nineteenth-century Jane Austen hero.'

'Oh hey, look, you don't have to explain anything to me,' Cassie rushed out. 'Allegra is nice.' *And obviously into you*, but she didn't add that bit.

'We are in contact occasionally because of the house, but it won't ever be anything more.'

'As long as I'm not in your way.' She'd meant to say 'we' to incorporate her children.

'Never think that, because it's not true.' He caught a hand to halt her. She stared up at the flecks of gold around his irises, that intense and direct gaze. 'You are a non-negotiable in my life. Always.'

'Pippa just wants you to be happy,' she said quietly, aware of the heat of his fingers, his eyes holding her more firmly than his hand. 'We all do.'

'Well, that's nice of her.' He stepped back and she missed his touch the moment it fell away. 'But I'm not going to find it with a twenty-nine-year-old land agent who thinks that black and white movies are a waste of time.'

Isla and Rory came home about eight and Cassie caught up with them in the kitchen. An online shop had arrived earlier, which meant she could stock the fridge and wouldn't be relying on Raf to keep them fed.

'Raf and I are doing a movie tonight, the first of forty he wants to watch over the next year,' she said casually, filling a bowl on the table with apples, oranges and bananas. 'And he's said you two can pick tonight so we can watch it together.'

'What's on the list?' Isla's head was bent over her own phone. Like all teenagers, she and Rory could hold a conversation and keep up with whatever they were doing on their screens.

'Here.' Raf pushed his phone across, and she and Rory abandoned theirs to look. 'You probably haven't seen that many, and most of them are classics everyone should watch at least once.'

'*When Harry Met Sally* sounds okay,' Isla said, sliding his phone back. 'I've heard of it, even though it's, like, pretty ancient. Mum loves a romcom.'

'Isn't that a Christmas one? I thought it was set at New Year.' Cassie absolutely was not going to look at Raf. The very last movie she wanted to watch with him was one about old friends who eventually fall in love and find their happy ending.

'You're killing me, Isla, seriously.' He laughed as he slowly shook his head. 'It's 1989, so barely even vintage, and the story is timeless.'

'What's it about?' Rory got up and collected Flynn's water bowl to refill it.

'It's a funny story about two people who are friends for a long time,' Cassie said quickly. 'Anyway, if you two want to chill in your rooms, we can watch it another time.' Like, never.

'But you're always telling us to stay off our phones.' Isla raised her chin an inch. 'And that watching a movie together is a collective experience. I don't mind.'

'Sorry, Mum.' Rory shot her an apologetic glance, Flynn's hopeful stare on him. 'I said I'd go online with Jacob and Alfie.'

'What time are we starting?' Isla jumped up, grabbing an apple.

'Thirty minutes?' Raf checked his watch.

I can do this, Cassie thought desperately. *It's only a movie.* 'Rory, don't stay online too late, okay? I'll come and say good night later.' At home the Wi-Fi went off at ten p.m., but for now, she could loosen the brakes, seeing as school had finished for the summer.

'Okay.' Rory returned a moment later with Flynn's bowl, and the wolfhound eased himself to his feet. Rory patted him and took off after Isla, thundering along the passage to the stairs.

'I wasn't expecting Isla to choose that one.' Raf held up his hands and she shrugged.

'It's fine. I like it, and I haven't seen it for ages.' At least she knew what to expect. She stood up and gathered the empty snack wrappers Rory and Isla had left behind. Usually she was firm about clearing up after themselves, but she would excuse them this once.

'We can open a bottle of wine if you like.'

'Lovely.' Could she drink the lot? Cassie wondered about spending the next twenty-seven minutes in her room, giving herself a stern talking to about why she didn't approve of friends becoming lovers. In her bathroom soon after, she ran a cool flannel over her skin, a face flushed pink staring back.

Downstairs in the television room she found Raf already there. He poured her a glass of wine from the bottle he'd opened and passed it across.

'Thanks.' She wasn't quite sure where to sit. The best view would be on the new L-shaped sofa, where she usually found Isla and Rory slumped if they weren't at the fridge or in their rooms. She settled at one end, it was plenty big enough not to be anywhere near Raf, and Isla flopped in the centre when she joined them. There wasn't going to be any cosying up here for Cassie, not unless it was snuggling with her daughter.

Flynn also had his own bed nearby, and he folded himself into it as Raf chose the opposite end of the sofa, one ankle crossed over the other. She found it impossible not to be aware of his every little move: long fingers holding the stem of his glass. The curve of a bicep revealed by his T-shirt when he leant down to run a hand over Flynn near his feet, and the breadth of his shoulders, something she'd never paid any attention to before Australia. Somehow she was halfway down her glass of Soave already. Isla put her phone to one side and grinned at Cassie as she folded her legs beneath her. He hit the remote and the familiar opening credits of *When Harry Met Sally* appeared. The jaunty song began, Harry Connick Jr crooning 'It Had to Be You'. She squirmed in her seat, thumping perfectly arranged cushions.

The kiss. Oh hell, how could she have forgotten the kiss? The characters of Harry and his girlfriend drawing out a very thorough goodbye as Sally pulled up in a car alongside. It went on and on, the camera panning around the couple oblivious to everything else. Cassie was scarlet and she slid a hand over her face. The hot flush wasn't a pretend one either; her skin felt nuclear. Maybe it was her age and not having to watch this with Raf at the other end of the sofa. She'd be checking his list twice before she agreed to watch any more of his bloody birthday movies.

She was very glad Rory had decided to sit this one out, and Isla was already glancing at her phone. Better that than all four of them having to watch this couple kissing for what seemed like forever, until Sally cleared her throat a second time. Harry's girlfriend finally realised she was there and introduced Harry. Really, that dodgy fringe ought to have been enough to put anyone off; Sally should've known better. Then another kiss for the road, before Sally blasted her horn and Harry finally got in the car.

The orgasm scene was excruciating. If Isla weren't here, then Cassie might have been in her underwear by now, purely for temperature reasons. She stared straight ahead, smile frozen in place as Sally brought the cafe to a standstill with her pretend performance for Harry. Raf hadn't moved either, and when Cassie risked a sideways glance, his face was set like granite, one finger tapping idly against his empty glass, a muscle flickering in his cheek. She was well down her second now and he'd just finished his first. The conversations between the characters, their fights and their feelings; so much of it seemed to be pointing a finger straight at them.

She always cried at the end and caught Raf swiping his face too, a gesture that sent a rush of something straight to her heart. She wasn't going to call it love, not beyond the friendly feelings she already had for him. The rest was a crush, and it would pass, as crushes generally did. But why did he have to have shoulders like that and those arms, covered in the tattoos revealing the story of his life? Why did he smile at her the way he did, when she was trying so very hard to be sensible? Almost every scene in the movie had dragged her back to those moments of madness with him in Queensland. Isla said good night and vanished, her duty done.

'One down. Thirty-nine to go.' Cassie wiped her forehead for about the tenth time, thankful he couldn't see the clattering of her pulse. Maybe he could hear it, she certainly could. 'Time for bed.' She leapt up so quickly she whacked her knee on the coffee table and grimaced as she tottered back.

'Are you all right?' Raf was on his feet, and he caught her arms.

'I'm fine,' she muttered. 'You can let go.'

She looked up and instantly realised her mistake. His eyes had deepened into dark pools, confusing her senses and leaving her drowning. She'd kissed very few people in her life, while he was an expert. She'd known it from the way he'd held her that night: one hand on her face, the other on her back, pulling her into him, hard and soft all at once. His mouth demanding more, asking her to meet him, to match him and never let him go. She'd wanted to hold him forever then, to lose herself in his strength and the desire she hadn't felt in so very long.

He ran a slow finger down her face, and it took every scrap of strength she possessed not to capture it between her lips and have him follow where she led. She knew what he wanted; his gaze and the catch in his breath couldn't be any clearer. She made herself step away, restoring the distance and clinging to her future as his friend for all she was worth.

'I have to go,' she said shakily. Her arms felt cold without his hands on them, her heart bereft at what she had to do.

'Cass…'

'Please don't make this any more difficult than it already is, Raf,' she whispered. 'I'll see you tomorrow.'

Chapter Thirteen

Gradually Cassie's days eased into a new routine, one where she took Flynn out early for long walks while Rory and Raf cycled together, and Isla went to Home Farm to help Harriet. Then Raf settled to work, something Rory teased him for, unused to this more professional version of his godfather. After spending some time working on ideas for the distillery brand, Cassie made sure she was around for the children in the afternoons, even if they sometimes made plans which didn't involve her. She included Alfie and Jacob whenever possible too, visiting a ruined castle, a museum about life in the Dales and a theme park an hour away. They had a blast, on and off rides all day, and at home she kept the fridge stocked to feed whoever was around at mealtimes. Her mind was slowly detaching itself from the pressures of her career, and if she wasn't uncomfortably aware of her feelings for Raf, she would be as close to content as she felt it was possible to be.

Rory was full of plans for a fishing trip with Gordon once his grandparents had returned from their holiday in Bath, and Cassie was looking forward to helping Fiona straighten out their new house. Soon Isla and Rory would be heading to Italy with Jas, and her anxiety flared every time she thought of it. They were so excited about spending a week with their grandmother, and Cassie couldn't quite picture those days without them yet, the change in routine and responsibility she wasn't used to.

Already London was fading into the past, distant and separate from the lives she and the children were living now. Their Galloway holidays had brought an escape from the city, but Hartfell was different again, especially without the prospect of returning to her job. She made sure to remind herself that this summer was an interlude, a pause on their usual commitments. But it didn't always feel that way, when she woke to the view from her bedroom window every morning and escaped outdoors with Flynn, absorbing the beauty of the landscape until it seemed to have seeped into her bones.

She joined Pippa and a small group of women who met early one morning each week to connect and make space beyond the demands of their everyday lives, their walks often including a wild swim and a bite to eat together afterwards. Cassie missed her sea swims, and she found the river bracing and sharp, but invigorating and energising too. Company on these mornings was a given, conversation optional, and everything they shared remained within the group. Each woman had experienced loss, health issues and family difficulties in some form, and she was grateful to have been made welcome and have the opportunity to share some of her own story.

Friday and the launch of Jago Lynch's new work at the gallery arrived, and she wasn't sure how she felt about seeing him again. She was looking forward to supporting Pippa at the event, and celebrating another milestone in the gallery's development, but there were nerves, too. Jago had sent her a message letting her know he was looking forward to catching up, and that he hoped she would find his work and the evening of interest. She liked his tone, keeping things vaguely professional and not too personal. She also privately agreed with Pippa that he *was* hot, something she hadn't shared lest her best friend ran away with the knowledge. But still Cassie couldn't get her head around the thought of a future date with someone new; it just didn't seem to fit. And although Jago might be a good place to start if he was interested, she was also aware of Pippa's professional relationship with him and wanted to avoid muddying any waters.

Waking early, an idea had dropped into her mind about Raf's birthday. Pippa loved it when Cassie messaged to share her thoughts, and they decided to keep the theme a surprise. It wouldn't be the big party he'd wanted to avoid, but a fun evening she hoped he would enjoy. Tonight Harriet and Alfie were coming over to keep Isla and Rory company while she and Raf were at the launch, and she would leave a chilli in the slow cooker so they could help themselves. Raf was planning to go straight to the gallery after a meeting at the distillery with Kenny and their small on-site team.

With Isla spending the day with Harriet at Dorothy's, helping bring in the store of next winter's hay into the barns, Cassie distracted herself from thoughts of seeing Jago by taking Rory and Jacob to an unusual garden set in the grounds of an old house, transformed by tunnels, follies and underground chambers. The boys loved it, and she was happy to wander round at her own pace and leave them to explore on their own.

Back at the house, she got ready for the evening ahead. Pippa had arranged caterers for the launch and Cassie couldn't face a thing to eat before she left, the teenagers tucking into a first portion of chilli and nachos. Raf had offered to collect her, and she had said not to, that she would be fine walking to the village, something she half regretted when she set out in her wedged espadrille sandals. Most days now she was in boots or trainers, another switch from her working life.

When she arrived the gallery was already busy, with guests milling around the ground floor and admiring Jago's wildlife sculpture, cleverly positioned by Pippa and her assistant. Waiting staff offered drinks and canapés and Cassie accepted a glass of champagne as she sought out Pippa, finding her in the largest of the two galleries with Jago beside her. The two women embraced, and Cassie turned to greet him, holding her glass awkwardly. She'd chosen her black-and-white summer dress with care, and suddenly she felt too visible, too aware of his scrutiny and unused to attention from someone she barely knew. She hadn't dated since her early university days before she and Ewan got back together, and the disconnect from those few months felt insurmountable as she batted away his compliment about her appearance. Her heels added a little extra height, and her gaze was level with his, something else she wasn't used to. She made herself shake away more comparisons with Raf; everything was different with him.

'Congratulations, Jago, your work is stunning and there's clearly lots of interest.' She froze at the unfamiliar pressure of his hand on her shoulder when he leant forward to kiss her on both cheeks. She couldn't fault his own appearance, a well-cut plum jacket worn over a crisp white shirt and indigo jeans.

'Thank you, Cassie. It's so good to see you again,' he said, his hand still on her shoulder. She shifted fractionally, and it fell away. 'Pippa tells me you've been instrumental in getting half these people here.'

'Oh, hardly.' She swallowed some more champagne as Pippa's attention was claimed elsewhere. Raf was driving them home later, so she was safe to enjoy a drink. 'I just contacted a few people I know. Your work is clearly the main attraction and speaks for itself.'

It was the right thing to have said, and his smile became a grin. Was she imagining that he'd drawn himself a little higher, too? Probably, and she instinctively took a half step back when he leant in.

'Duty calls. I think I spot one of my collectors.' He winked, and she nodded quickly. 'But let's catch up later, yes? I'd love to show you around properly.'

'That sounds nice.' She refrained from pointing out she could see most of his work from where she stood. She'd agreed in the spirit of moving on and testing the dating pool, as it were. She wandered out to the terrace and found Edmund, happy to catch up on his news as they chatted about the village and how she was enjoying the summer here so far.

She didn't need to see Raf to know the moment he arrived. A murmur flew through the crowd, and she stilled as every single sense flared into complete awareness of his presence. He spotted her above the heads in between and grinned before greeting those he knew, instantly waylaid by a crowd clamouring to say hello. Whether it was the band, his years modelling or just his fame, Cassie had no idea. He carried an aura and a vitality that drew attention with ease, and almost every eye, including her own, was on him. It had only been a few hours since she had seen him, so how could she possibly have missed him? Then Allegra was there, kissing Raf on both cheeks before introducing the older couple, presumably her parents, hovering nearby.

Cassie was caught staring when his gaze sought her out again. His lips pursed in the half smile she knew so well before his attention was claimed by Pippa, and she turned away. Her body was poised and utterly aware of his, as surely as if he had touched her. She spotted Gil, thankful to have a distraction, and squeezed through the gallery to join him. Dorothy was alongside him, having made a rare social appearance, still in her wellies and suit trousers. She spoke kindly to Cassie about Isla's riding and how much help she was providing around the farm.

Again Cassie was glad they had come to Hartfell, Raf's disturbing presence somewhere behind her notwithstanding. A quick glance revealed Pippa introducing him to yet more guests, and Cassie checked her phone, making sure there were no alerts from the teenagers at home. She noticed a small bronze of a kingfisher perched on a stem, wondering if she might indulge if there was no red dot by the end of the evening. Gil excused himself to find Pippa, and Dorothy announced she had seen quite enough animals rendered in metal and was returning to her real ones.

Eventually Raf fought his way to her side and Cassie was rapt when he bent his head, skimming her cheek with his mouth. It was no more intimate than his greeting for Pippa earlier, and yet her breath still caught as warmth stole through her body. Was she imagining his eyes lingering on her, the flare of yearning and pleasure in them? Yet more people were arriving, and they were pressed together as guests moved through the throng. A photographer was busy too, and she melted when she felt the touch of Raf's hand on the small of her back as they faced the camera. Her own smile was more distracted, one hip pressed against him. The photographer moved on, and his hand remained on her back, implying a possessiveness she would have abhorred in anyone but him.

'Do you want to get out of here?' His suggestion and those low words skimming her ear sent her imagination into overdrive. 'We could have a nightcap at home if you like?'

'I can't.' He had made that sound so intimate, even though they sat on the terrace together most evenings while the kids did their own thing indoors. 'I promised Jago I'd stay so he could show me his work.'

'Ah.' Raf's hand slid from her back and he nodded slowly. 'Then I should let you go.'

Cassie nodded dully. She wanted exactly the opposite, to leave right now with him and let the night and his company take them where it would.

'Call me if you still need a lift home. Don't walk back on your own.'

She accepted another glass of champagne as a waiter appeared, and Raf turned away. It was almost impossible not to follow him with her eyes, her body still clamouring for more of his touch. Gradually guests began to drift away, and she had no need to check if he had left; her senses knew it. She went to view the kingfisher again and found it was still available. She wasn't sure if she wanted a permanent reminder of tonight and chose to sleep on it before deciding. Jago was surrounded every time she looked, and when they did eventually catch up, he apologised and suggested meeting another time. She agreed, sharing a goodbye when his taxi arrived.

She helped Pippa and Gil tidy up and they ran her home, so she didn't have to call Raf. He'd left a light on in the kitchen, the house silent, and she gave Flynn a cuddle before letting him into the garden. He was happy to settle

183

back in his bed, and she went upstairs to say good night to Isla and Rory. From the sounds at the end of the corridor, Raf was in his music studio, and she had no wish to disturb him.

In the morning she discovered that he and Rory had already taken their bikes out. Isla was heading to Home Farm, and she grabbed some fruit and snacks, stuffing them into a rucksack. Over breakfast Cassie learnt that she and Harriet were getting Hero the foal used to being handled under Dorothy's expert guidance and taking it in turns to ride her dapple-grey cob. He was proving very steady and sensible, according to Pippa, who had watched one morning.

After her walk with Flynn, Cassie set up her laptop on the kitchen table. During the week she'd had some thoughts about how she might help position the distillery's brand, and she opened a browser. She brought up a website for a hotel which had reopened under new management six months ago following a refurbishment. The hotel was exquisite, exactly the type she was used to working with. Set in landscaped gardens with a brand-new spa in the old stables, it offered high-end luxury and fine dining alongside home comforts. She'd already noted a select few special events: themed evenings with carefully curated menus celebrating a local author, and a famed athlete, champagne tasting with a top brand, wellness weekends set around the spa, and intimate chef's table dining experiences. All perfect for what she had in mind. She sent a connection request to the managing director via her professional networking platform with a brief message introducing herself and the distillery, before following them on Instagram.

Lost in her work and checking out local lifestyle magazines, with Flynn in his basket nearby, she didn't hear Raf and Rory return until they burst into the kitchen from the boot room. Flynn leapt to his feet with a startled bark, before his tail began to wag and Rory rushed to greet him. Cassie's heart softened towards the wolfhound yet more as he nudged Rory to continue. Rory grabbed something from the fridge and offered a last stroke before heading to his room. Practicalities over how they might manage their own dog seemed less important when measured against Rory's increased happiness. He loved to help, making sure Flynn was fed and taking his turn to clear up after him in the garden. Flynn was proving himself to be quiet and calm for the most part, as gentle as he could be for a dog his size. He liked to approach when he wanted a cuddle, and she was aware it wasn't only Rory who had fallen in love with him. He was often at her side, padding through the house.

'Morning. How are you getting on?' Raf smiled and she was doing it again, thinking of his hand on her back last night. His gaze darkening with desire as he'd caught her eye across the gallery, the blaze igniting her skin as she'd waited for him to make his way to her side.

'Yeah, really well, thanks.' She looked at her laptop instead. 'I've emailed a couple of magazine contacts and one of them is definitely interested in running a feature on the distillery. There is a catch, though.'

'Let me guess.' His back was to her as he found a glass and filled it with water from the fridge. Even in muddy Lycra, all sweaty and hot with messy hair, she still found it so difficult to ignore him. He turned and held up the glass questioningly.

'No, thanks, already got one.' Some ice wouldn't go amiss, though.

'They want to include me in the feature?'

'Yep. Sorry.' It was hardly surprising, with his background and looking the way he did. Another gin distillery might not be news, but Raf Jones taking an interest in one could be.

'Hey, don't be sorry. It's not your fault; it goes with the territory.'

'So will you think about it and let me know? They suggested Christmas, so there isn't much time to decide.' She imagined him lounging on a sofa, the house beautifully decorated and welcoming for the festive season, no tie, white shirt, formal jacket hooked over one shoulder. She blinked rapidly. She was getting far too carried away with her own fantasy.

'Why are you shaking your head? Don't you want me to do it?' He pulled out a chair, settling opposite her.

'What?' Cassie blushed furiously, and his mouth curling into a lazy smile told her he had seen. 'No, of course not! I just wasn't sure. You left that world behind a long time ago.'

'Yeah, but I don't mind the occasional shoot. If it's for the good of the distillery brand, of course.' His gaze on her was watchful, and it felt impossible to hide anything from him, even her own thoughts. 'If my publicist promises to be there to hold my hand and deflect any awkward questions.'

'Raf...'

'What? That's not an unreasonable request.'

'No, but we both know I'm not really your publicist.'

'For the summer you are.'

She could hardly refute that when it had been her idea. He grinned as he leant back, knowing he had won. 'So last night was a success. Pippa looked thrilled and I spotted quite a few red dots.'

'Yes, it was fun,' Cassie said casually. 'I love the peace and solitude here, but it was nice to go out for a change.'

'Do you miss London?' Raf rested an arm on the table, his other hand stroking Flynn, who was sitting nearby, huge head on Raf's thigh.

'Less every day,' she told him honestly. 'We miss our friends, but it really does feel as though the most important people in our lives are here now.' She waited a beat. 'What about you?'

'Do I miss it?' His mouth eased into that smile she knew so well, and heat curled in her stomach. 'Barely. Mostly I'm there to see you.'

'And the kids, obviously.'

'Obviously.'

She knew how important Isla and Rory were to him, and yet his eyes were telling her it was more than that. Every day she sensed they were moving towards something else entirely. He reached across the table, his thumb skimming the fingers on her left hand.

'You're not wearing your wedding ring.'

'No. I took it off last night.' Cassie was unsurprised that he had noticed. Her finger looked so empty, and she'd felt almost naked, as though the ring was a barrier fending off the rest of the world. 'It just seemed time.'

'Does it change anything?' Raf's voice was so low that her head jerked up, wondering if she had misheard.

'Like what?'

'How you feel, moving forward.'

187

She knew what he was asking. Did she still feel married, attached to a relationship with his best friend which had endured twenty years. 'It's too soon to say. Probably not much different right now.'

She dragged her mind to safer ground before she allowed herself to fall into that look and where it might lead. 'Do you remember the hotel I told you about, the one with the spa in the stables?'

'I do.' Raf's gaze never left hers, and she was certain he had seen straight through her abrupt shift in conversation.

'I'm waiting to hear back from them, but if they're interested in the distillery, then I think it could be a great fit. Vince mentioned when we met the other day that right now you only sell to the pub and, of course, that makes your brand exclusive. But with the distillery increasing capacity, you're going to need to widen your reach, and the hotel could be ideal. Produce a flavour that's exclusive to the hotel, and if everyone agrees, you could also take part in the occasional event. Exclusive tastings, meet the makers, new product launches, that kind of thing. What do you think?'

'I think you're brilliant and I'm grateful for your help. I love the idea of an exclusive gin for the hotel, and I'm sure Kenny and Vince will too.' He downed his glass of water. 'Right, I'm going to shower.'

'Before you do,' she said idly, 'would you mind sending me a copy of your movie list? I'd love to see what else you've got on there.'

Hopefully, he would assume she was simply keen to avoid sitting through any more romcoms with him rather than suspect her interest was connected to his birthday. Plans were moving on, and Pippa had suggested that Cassie take Raf somewhere for the day so she could set up while he was safely out of the way. Cassie had found an off-road experience for the four of them, so Isla and Rory could have a go on quad bikes, and she and Raf would drive Land Rovers.

'Sure.' He disappeared, and Flynn gave a little whine. He turned to Cassie, plonking his head on her lap instead, and she smiled. He might be missing Raf, but it seemed he was staying with her.

She switched her mind back to work instead of picturing Raf soaking wet upstairs. Distraction aside, it was fun to put her experience to good use without the usual pressures. She emailed the magazine, letting the editor know he was interested. The managing director of the hotel had already accepted her connection request, and an email popped into her inbox shortly after. Raf was back in less than thirty minutes, and she'd switched to an online food shop.

'So how would you like to have dinner at the hotel?' she said casually, saving her basket. 'The hotel has already replied, and the chef patron has sent an invitation to try the tasting menu, to see if you like what they do.'

'On my own?' He frowned as he opened the fridge and removed a pot of blueberries.

'No, not on your own.' Cassie cleared her throat. 'He was kind enough to include me in the invitation as well. It would be a great way to experience the hotel as a guest, and it's so generous of him to suggest it,' she rushed on, ignoring Raf's widening smile. 'We can have a table at seven p.m. next Friday if you're up for it. I know it's the evening before your birthday, but we might be waiting weeks if we say no.'

'I'd love to.' He closed the fridge door, leaning against it to regard her. 'So like a date, yeah?'

'Not a date,' she told him firmly, even though she longed to say yes. It would be all too easy to let such an evening resemble a date, if they chose. 'It's work, Raf. Let's not forget that, even if we do have an exceptional meal to look forward to.'

'Work. Right.' The mischievous grin still lingered. 'But we get to dress up?'

'Of course. It's smart casual, no shorts or trainers.' Cassie mentally ran over the clothes she had brought with her from London, searching for something which would be suitable for a professional evening she hadn't expected. She'd left most of her work outfits behind.

'Then I'm definitely in.'

'And you don't mind the idea of taking part in a few events later on?'

'Not if...'

'I'll be back in London, Raf,' she told him quietly. 'You really don't need me for that.'

'Yeah, but you could come up.'

'What if you don't keep the house?' She wondered about this daily. Already she felt so at home, and it was clear he did too, despite the faded 1980s décor and almost total lack of contemporary comforts, such as underfloor heating and a wireless speaker system in every room, something Rory had told her Raf was looking into.

'I'm thinking about that. Cassie...'

'Jago's asked me to have lunch with him,' she blurted out. She didn't know what Raf had been going to say, but the question had been clear in his eyes. He wanted more and she wasn't ready to say yes, and so she'd rushed out the first thing in her mind that could place a barrier between them. 'He was busy last night, and he didn't get to show me his work.'

'Right. So when are you seeing him?'

'Today, actually, while he's still around for the opening weekend.' She snapped her laptop shut and leapt up. 'I should probably get going. I hadn't realised how late it is. I don't want to keep him waiting.'

'Well, I hope you have a nice time.'

'Thanks.' Cassie was already regretting it. There was simply no point, not when her heart felt as it did. But she'd agreed because maybe it would be another small step into a world in which she dated again. Began the process of putting that kiss with Raf behind her for good.

'So I'll see you later, then.' He made for the door, Flynn at his heels, before turning to face her. 'Cass?'

'What?'

'Be careful, yeah?'

'Of course I will. You don't mind?' Her toes curled. It was exactly the wrong thing to have asked him. To discover if, and how much, he really cared about whom she saw.

'Why would I mind?' His eyes narrowed, and he shrugged. 'It's a good thing, right? Moving on.'

Chapter Fourteen

It's not a date, Cassie muttered crossly for about the tenth time. But it didn't feel that way as she got ready in her room on Friday night, a week after the launch. Anticipation made her clumsy and she'd had to apply eyeliner a second time when she messed up the first. She checked her image in the full-length mirror, satisfied with the woman staring back at her.

Without the kids in the house, still at Home Farm, her strappy nude heels tapping on the stone staircase seemed to echo in the unfamiliar silence.

She opened the sitting room door, and when she saw Raf, she knew she'd got it exactly right. Her plum dress was sleeveless, a high neck rising above a pleated chiffon bodice, the elegant simplicity of the top flowing into a layered asymmetrical skirt in lighter shades of mauve and heather. It was sophisticated and sexy, and a slim bangle in platinum around her wrist and her twenty-first birthday necklace were the only accessories she wore. She touched her wedding ring finger, still empty and strange. She was slowly getting used to its absence, aware it was another step in putting her marriage and not her memories behind her.

'You look incredible,' he murmured as he crossed the room. In her heels, he had only to lower his head to place his mouth against her temple.

'So do you,' she whispered. There was no point in pretending. She hadn't often seen him dressed so formally, more used to the casual, everyday man who lived in shorts and jeans, or cycling kit. His suit was burgundy with a tailored white shirt underneath, and she loved that he'd chosen black Oxfords and gone for a classic look. The top two buttons of his shirt were undone, giving a tantalising glimpse of the angel tattoo beneath and suggesting a playful contrast to the formality of his clothes.

She drew her phone from her bag, needing something to do. 'Is the car here? I thought I saw lights on the drive.'

'Yeah, I just got a text. Shall we?' Raf held out an arm, and she slid hers into the crook at his elbow. 'Did the kids get back to Pippa's okay?'

'Yes, she messaged to say she was feeding them, and she'd drop them back when we get home. We shouldn't be late,' Cassie continued blithely. 'It's only a work dinner.'

But it didn't feel that way when they emerged into the still-warm evening, birdsong clear and cheerful in the trees opposite the house. A black car was waiting, and the driver got out, holding open the back door. She thanked him as she slid onto cool, cream leather seats. Raf followed, and as the door was shut, she couldn't have explained why she suddenly felt so enclosed, so alone with him. Even though they only spoke about ordinary things, he felt so present at her side, the atmosphere charged with everything she couldn't share.

The hotel was only eighteen miles away, but meandering country lanes meant it was a forty-minute drive through the remarkable landscape she had come to love. Eventually the car turned between stone gateposts onto an immaculate drive lined with stately lime trees. The driver was quickly out to open the door and Raf took her hand as she emerged, letting go once she was beside him. He thanked the older man and arranged to text when they were ready to return home.

Painted in a creamy off white, the hotel had four deep sash windows either side of a portico and front door, appearing more intimate and snug than Cassie had expected from online images. Tall stone pots either side of the door were filled with agapanthus flowering midnight blue, and it was the only splash of colour beyond the lawns and mature evergreen shrubs.

'Did I mention they have their own charcuterie on site?' She looked up and his lips pursed in a wry smile. She quivered when he placed his hand on her back as they made for the entrance.

'I don't think you did, no. I have to confess, the finer details of what the hotel offers aren't at the forefront of my mind right now.'

'Well, they should be,' she told him sternly, trying not to fall into the tease he was suggesting, utterly aware of his palm, every single finger, on her chiffon dress, the skirt fluttering around her legs. 'It's all about the details.'

The front door opened and a middle-aged woman in a navy suit emerged to greet them, alongside a younger man. Cassie recognised her as the managing director with whom she had communicated online, and she sensed Raf slipping effortlessly into his more public self as the introductions were made and the woman's face lit up with the usual awe and interest. Sasha was the maître d'hôtel, she explained, and he and his team would be looking after them this evening.

Inside, glasses of vintage champagne were offered and Cassie sipped hers slowly. She didn't want to be tipsy before they'd even sat down. She already knew that the hotel had once been a country home for a wealthy industrialist family and it had retained that same sense of intimacy and comfort, contemporary design in creams, greys and accents of colour sitting well alongside period features. Henry, the chef patron, appeared in his whites, no doubt alerted to their arrival. He kissed her on both cheeks before shaking Raf's hand vigorously, exclaiming his delight that they were here and interested in partnering with his hotel. A small, neat man in his mid-forties, Cassie liked him at once. Henry had a long career in fine dining and a reputation for innovation and elegance. He assured them of his every attention and promised that he was leaving them in the capable hands of his team and hoped they would have a wonderful evening.

'We thought you might prefer the seclusion of our private dining room,' Henry said. 'It was the original library and has a beautiful view of the walled garden. It lends itself perfectly to hosting intimate events, and we like to think it offers an atmosphere of refined elegance and exceptional service for guests wishing to elevate their experience.'

Raf thanked Henry, and although she was relieved at not having to sit opposite him and make conversation in front of other guests, Cassie wasn't sure how she felt about their eating alone. Henry disappeared, and Sasha led them along a corridor past the dining room on the left. Cassie noticed a few guests gaping at Raf and pretending not to, presumably trying to work out if it really was him, or he was just familiar in some way. Thankfully there were no raised phones, and she glimpsed a sweep of perfect lawn leading to a small lake surrounded by ancient trees and beautifully planted borders.

Sasha moved aside to let them enter once he'd opened a door, a waiter following with their champagne. Cassie found herself in a panelled room, its subtle lighting and darker tones immediately suggesting that intimacy Henry had mentioned. The artwork was exquisite, and she made a note to mention it to Pippa, who might have something to offer in the future. The walled garden beyond the windows was a dazzling and exuberant display of mid-summer colours, forms and textures, and she recognised a professional hand at work. Sasha explained that the kitchen garden was extensive and they grew much of the hotel's produce in the grounds. A gleaming circular table which would sit twelve with ease had been moved aside, and Sasha pointed to a much smaller one to the right of a stone fireplace, beautifully set for two in the curve of the bay window.

Cassie murmured her thanks as he pulled out her chair. She sat down, aware of him repeating the gesture with Raf opposite. Napkins were flared, champagne glasses topped up and menus offered, and she found it impossible to meet Raf's gaze once they were alone, the room seeming to echo with all the words she couldn't say.

'So what do you think?' she asked, jumping into the silence. 'Everything I've seen so far suggests the hotel would be perfect for the distillery and would elevate your brand beyond the pub.' She removed her phone from her bag and took a couple of photos so she could refer back later on.

'I agree. I really like it.' He tilted his champagne glass towards her. 'You obviously impressed them enough to pull out all the stops.'

'We both know that's down to you, Raf. I'm just the messenger.'

The door opened to reveal their waiter bearing canapés, and Cassie almost moaned when she tasted tiny scraps of sourdough served with a smoked tomato emulsion and plump green olives. Suddenly she was starving after skipping lunch, and the canapés swiftly vanished as they both tucked in.

'Can't wait to see what's next if that's what they can do with bread.'

'Quite,' she murmured. The champagne had hit her bloodstream, and every sense was elevated, sitting opposite him like this. 'There's a wine flight too, but we probably shouldn't drink too much seeing as it's your birthday tomorrow and we're going off-roading with Isla and Rory.'

'Yeah?' Raf's face lit up, and she loved that she had surprised him. 'That sounds cool. So what else are you planning? I know Pippa's up to something because she said that she's taken me at my word and hasn't arranged anything. I know my sister too well to know that's just not true.'

'I couldn't possibly say.' Cassie arched a brow, feeling playful after the champagne. 'All will be revealed tomorrow. Patience.'

'It's a virtue I'm becoming more familiar with,' he replied drily.

'So how do you feel about turning forty? It's not an age I associate with you yet. Far too grown-up.'

'I'm fine with it, weirdly. I'm ready to embrace everything the next decade brings.'

Their canapé plates already cleared, Sasha returned with their first course proper, which he explained was roasted scallop served with radish, cucumber sauce, a hint of green chilli and finished with cumin. The wine accompaniment was a Reisling from the Columbia Valley in the United States, chosen to offset the scallops' natural sweetness.

Conversation became simpler as they moved through the menu and wine flight, chatting about the distillery, family and the village. Nothing about the end of summer and Cassie's return to London to begin studying for a new career. When they had feasted on lobster, salt-aged duck and lemon sole, she leant back with a sigh.

'That was incredible. If we didn't still have strawberry and chocolate courses to come, I don't think I could eat another thing.' Even the wine hadn't been enough to dull her senses, heightened every single time her gaze met Raf's across the table.

'Me neither.' He toyed with the almost-empty glass in his hand, long fingers tapping a lazy beat against the crystal. 'How was your lunch with Jago? It's been a busy week, and I haven't seen much of you.'

Raf had been at the distillery or studying online most days. Some nights, lying alone in bed, she'd heard faint music from his studio, guitar chords echoing along the corridor. She hadn't gone out of her way to avoid him, but she hadn't sought him out, either. It had helped, not seeing him, with the longing she constantly tried to suppress.

'Oh, that.' Last Saturday already seemed an age ago, and her mind ran over the lunch she'd shared with Jago at the gallery. 'It was fine.'

'Fine?'

'Yes. Pleasant. But I don't think I'll be seeing him again.'

'Oh?'

She hadn't shared the full details with Pippa in case they had any bearing on her best friend's professional relationship with Jago. Pippa had been only too happy to hear that Cassie and Jago were meeting, and in the debrief which followed, Cassie had said that they were both busy and it had helped her realise she wasn't ready to date anyone new yet. It was a version of the truth, and another lesson in not altering relationships from their origins lest anyone be forced to choose later on.

'I think he felt sorry for me,' she said eventually. She picked up her wine glass and put it down again when she realised it was empty. She didn't have to share this with Raf either, but she worried that the fault lay entirely with her and she had little to offer anyone else in the future. Perhaps it wasn't fair to compare a stranger's scant knowledge of her life with the man sat opposite, when they had known each other for so long. So why couldn't she revert Raf to what he had been to her before and allow a return of some peace of mind?

'He felt sorry for you,' he asked incredulously. 'Because of Ewan?'

'No, not that. I got the impression he thought he was doing me a favour by suggesting lunch. That maybe because I'm a widow, my life is quite empty, and he could help liven things up a bit. He managed to turn every question into an anecdote about himself, where he had been, who he knew,' Cassie replied quietly.

'He's been divorced twice and I know that's hardly a red flag, but he did seem to lay the blame squarely with his ex-wives because they apparently couldn't cope with his success. He made sure to tell me which of the great and the good collects his work, and he ended with asking if I'd be interested in acting as his publicist. Not that he really sees the point of one, given his success, but they have their uses, and as I was currently at a loose end and on my own...'

She tailed off. It felt disloyal to Pippa, even saying the words out loud. Raf swore furiously and she looked up in alarm. His eyes had darkened with a danger she had rarely seen. 'Promise me you won't tell Pippa?' she said hastily. 'He didn't do anything inappropriate or threatening. He's just obsessed with himself and he's hardly alone in that. Underneath he's probably very lonely. I thought maybe it was me. I'm so out of practice at these things.'

'Do you want me to go round and bash one of his bloody sculptures into smithereens? Worst case I have to pay Pippa for it. It'd be worth it just to see his face, smug bastard,' Raf said angrily. 'I knew there was something off about him. And it's totally not you. You're amazing and he's a fool if he can't see it.'

Cassie laughed, holding his compliment close. Telling Raf had made those sixty awkward minutes seem much less significant. 'Please don't. Pippa was so happy after the launch and I'm not about to spoil it for her. It's not like he's going to be around that much, and I've deleted him from my contacts.'

'I'm glad to hear it. And if he ever bothers you again, I'll...'

'I can manage him, Raf. I've come across far worse in my career,' she told him softly. 'Would you really do that for me? Bash one of his sculptures?'

'Dead right I would.' Raf drained his glass and a wicked smile followed. 'And I'd love every single minute.'

'You're very bad.' Somehow that came out much huskier than she'd intended. She saw the reply flare at once in his eyes as they narrowed, and he laughed softly.

'You have no idea,' he murmured. That tone, those few words, his look, were more than enough to ignite every nerve ending and a swift kick of desire landed in her stomach. She watched as he touched the napkin to his lips.

'You've missed a bit.' A golden teardrop of wine was caught on his mouth and suddenly she couldn't take her eyes off it.

'Seriously? What am I, five?' He quirked a brow, that lazy smile lingering. 'You do it. I might miss again.'

'Me!'

'Yep. You.' He tugged the napkin from her grasp and dropped it out of reach. Her breath caught at this new game, eyes locked on his bottomless brown ones, and she knew, then. That whatever they told each other about remaining friends and nurturing an affectionate relationship for the sake of her children and their families, they had blown it right out of the water with one single kiss eight months ago. That night in Australia, her desire and her feelings for him had hit her without warning, and whenever he was near, it was almost impossible to think of anything else. She wanted to repeat that kiss over and over. And he knew it. Every look, every touch on her body, told her he wanted the same.

Her finger trembled as she touched it to the corner of his mouth, heard his sharp intake of breath as she caught the teardrop. Without her napkin she had no alternative and her lips parted to lick the wine from her finger. His stare never left hers and Cassie didn't think her pulse had ever pounded so hard in her life. The door behind them opened and she leant back so quickly her chair rocked as Sasha appeared.

She tried to absorb everything he was imparting about their first dessert course and the accompanying wine, but his words were a blur, her mind stuck on those last few moments alone with Raf.

'Cass, there's something you should know before Pippa finds out and lets it slip.' Sasha had left, and Raf's spoon was poised above a caramel and chocolate tart so delicate and beautifully presented she almost thought it would be a shame to eat it.

'I had a drink with Allegra at the pub today. I was already there to meet with Kenny and the timing worked, that's all.' The playfulness from before had vanished and Cassie was poised for bad news. 'I've made an offer on the house, and I heard this afternoon that it was accepted.'

'Raf, that's amazing,' she exclaimed. 'How brilliant, I'm so pleased for you.' Whatever their own future held, it was a thrill to think of him remaining in the house she had come to think of as a home from home. 'Have you told Flynn? I'm sure he'll be over the moon to find out you're staying.'

'Not yet,' he replied drily. 'I wanted you to be the first to know.'

'Well, that's nice, thank you. Congratulations. Pippa will be delighted.'

'Yeah. But how do you feel about it?'

'Raf, much as I love the idea of you staying in Hartfell if it makes you happy, it doesn't change anything for me or the children,' she said quietly. 'We have to go home at the end of summer. But maybe we can stay for the occasional holiday or weekend. Isla and Rory would love that. As friends.'

'Is that what you think we are?'

Cassie didn't have the chance to reply as their second dessert course appeared, followed by coffee and a tempting tray of perfect petit fours. Then Henry, the chef patron, arrived, and Raf assured him that the tasting menu had been superb, and he and his business partners were definitely interested in working with the hotel. She was pleased to have brought the two together and added her own suggestions to future plans. So there was no reason to feel sad that she wouldn't be around to follow the partnership to its fruition and offer help in the future, when she would be back in London.

The intimacy of the conversation with Raf was lost when they were taken on a tour of the wine cellar and the spa. She wished she could immerse herself in the bubble pool and let the water do its work to smooth away all her worries over the future and how she felt about Raf. Their driver returned, and as the car took them home through the darkness, the silence was charged with an atmosphere she recognised. In so many ways, this evening had felt like a date, and she refused his suggestion of a drink in favour of escaping to her room. Something had shifted between them again, and she would confront her feelings once his birthday celebrations were over and she'd had more time to think.

Chapter Fifteen

Cassie was first up in the morning, and she took Flynn for a quick walk around the meadow. When she returned, Isla and Rory were preparing a surprise breakfast in bed for Raf. She fed Flynn as they made French toast with berries and yoghurt, and she nipped out to the garden and picked a rose to go in a vase on the tray. She doubted he'd ever been given flowers from his own home before, a thought which pleased her.

Isla and Rory insisted that she come upstairs too, and Rory knocked loudly on Raf's door. He rearranged the pillows as he sat up and grinned as the teenagers launched merrily into 'Happy Birthday'. His gaze met Cassie's above their heads, and she was glad he reached for a T-shirt to cover the bare chest she had no wish to be distracted by right now. Flynn had followed them up as well, seeming to realise it was a special occasion, and he ambled over, nosing at Raf's hand until it was on his head.

'Thanks, guys, this is a very unexpected and welcome treat.'

'You're always doing nice things for us, so we wanted to do one for you.' Isla settled the tray on his lap then clambered onto the end of the bed, facing him.

'I love it, it's much better than nice. And you've made me my favourite breakfast.'

Rory held out two gifts. 'Happy birthday.' He joined his sister, which left Cassie hovering awkwardly. 'I know you're opening presents tonight, but we wanted you to have ours now.'

'Thank you.' Raf accepted the gifts. 'I'm intrigued. One of them sounds noisy.'

'Mum, sit down.' Isla patted the bed, and Cassie found a spot near the edge, curling her legs beneath her. 'Aren't you going to wish Raf happy birthday too?'

'Oh, yeah.' She laughed, as though it had simply slipped her mind. 'Happy birthday.'

'Thank you.' Ordinarily they'd never used to celebrate anything without sharing a hug, a friendly kiss. But she wasn't about to scramble over the bed and land in his lap in front of the children.

Isla and Rory were impatient for him to finish eating so he could open his gifts. Cassie had no idea what they'd chosen; they'd dipped into their own savings to buy them. She took the tray away once he'd emptied the bowl and he opened Isla's gift first, unable to resist a loud chuckle when he found a pair of brown leather slippers and a pipe Isla pointed out was made of chocolate. He drew her close for a hug, telling her it was perfect now he had his own home and was badly in need of slippers to keep him comfy in his old age. Rory's gift was a Lego set of a classic Land Rover, not dissimilar to the real one on the drive.

'I hope we can build it together,' Rory said earnestly.

Raf promised they could, and then it was Cassie's turn. She handed him a small, gift-wrapped box. He took his time to unwrap it, and when he opened the box and lifted out the leather bracelet inside, she tried to bat away its significance.

'I know you've already got bracelets.' She pointed to his left wrist, as though he might've forgotten there were several wrapped around it. 'But I saw this, and it felt right…'

He raised the two strands of dark brown leather held together with a silver bead ring to admire it and turned it over to read the words inscribed on the ring.

'What does it say?' Rory shuffled up for a closer look.

'It's the opening lyrics of our last number one single.' Raf found his phone to enlarge the image so Rory could read it, too. His eyes met Cassie's over her son's, and she read the surprised delight in them. There had been plenty of number-one singles and albums down the years, and she'd chosen this one because although he'd been credited, with Jonny writing the music, she was one of the very few who knew that Raf had written every line. Most of the recent Blue at Midnight songs were a collaboration, and he preferred to keep it that way as far as the world was concerned.

'That's really cool, Mum, I love it.'

'So do I,' Raf said softly, and there was nowhere else for Cassie to go when he leant across, not unless she threw herself off the bed. 'It's perfect.'

His lips were gentle against her cheek when he kissed it, the rough scratch of his beard brushing her skin. One arm went around her, and her pulse spiked again as he drew her close. She allowed herself a moment to indulge the pleasure her gift had brought him, then eased free.

'I'll take your tray down,' she said casually. 'Come on, Flynn, let's give the birthday boy some peace.'

They left for the off-road experience after a light brunch, Cassie driving. Raf was busy on his phone, replying to the birthday notifications still pouring in. He'd mentioned that he'd been invited to take part in an interview with a music magazine, reflecting on the end of his career and talking about new plans, but he'd turned it down for now. Calls also came from Jonny and his half-brother and sister in Australia, as well as his sister Tilly in her Greek B&B, and he was still chatting with her when they finally arrived at the off-road centre.

Once they'd sat through the safety briefing, Isla and Rory couldn't wait to get out on the quad bikes. They adored the experience, belting along muddy tracks as fast as they were allowed. Rory was a natural, and Raf was at his side as Cassie and Isla kept up a few lengths behind. When it was time to drive the Land Rovers, Rory opted to join Raf while Isla sat in the back of Cassie's vehicle. She enjoyed it more than she'd expected, climbing steep and rutted mounds and slithering down the opposite side. They shared high fives when they were done, and she checked her phone after a coffee, making sure Pippa was ready for them to return. As they approached the house, Isla insisted on blindfolding Raf with a scarf so he couldn't sneak a peek or identify guests from their cars outside.

Isla and Rory tucked their arm through his as they led him past the house and into the walled garden, with Cassie in front. She'd texted a five-minute warning to Pippa and couldn't stifle a laugh when five dogs came charging across the lawn. Lola and Maud were followed by Flynn, Bramble and Briar, and she turned around to see the children removing Raf's blindfold as the opening notes of Stevie Wonder's 'Happy Birthday' hit the outdoor speakers. They were first to hug him before they took off, and with everyone else approaching, Cassie only had a moment.

'I hope you don't mind,' she said softly. 'But watching one of your movies all together seemed like a nice idea, and everyone who loves you wanted you to have a special day.'

'Mind?' His hand caught hers as she went to step aside. 'It's perfect.'

A huge screen was set up at the far end of the lawn, surrounded by rows of fairy lights running along the rows of chairs facing it. A gazebo stood to the right, the tables inside it made from old beer barrels Pippa had borrowed from Kenny and Vince, set amongst more chairs and a couple of sofas scattered with cushions and blankets. A firepit was burning, the orange glow reflected in the sun beginning to slide behind the fell, and Pippa was the first to reach her brother and wish him well. Then it was Harriet's turn, followed by Alfie and Jacob, who shook his hand, then Gil and his two sons, Joel and Luca. Fiona and Gordon hugged Raf as well, and Kenny and Vince were here too, a flying visit before service at the pub. Cassie was keen to make herself useful after missing the preparations while they'd been out, and Fiona came to help.

Yesterday at Home Farm she and Pippa had made spiced pork belly and a butternut squash version roasted the same way, which they served with black beans baked with feta cheese, coriander and tacos. Pudding was individual servings of ice cream in tubs to eat with popcorn during the movie, and afterwards they'd light the candles on the chocolate birthday cake Violet and Daphne had sent. Gil was in charge of the projector to screen the movie, and it was his and Pippa's birthday gift to Raf so he could watch more movies outdoors.

The food soon vanished, and the teenagers went indoors hunting for leftovers. Cassie made sure everyone had drinks and was comfortable when they sat down to watch the movie a bit later. The fairy lights glittered through the dusk in their snug cinema, and her heart lifted again when she saw Isla and Rory laughing with the others. They'd been right to celebrate Raf's birthday this way, and she knew it from his gaze constantly finding hers. He'd tried to persuade her to confess which movie she'd chosen as she took her seat next to his, but she'd playfully refused and told him to wait.

His hand found hers through the darkness to squeeze it when the opening credits of *E.T.* began to roll. Thankfully, the teenagers didn't grumble about watching a movie so old, and she had to brush away a tear more than once. It always got her; it was such a sweet story of friendship and fun. Once it was over, the younger ones huddled together with the last of the ice cream tubs, Cassie went to fetch the cake, and Pippa offered to help with replenishing drinks. In the kitchen she opened the high cupboard where she'd hidden the cake. There were too many dogs around to leave such a tempting treat within reach, and she heard Pippa behind her.

'Isn't it a wonderful evening? Thank you for everything you and Gil have done. Raf seems thrilled and I'm so happy we managed to surprise him.'

'You definitely did surprise me. And I love every single detail, so thank you.'

'Oh, hey!' She slammed the cupboard door, hoping Raf hadn't spotted his cake or the black and gold fortieth birthday topper. She whirled around to see him propped against the table, hands resting on it. 'I thought you were Pippa.'

'I offered to help you instead. Pippa told me all this is down to you.'

'It absolutely isn't. Pippa's done as much as me, and she and Gil have been setting up half the afternoon.' Cassie cleared her throat. 'So would you mind fetching more champagne, please?'

'In a minute.' He was wearing a pair of vintage 501s with a turn up and the black retro T-shirt Tilly had sent him, the year of his birth emblazoned across it in blue, yellow and pink. He looked dangerous and desirable, and suddenly far too close. 'I wanted to see you first.'

'Oh. Well, if you're going to thank me again, there's really no need.' She laughed, hoping it didn't sound as forced as it felt. She didn't need to hear that rough note in his voice or allow herself to fall into that dark brown gaze.

'You do so much for us, and a nice birthday was the least I could do in return. And now you can tick another movie off your list. Why don't you go back outside? I'll get the champagne.' She wanted him in the garden when the cake was carried out, candles blazing and everyone singing.

She went to the fridge and opened the door, a welcome blast of cool air following as she removed a bottle of fizz. Raf hadn't budged, and as she went to pass him, he caught her hand. Cassie meant to free herself, to restore the distance she worked hard to maintain, but instead she was breathing him in, the scent of amber and something spicier in his cologne, alerting her to danger. She'd drunk a couple of glasses of champagne, nowhere near enough to make her take total leave of her senses, and yet…

'Are we ever going to talk about that night and what it meant?' he asked softly. She could barely think with his fingers idly stroking hers, tracing a pattern her mind couldn't follow. Even her cotton shirt suddenly felt way too hot. Slowly, she looked up. His gaze was burning on hers and she daren't tell him the truth: that she couldn't get past that night and their kiss, and she wanted more. So much more, and somehow her fingers were still around his, the heat of his touch lighting a blaze across her skin.

'We are past it,' she muttered. 'We're friends again and that's all we can ever be. Nothing happened.'

She repeated the mantra that lived in her head, the one she clung to when she woke in the night dreaming of Raf and all she wanted to share with him. But something *had* happened in Australia, and it wouldn't go away, no matter how often she tried to force it, tormented by the memory of being in his arms and how he'd felt against her, his mouth demanding and insistent and perfect on hers.

'And what if I don't want to be friends with you anymore? There isn't anyone who gets me like you do. No one who makes me feel the way you do.'

She'd never heard his voice like this, so low and somehow lazy, planting every single word deep in her heart. She couldn't offer any resistance when he eased her between his legs and took the bottle. Cassie was melting, longing to fall into his embrace and have him hold her in all the ways she dreamt of. He ran his hands very slowly from her shoulders to her wrists, and her limbs were turning to liquid, heat pooling in her body and demanding satisfaction with every brush of his palms. His own breath was ragged and uneven, and she was desperate to repeat every lesson she'd learnt that night in just one kiss.

'Do you want me to stop?'

'Raf, please,' she told him helplessly. She couldn't hold back a gasp when his languid gaze fell to her mouth, her lips parting as willingly as if he'd skimmed them with his own.

'Please stop, or please don't?'

'What is it you want from me?' she whispered. She knew his reply before he uttered it; she wanted exactly the same. But after that, what would their friendship be then?

'Everything,' he told her roughly. He took her hands and placed them on his face, the beard grazing her skin in the way she found so tantalising. 'Tell me you don't feel it too, Cass, and I'll walk away. Tell me what's in your heart.'

'I can't.' There were only a few scraps of sense remaining, and she was clinging to them, her last little bit of composure before she fell too far. She would have nowhere left to go if she told him that.

'You know I wouldn't be touching you like this if I thought you didn't feel the same.'

Cassie inched towards him until his thighs were pressed against hers, holding her in his orbit with eyes revealing even more than his words and uneven breath had. Her thumbs were stroking his face, mesmerised by the gold in his gaze and longing he'd never revealed so nakedly before. He turned his face to catch her thumb between his teeth, and she bit back a cry as his lips closed around it.

'Do you want me to stop?' he repeated.

'You know I don't,' she whispered. She couldn't disguise her body's reply any more than she could walk away, and she slid her thumb free to cup his face. 'But what about when it's over? My children love you, Raf, they need me to be your friend. I can't sneak around behind their backs.'

'And why would it have to be over?' He frowned. 'You think I haven't changed, that I can't commit? Is that it? I know it's complicated, but we didn't do anything wrong when we kissed. Let me be there for you, and Isla and Rory. My life is different now, and I'm done with the band, travelling, the bullshit that comes with it. This is who I am, Cass. The man standing here, asking for a chance to stand still with you.'

His hands were on her shoulders, sure and firm, and she was falling. Falling into his strength and confidence, the desire he had made plain. But her body was screaming that it wasn't complicated it all. That their next move was very simple and she only needed to touch her lips to his again, and she would be flying and falling all at once.

'I'm frightened of never feeling this way again, and terrified of taking another step,' she told him with a trembling voice. 'But please don't say something you don't mean. All I need is to look after my family. I don't know how to make room in my life for anything else.'

'I meant every single word, and one day I hope you'll feel differently. And I'll be there, waiting for you.' He dropped the words against her ear, and she clutched his arms as his lips skimmed her neck. There was such certainty in his promise, and she wanted to tell him not to wait, that maybe she'd never be ready. But she couldn't disguise how she felt; it simply wasn't possible when he made her feel so alive, hopeful and happy.

Footsteps were approaching along the passage, and Cassie leapt back just before Fiona appeared, a blush staining her cheeks scarlet.

Chapter Sixteen

After that conversation with Raf, Cassie moved through the next week on autopilot as the children's holiday in Italy approached. She had coffee with Pippa at the gallery, debriefing his birthday and burning up every time she thought of those few moments alone with him in the kitchen. She cleaned for Fiona and Gordon, cooked meals for their freezer to help lighten their load, and swam in the river with the Wednesday walking group. She walked Flynn and wrote her journal, trying to disguise her exhilaration and the sense that she was on the brink of another life-changing decision. Raf was polite and friendly, and she found excuses for things she needed to do if Isla and Rory weren't home. Their own excitement about Italy was building, with Jas arriving on Friday afternoon, ready for the flight on Saturday.

Jas brought another level of energy to the house, and Isla and Rory couldn't wait to show her around. Cassie did her best to disguise her anxiety over the children travelling without her, but she trusted Jas and knew she would take good care of them. The next morning Isla and Rory wanted Raf to come with them to the airport. Once Cassie had seen them safely checked in, she wandered back to the car with him in a daze. For the first time in her life after Ewan, the children were away without her, and she felt a bit lost. Maybe the sense of freedom would kick in later. She and Raf watched a movie in the evening, no sense of intimacy or awkwardness as they sat through *Rain Man*. She'd invited Fiona and Gordon over for lunch on Sunday as Pippa and Gil were taking Harriet, Joel and Luca to meet friends of Gil's.

They ate on the terrace, and afterwards she was in the kitchen, supposedly making coffee, when Fiona found her staring blankly through the window.

'Are you all right?' Fiona touched a hand to her shoulder and Cassie spun around. 'I know you're worried about Isla and Rory, but they'll have a blast, and Jas is perfectly capable.'

'I'm fine,' she said automatically, waking up the coffee machine again. 'I know you're right, but there's still that stupid voice reminding me of all the ways it could go wrong.'

'Believe me, that voice never quite goes away, no matter how old they are.' They shared an understanding smile. 'And you're only a couple of hours away in the very unlikely event of them actually needing you. It's a mum thing, but please, try not to worry.'

'I will, thanks.' She may as well try and stop breathing, but the sentiment was the right one. 'Coffee will be ready in a minute.'

'I hope you don't mind me asking, but is everything all right between you and Raf?'

Cassie nearly dropped the espresso mug she'd been holding. She shoved it in place as the coffee machine went to work. Oh hell, she should have known Fiona would notice. 'Of course it is. Why would you think otherwise?'

'I'm not sure, you just seem… a little tense, I suppose. As does he. There are a lot of things that aren't my business, and I simply want to know that you're both okay.'

'We're fine,' Cassie assured her. 'Really, we are. I'm distracted about the children, that's all, but it'll pass. I didn't sleep that well last night.'

'And you're certain there's nothing else worrying you, something I can help with?'

She longed to confess, but she could never do that, not to her mother-in-law. To share this secret she carried and have Fiona tell her that it was wrong to feel the way she did about a man she'd known most of her life and had never thought of in the way she did now. Fingers trembling around the cup of espresso, she set it on a tray.

'Nothing else,' she said firmly. 'Why don't you join the others, and I'll bring the coffees in a minute.'

'Before you do...' Fiona hesitated. 'I promise we're not ganging up on you, but I spoke with Pippa this morning and we thought it would do you the world of good to get away and have a complete rest while Isla and Rory are on holiday.'

'Away?' Cassie's brows shot up as she stared at Fiona before she managed a laugh. Until this summer her life had been built around her family and her career, and she was still getting used to not working full time, her body adjusting to a new rhythm. 'But I am away, I'm here. And I don't need a rest. I'm fine.'

'I disagree,' Fiona replied in a tone that Cassie recognised. 'Pippa's already had a word with Jonny, and the house in Majorca is free. There's a flight tomorrow and we made an executive decision and booked two seats.'

'A flight? To Majorca? Why would I go there?' She laughed again, because the suggestion was crazy and ridiculous and... 'What do you mean, seats? Is Pippa coming with me?'

'No, Raf is. Pippa rang him and he agrees the rest would be good for you.'

'But he never said!' Cassie's chest felt tight, the pulse in her throat pounding. Her mind raced to the old Mediterranean house Pippa's dad had owned since his children were young, where they'd all retreated over the years. How could she be there with Raf, swimming in the pool, lounging in the heat of the day and those long, still nights. He'd tried to speak with her earlier and she'd put him off, making some excuse about being busy with the lunch. 'Absolutely not. Besides, there's you and Gordon to consider. I'm supposed to be keeping an eye on you.'

'No arguments.' Fiona held up a hand. 'Pippa and Gil will look after Flynn. Plus the last time I checked, Gordon and I were a pair of reasonably fit and capable sixty-somethings who are more in the habit of keeping an eye on other people rather than needing my delightful daughter-in-law to watch over us. So please go while you can, it will do you good. You can fly to Italy from Majorca just as easily as you can from here if you have to.'

'Fiona, it's…' Cassie was wavering, searching for a reason to refute all arguments and anchor herself to this house, where it was easier to avoid Raf than in a sunlit villa high in the hills above the Majorcan coast. 'I don't know whether to laugh, cry or be cross. Don't I get any say in this?'

'It is, my darling, a done deal. I'll even drive you to the airport myself. Now let's have our coffee and then we'll leave you to pack.'

—

The flight on Monday afternoon was uneventful, other than Cassie alternating between anxiety at Isla and Rory being away and spending the next five days alone in a villa with Raf. They would be flying back on Saturday, due to land a few hours before the children, and she'd already decided the weekend couldn't come soon enough. Before they'd left she'd tried to persuade Pippa to abandon the plan as well, but her best friend was having none of it; she and Fiona had united against her. Only Cassie, and no doubt Raf, understood the next few days were likely to do nothing whatsoever for her wellbeing. She'd loathed saying goodbye to Flynn, promising she'd walk him again just as soon as she was home. Harriet had promised to send regular updates, but Cassie didn't dare think about the end of the summer when she would have to leave him behind for good.

There hadn't been time to buy any clothes suitable for a few days in the Med and have them delivered before they'd left. Almost everything she'd brought from home had been with a Yorkshire summer, not a Mediterranean one, in mind. She'd picked up a few things at the airport, focusing on reading by the pool all day and not stripping down to a swimsuit with Raf around.

A car was waiting when they retrieved their bags, and despite her reservations, outside she was transfixed by a cornflower-blue sky and the heat seeping into her body, staring at dry and rocky mountains dusted with green. Traffic and tourists were plentiful as they skirted the city and headed northwest towards a harbour town close to the villa. She was utterly conscious of Raf at her side, his suntanned legs bared by cargo shorts, the growing silence punctuated with casual comments as he pointed out local landmarks. He'd assured her he planned to work much as usual while they were away, continuing with his online training course. So at least he would have that to keep him busy.

She'd forgotten how dazzling the house was, and as the driver approached it, a pair of rustic wooden gates slid open. Nestled amongst evergreen hedges and colourful planting, stately olive trees bordered a gravel drive leading to a terracotta stone building, welcoming and warm, cream shutters framing every window above more olive trees in pots, dark green against hot-pink rock roses planted between them. High stone walls enclosed the boundaries, the hillside beyond dotted with trees and rocky crags. The heat hit her again as they got out of the cool interior of the car, and she turned her face up to the sun to enjoy it for a moment.

'Ready to go inside? It'll be cooler on the terrace.' The driver had retrieved their bags, and Raf thanked him.

So this was it. They were alone here, with this incredible hideaway all to themselves, and she had no idea how she was going to manage for five days. And those sultry Mediterranean nights.

'I'd love to.' The nervous note in her reply suggested something other than the casual comment she'd been aiming for, and she cleared her throat.

Raf stood back so she could enter the cool white hallway, and her exclamation was one of pure pleasure. Oak and wicker furniture was rustic and simple, and she recognised two of Pippa's paintings on the walls. A formal sitting room was to her right, with a pair of white sofas scattered with blue cushions. Ahead two glass doors opened onto the gleaming kitchen, a corridor to the left.

'It's so beautiful,' she said, risking a glance at him. 'I'd forgotten how much.'

'Yeah. The bedrooms are along there.' He pointed to the corridor, and Cassie couldn't miss the brisk note in his voice. 'You can have the master; there's a private terrace and a path leading to the pool.'

'Raf...'

'Don't even think about protesting.' He shot her a smile as he put their bags down. 'You came here for rest and relaxation, and it's my job to see that you get it.'

'Is that what Fiona and Pippa told you?'

'No, I decided all by myself.'

'But where do you usually sleep?'

'Anywhere.' He shrugged as they headed for the kitchen. 'There are four bedrooms, usually we crash wherever we can. I'll probably take the room upstairs; the rest are down here.'

At least that meant there would be a staircase between them. They hadn't spent a night in such close proximity since Australia, and she couldn't afford to think about that now. Their conversation on his birthday sat wedged between them. Cassie thought about it constantly, trying to balance her desire against the future. But she was a grown-up; she could do this.

'Maybe you'd like a nap when I've shown you to your room?'

'I'm not a toddler,' she told him exasperatedly. 'I can't let myself get used to sleeping every afternoon. Wow, this isn't how I remember the kitchen.'

'No, Dad extended it after Phoebe and Freddie were born, and it had an upgrade last year.'

Oak cabinets and pale marble tops gleamed against more white walls, photos of the family over the years scattered in the spaces between. This home, away from Jonny's life in the band, had been the children's solace after they'd lost their mum. A home where they could just be a normal family and hold one another close.

Windows offered views of a glorious garden, with more lush planting amongst evergreen hedging and low stone walls framed by lavender. Raf went to the bi-fold doors, opening them wide onto the terrace and a pergola smothered in passion flowers, three sofas nestled beneath it. Beyond that stood a glass-topped dining table and eight chairs, the terrace bordered by another lavender hedge and tall agapanthus in terracotta pots, vivid blue against green. But it was the rectangular pool that captured her attention and had her rushing outdoors. Surrounded by neat lawns and wide stone paths, loungers sat on three sides of the pool beneath closed parasols.

'It's so beautiful! Maybe Fiona and Pippa had a point, I can't wait to swim.' Cassie kicked off her pumps, the stone hot beneath her feet. 'Thank you for coming with me.' Already the sun was doing its work, loosening her shoulders, easing her mind.

'You're welcome,' he said impassively. 'So why don't I take your case to your room, and you can change and do just that.'

'Thanks.' She wasn't going to think about the last time he'd seen her in a swimsuit, that night on the beach in Galloway when they'd talked, and he'd given her his T-shirt to keep her warm. 'I might never want to leave here.'

She followed him to her room, already in love with the space for as long as it was hers. She went to the doors and opened them to discover the private sitting area he'd mentioned, beneath a canopy. A neat wrought-iron patio table and two chairs were surrounded by pots filled with rosemary and lavender, their scents perfuming the air. To her right stood a trellis smothered in abundant bougainvillea winding its way to the sky, separating her patio from the terrace further along. Barefoot, she followed the stepping stones set into the grass until the shimmering water of the pool was revealed.

'I think I've landed in paradise.' She laughed softly, scrunching her toes against the grass. 'I adore it.'

'Good.' Raf backed away. 'So why don't you have that swim, and when you're ready, I'll make us dinner.'

'Don't we need to go shopping first?' That hadn't even occurred to her, perhaps a sign of a new relaxation.

'Nope.' He flashed her a grin from the bedroom door. 'I had everything sent ahead and we have a housekeeper for when we're not around. There are some advantages to being a rock star, even an ex one.'

Cassie was still smiling after he'd left. He'd mentioned there was a regular market in the town at the bottom of the hill which sold everything, and she hoped to find a few more summer clothes. Her cut-off jeans were far too hot, so back in her room she took them off, opening her case in search of something lighter. She changed into the navy swimsuit she'd worn in her gym days, a practical design cut low on the legs and ruched, with wide straps running across her shoulders.

It wouldn't win any prizes for the sexiest swim wear, but she felt comfortable in it, slipping a loose blue and white kimono over the top, with sleeves that fell to her elbows and a gather around the waist to fasten it. She'd bought the kimono online ages ago and had never worn it, so it wasn't until she glanced in the full-length mirror that she realised it was made of a see-through mesh, revealing every curve she was trying to keep hidden.

There was nothing she could do about that now, and she stepped onto the terrace, dark glasses shielding her eyes from the glare. Beyond the shade of her canopy, the late afternoon sun was fierce as she strolled as nonchalantly as she could manage to the pool, trying not to think of Raf watching. She chose one of the loungers furthest away and set down a towel and suncream. She went to slide the kimono off and forgot to untie it, so after a minor battle with the belt, it eventually fell to the floor in a rustle of fabric.

The steps were at the opposite end, so she walked around the pool and sank into the water, deliciously cool on her skin. She forgot her discomfort as she began to swim, managing a few lengths to satisfy a vague sense that she ought to exercise. She flipped onto her back and shielded her face with a hand, still ineffectual against the glare. After fifteen minutes she returned to her lounger and dried herself, applying suncream before she lay down and closed her eyes.

'Hey. Sorry to wake you.'

'Huh?' Cassie blinked, squinting behind her sunglasses to see Raf sitting sideways on the lounger next to hers. 'How long have I been asleep?'

'About forty minutes. I brought you some water and a coffee. I wasn't sure if you meant to stay out here so long.'

'Thanks.' She sat up, casually reaching for the discarded kimono and draping it around her. 'I didn't mean to fall asleep, but it's so gorgeous, and it seemed a shame to be indoors.'

'It is, but your shoulders are already turning pink.'

'Oh!' She checked and pulled a face. 'So they are. Thanks for waking me, and the drinks.'

'You're welcome.'

'What time is it?'

'Almost six. I thought we could eat around seven if that works for you?'

Was she imagining the new distance in his gaze as he looked away, the cool note in those few words? Was he already regretting this trip, bored of babysitting her because her best friend and her mother-in-law thought she needed some time away. She very much doubted they'd have suggested Raf accompany her if they knew the truth about her betrayal and what she had done.

'That sounds nice,' she replied stiffly, taking a long drink of iced water. 'Raf, seriously, please don't feel you have to look after me, or cook every meal. I want to do my share.'

'Cass, you've always taken care of everyone else. Let me look after you.'

'Why would you do that?'

'Just because.' Aviator sunglasses were perched on his head, and he was busy on his phone, fingers running over the screen.

She picked up the book she'd brought, but the words were a blur with Raf on the lounger beside her. Once he'd finished his coffee, he stood and pulled the T-shirt over his head, diving into the pool in one fluid movement. The book was propped on Cassie's bended legs, but she stared as he sliced efficiently through the water. She swallowed when he hauled himself out, aware of him strolling towards her, picking up a towel and running it over his body.

'I think I've been out here long enough.' She stood hastily and gathered her things, too rattled even to slide the kimono around her shoulders. In her room she took a cool shower and moisturised her pink body, heart clattering at the thought of the hours ahead with Raf. She chose a green maxi dress and returned barefoot to the kitchen, hoping to beat him to it. But he was already there, and he glanced up from the marble island in the centre.

'Cocktail?' His hair was still damp, and he'd changed out of the swim shorts into cargo ones, a casual shirt half buttoned. 'I thought you might like a negroni.'

'I'd love one, thanks.' She pulled out a stool at the island, watching as he deftly mixed their drinks, thanking him when he slid a glass across. The twist of orange was sharp against vermouth, Campari and gin when she tasted it. 'I could get used to bad habits like this. Cocktails before dinner, eating al fresco.'

'But it's never the same at home, is it?' His own smile was wistful as he sliced plump ruby-red vine tomatoes, layering them on a plate with mozzarella and basil before drizzling them in salt and olive oil, and her mouth watered greedily.

'That looks incredible. I could eat the lot.'

'I can always make more. And it's just a salad, nothing special.'

She thought of the pool earlier, and how she'd wanted to join him in the water, to press herself against his wet and nearly naked body. Already her resolve to be careful around him was weakening. She couldn't help but recall the kiss they had shared in Australia and how he'd held her close on his birthday in the kitchen with barely even a touch, just the heat of his words and his stare. She twirled her glass between trembling fingers, afraid he could read her desire for him laid bare.

'It's ready.' Raf gathered a few scraps and dropped them into a bin. 'Shall we eat on the terrace? It's perfect out there now.'

'I'd love to.' Cassie leapt up from her stool, almost knocking it over in her distraction. He directed her to the appropriate drawer for cutlery and soon they were sat beneath the passionflower vines clambering amongst the pergola. A breeze was faint but welcome, and in the distance she glimpsed the tall spire of the church and rooftops in the town below, the deep blue of the sea rippling beyond the harbour.

Along with the salad, there was fresh crusty bread, olive oil in a jar without a label that he explained came from a neighbour, cured ham and roasted vegetables. She was ravenous, and they finished everything, including the chilled bottle of Albarino he'd opened after cocktails. As the evening moved on and darkness fell, they moved to the sofas. Conversation became easier and they were laughing and teasing one another about a story from long ago.

Her phone pinged with a message notification, and she saw it was from Jas. She slid the phone across to show him. 'I don't think anyone's missing me. My mother's taken the kids out on a friend's boat and they're obviously having a fabulous time.'

'Rory looks so happy.' Raf scrolled through the images before returning her phone. 'You're not missing them too badly?'

'Not as much as I expected. I know they're in great hands with Jas, and my mother's not entirely without sense.' Cassie gestured to the terrace, the pool and the view. 'Maybe it's being here. Holidays always feel like leaving real life behind.' She paused, blinking back a moment of sorrow. 'It feels strange, if I'm honest, to realise I'm becoming more redundant in their lives now they're growing up, especially after everything...'

'Hey.' His hand covered hers. 'Look at me.'

She almost didn't dare for fear of what she'd find. His gaze was full of compassion and something else, something dangerous she'd seen before. She squeezed her eyes together to prevent a tear from escaping. There had been so many, but sometimes they still caught her unawares, often in moments that she recognised were happy ones, too.

'You're doing so great and the kids are amazing. You've come such a long way.'

'Thank you for saying that. It still takes my breath away sometimes, when I remember this is the rest of our lives, and Ewan isn't coming back.'

'I know, I get it. It was years before I finally accepted my mum was really gone.'

'I'm sorry.' She threaded her fingers between his and squeezed, wanting him to understand she was mindful of his own loss, too. That it wasn't all about her.

'It's okay, we all have to do what we can to carry on. I think Pippa and Fiona were right about you coming here. I want you to be happy.'

'I am, really.' She slid her hand away. It was the truth, and she was gradually learning to accept it. 'I just need some time to adjust to not being a mum twenty-four seven. I think I'll head to bed. Sorry, do you mind if I clear up in the morning? The wine's really caught up with me.'

'No, you go.' Raf stood and she waited to see if he would come around the table to kiss her good night. Once, she would've hugged him, an ordinary gesture between friends, and she glimpsed the same thought lingering in his gaze before she made herself walk away. Being so close to him when they were completely alone here would be a step too far. Danger lurked in every single look, every accidental touch.

'Night, Cass,' he murmured. 'Sleep well.'

'You too.'

In her room she freshened up and changed, still restless after she'd got into bed. Sleep was something that came and went now, and she'd tried most things to help. When she did wake in the night she'd learnt not to fight it, but to accept the wakefulness and understand that sleep would eventually come again. Usually she wrote in her journal, and in the morning she'd wonder at the thoughts she'd recorded, the worries her mind seemed to find in the hours of darkness.

She dozed off and woke later with a start, her lamp still bright and the book in her hand. She set it aside and got up, opening the doors onto the patio, the white muslin curtains wafting gently. Stars glittered above her, a pale moon reflected in the pool. She walked towards it, the night air cooling her warm body, and halted abruptly when she saw Raf sitting on the terrace.

His head was bent over an acoustic guitar, fingers finding the chords as he played. Cassie wanted to back away, to leave him to his solitude and respect his privacy. But the words and music drifting on the darkness formed a song, and she froze. It seemed as though his heart was laid bare as he sang of a love he had to leave time and again, the lyrics and the tune piercing her soul. When it ended, he looked up.

'I didn't know you were there.'

'I'm sorry,' she blurted out. 'I wanted some air. I didn't mean to disturb you.' She hesitated. 'You sounded incredible. Did you write it?'

She didn't need his brief nod; she'd known it already. 'I was just playing around. Couldn't sleep.'

'I love it, because you wrote it.' Her feet were walking her towards him as though she had no control over where they might step. 'It was beautiful.'

Shoulders hunched over the guitar, his arms resting on it, Raf's stare was fixed on her, lit by a faint glow from the kitchen. She crouched down and took his hands.

'Please tell me you're not writing songs like that and still hiding them away?'

'What else am I meant to do?'

'Share them,' Cassie told him simply. 'Let other people listen and understand what an incredible musician you are. You earned your place, Raf, you're brilliant. I hope you know it.'

'And what if no one else thinks that?' His laugh was a brief one. 'Half my life I've got by on how I look and who my dad is. Being at the back on the drums was my safe place.'

'At heart you're a musician, and I don't think I truly realised that until just now. You have a wonderful voice and so much to say. Please don't forget that.'

'Maybe one day I'll believe in myself as much as you do.'

He freed her hand to cup her face, pulling her into his gaze and the promise she found there. He stood and tugged her upright, until she was between his legs. She was poised for Raf to make the first move, one she needed to give her confidence and let her know this would be okay.

'You should go back to bed,' he muttered. He let go and stepped past her, shattering the spell.

'Is that what you want?' she whispered.

At the door he turned, his face revealed by the moonlight. 'You know it's not. But I need you to be as sure as I am, to feel what I feel. I understand it's different for you, and I don't want any more regrets if we do this.'

Chapter Seventeen

Cassie wasn't expecting to sleep in until nine a.m., and she reached for her phone to make sure she hadn't missed anything from Jas and her children, relaxing back onto the pillows to enjoy the new images they'd sent. There was a message from Raf, too, letting her know he'd gone down to the market in town and hadn't wanted to disturb her. She sent him a quick reply and put the phone aside. Sun was shimmering through the white curtains, and she hurried out of bed to open the doors onto her patio and welcome the day.

Mornings at home were usually frantic ones, time somehow seeming to slip away twice as fast as she'd got ready for work and seen Isla and Rory off to school. Here it was so different, the grass damp underfoot, the path around the pool already hot beneath her bare feet. The water looked so inviting, shimmering against blue tiles reflecting the sky, and she threw a glance at the closed kitchen door, the empty terrace. Really she ought to go back for her swimsuit and suncream, but the house was silent and Raf was at the market. She was alone, and she'd only be in the pool a few minutes.

She swiftly removed her white silk camisole pyjamas before she changed her mind. She walked down the steps, the water delightfully cool. She'd skinny-dipped plenty in the past and it was wonderfully freeing to swim naked now. But she had no idea when he would be back, and Cassie didn't want to get caught out. Not after last night, and how they'd parted. She left the pool and stood beneath the outdoor shower, rinsing the chlorine away. Already the sun was hot, and she tipped her head back, shaking the water from her hair.

Her pyjamas were on a lounger, so she darted across the terrace, leaving wet footprints on the path. She grabbed them and pulled the shorts on, hopping in her haste, and dragged the top over her head just as the bi-fold doors opened and Raf stepped out. There was nowhere to hide, not unless she dived straight back in the pool. She faced him nonchalantly, trying to pretend that her pyjamas weren't already soaking and clinging to every curve.

'Morning. I hope I didn't wake you. So how did you…' The shopping bags slid from his hands and crashed onto the terrace. 'Sorry. I didn't realise you were… Er, that you…'

'Have been swimming,' she finished for him, gesturing to the pool as though he might wonder where.

'In your pyjamas?' Aviators covered his eyes, but she didn't need to see behind them to recognise his distraction as a muscle flickered in his cheek. He'd seen her in a bikini not that long ago and this wasn't much different. Except that her bikini hadn't become transparent when it got wet.

'I didn't bring a towel. Or my swimsuit.' Her tongue felt strange in her dry mouth and she swallowed.

'Right.' Raf was staring at the shopping around his feet as though trying to remember how it had got there.

'It was too nice not to,' she continued hastily, trying to estimate how many strides it would take to leg it to her room and safety. 'I thought you weren't here.'

232

'I wasn't. I went to the market,' he muttered, bending to gather some of the shopping. Cassie felt she ought to help, except...: 'But now I'm back.'

'So I see. I'm sorry I missed it. The market, I mean.'

'You could come with me tomorrow.'

'I'd love to. So I'd better go and... change.' She raced back across the grass to her room. A glance in the mirror revealed wide eyes with dilated pupils and nipples perfectly outlined by the white silk. She might as well have been standing before him naked, and if he'd returned a few minutes earlier, then she would... She shook the thought away. They still had four days and three more nights to get through.

But with every hour they spent alone in this perfect hilltop hideaway, it became more impossible to deny what she felt. There was desire and longing in every shared look, the meaningful and easy conversations. The hours spent thinking of him, the truth of his own feelings revealed before they'd said good night. She understood the pull between them every bit as well as he did, but he was right; she needed time. Time to decide if she could actually do this, and how she would feel when it was over. Because she couldn't have him in her life in every way possible.

Perhaps he was part of her pathway to healing, the first man she had longed for as a single woman, one whose heart was gradually getting used to no longer being a wife. The sun, this house, the setting, Raf; all were doing their work in helping her mend, slowly loosening her mind from the worries that usually held it firm. He had promised he would always be there for her children, and she believed him. There was no reason to doubt it, even if their own relationship had irrevocably changed once this week was over. So this would be their secret, and she would never reveal it.

In the kitchen he was still putting away shopping when Cassie returned, changed into shorts and a shirt over her swimsuit. She made coffee, trying not to let her body make obvious the decision she'd made in her room. Would she really be brave enough to act on it, to let him know how she felt and what she wanted? Even the silence was screaming at her as they moved around one another.

'How did you sleep, impromptu music on the terrace notwithstanding? I hope I didn't keep you awake,' Raf remarked.

She thought of him playing beside the pool in the moonlight, singing of a lost love, someone far out of reach. The hours he'd spent in the past teaching himself to play the guitar and then the drums, how music had sustained him through the darkest days. And then his own story of loss following his break-up all those years ago, and the pain which had sent him around the world on tour time and again as he kept his distance from all that might unbalance him. She desperately didn't want him to be hurt again; neither of them deserved it.

'I slept better after we talked,' she whispered. 'Raf, your song, it was beautiful, truly.' She reached for his hand, and his eyes told her more as she placed it over her heart. 'I felt it, here.'

He must have felt the racing of her heart, and she caught the catch in his breath as his fingers skimmed her breast. She waited, watching him staring at his hand lying possessively on her chest. Slowly he raised it, her hand over his, until it was at her cheek, and he touched his forehead to hers.

'I wanted you to hear me, because I wrote it for you,' he muttered. 'Writing music is the only way I know how to fully express myself.'

'Raf, I… That's so amazing, thank you.' His hand fell away and hers with it, and she was relieved and sorry all at once. She still needed to take this slow.

'My pleasure. Let me make you some breakfast.'

'No way.' She placed a hand on his chest, her fingers brushing the tattoo revealed by his half-open shirt, and his eyes darkened a second time. She hadn't planned to swim naked and have him catch her soaking wet, but now that she had, it was as though she'd stripped away another layer of doubt. 'It's my turn. You can watch me work for a change.'

-

They spent the rest of the morning reading beside the pool, swimming and talking. For Cassie there was sleep too. A lightness seemed to have entered her mind, and whenever she woke, it was to see Raf nearby, insisting she needed the rest. Although she checked her phone regularly for news of Isla and Rory, a weight had been lifted and she felt lighter than she had in years, the ease transferring itself to her body made languid by heat and Raf's presence.

After a lazy lunch he sat on the terrace with his guitar, picking out chords or scribbling on a pad. She wanted to wind her arms around him and let him know how much his openness meant, but she held back, waiting, *needing* to be certain. His gaze told her everything written on his heart, and later he held her hand as she read. The connection felt both easy and profoundly moving. Slowly, gradually, she was moving into a new space in her life, and it was Raf she wanted beside her. She'd abandoned the navy swimsuit and changed into her tropical-print bikini instead, and one heated stare was enough to let her know he had noticed.

In the evening Cassie cooked a simple dinner they ate on the terrace with hunks of crusty bread he'd bought from the market, and she was sleepy again after a glass of wine. They called Isla and Rory in Italy, who were full of excitement about their plans, including a trek into the mountains and a pizza workshop. Then Raf suggested a movie from his list, which they watched indoors, curled up on the sofa, close without actually touching. They parted in the kitchen after he brushed her cheek with his lips, and she'd gone to bed smiling and alight with anticipation.

The next morning she was ready to leave at eight, their agreed time to head down the hill to the market. The sun was already high, and she laughingly told him she would be leaping into the pool to cool off the moment they returned. They had only three more nights before their trip would be over, and she tried to cling onto every moment, hold it close to her heart.

The small town was already busy when they eventually reached it, strolling along a narrow cobbled street which opened onto a central square, dominated by the church and its tall bell tower. Painted doors and balconies stuffed with plants made a colourful splash against dark railings, the height of the buildings helping to block out the sun, if not the heat. They followed tram tracks carved into the ground, which Raf told her ran from the town to the harbour. Buildings lined every side of the square, some set behind hedges and more railings, mountains rising behind them. Stalls were crammed into every scrap of space, shaded by white canopies, and Cassie shot him a smile, itching to explore. Tables lined the pavements outside cafes, already half full as people hurried past with laden bags bumping at their sides.

'You didn't tell me there was so much here!' She was glad she'd brought a large bag, although lugging it home up that hill wouldn't be much fun. 'How long have we got?'

'As long as you want.' He paused beside a stall hung with preserved meats, chunky red rings of chorizo suspended in the shade. He spoke rapidly and soon the stallholder was wrapping a couple and handing them over.

'I'd forgotten how well you speak Spanish,' Cassie said wistfully as they resumed their walk. Languages had never been her strong point. 'You sounded like a local.' She also hadn't missed how easily he attracted attention as surprised glances and a few double takes came his way. Was it his height and looks attracting interest, his fame, or was he simply known to some of these people after years of holidaying on this hillside?

Orange trees jammed in wide planters stood on the pavements outside the cafes, parasols open wide to offer shade. Fashion, food, plants, local arts and crafts; all were here, and she wandered from stall to stall, appreciating having the time to explore without two teenagers grumbling at her shoulder. She bought a sunhat and put it on immediately, pausing to let Raf adjust it. His hands skimmed her shoulders before he caught her hand and tugged her closer still, dropping a kiss on her cheek. At a stall selling dresses, she pulled one and then another out for a closer look, holding them against her body.

'What do you think?' She felt a little self-conscious, asking for his opinion. Even though she couldn't see his eyes behind the aviators, she had the sense they'd narrowed to observe her.

'The truth?'

'Of course.' She laughed. 'I can take it.'

'I'm not sure the green would suit you, but the other one is perfect.'

A soft cream cotton with narrow straps across the shoulders, the dress was emblazoned with deep blush roses and splashes of pale green leaves. It fell almost to her ankles and fastened across the left hip, the skirt a wide swirl that fanned out as she twirled. It was a holiday dress, the sort she didn't often get to wear. But here, in the sunshine of a bustling market lively with tourists and locals jostling amongst the stalls, Cassie felt loosened from her life at home.

'So shall I buy it?'

'Definitely. I think it will look great on you.'

'Maybe later.' She slid the dress back on the rail with an apologetic smile at the stallholder. 'I don't suppose I'd wear it much at home.'

After that their hands found their way to each other, fingers entwined, and occasionally she tugged him over to a stall to examine something. Raf readjusted her hat when he dislodged it and pulled her into his side, as though they really were lovers and this day had been made just for them.

They lingered over coffee and breakfast at a pavement cafe, watching the world strolling by, and bought enough food to last until they left on Saturday. Walking back up the hill was much harder, even with a light breeze, and Cassie was glad to return and put everything away.

In the mirror in her room, she noticed a suntan already developing. The face staring back looked more at ease, her skin smooth and clear, eyes glittering with something she recognised as desire. She changed into her bikini with the kaftan over the top and wandered out to the pool. He was on the terrace and her skin burned yet more as he watched her approach.

'I'm off to see a neighbour up the mountain, the one who produces the olive oil. Pippa wants me to bring some back. I was going to do it tomorrow, but he's messaged to say he won't be around. You want to come with me?'

'Do you mind if I don't?' Cassie raised her book. 'I'm feeling very lazy after that walk, and I don't think I'm ready to face another hill just yet. I thought I'd read and swim.'

'Sure, you go ahead.' Raf got up from the sofa and collected his phone. 'I'll only be an hour or so.'

The villa felt empty when he'd left, as though it had lost some of its energy without his presence. After a swim, she oiled herself and lay on her front to top up the suntan, chin folded on her hands. It wasn't long before she felt sleepy again, and she woke to the touch of his hand gentle on her shoulder.

'How long have you been out here?'

'I'm not sure,' she muttered. She raised her head, blinking, the sun bright behind him as he settled on the edge of her lounger, utterly aware of his proximity as he pushed sunglasses into his hair. 'Since you left. I swam and had a shower, then lay down here.'

'Maybe you need to move inside, or at least into the shade again.' He tapped her shoulder with a finger. 'You're burning.'

'I don't know what's come over me,' she said hazily, aware of his finger resting lightly against her skin. 'I just want to swim, sleep or sunbathe the whole time. And eat. The food is amazing.'

'It's your body's way of letting you know you needed a rest. And maybe some sun. Go with it, don't fight it.'

'Do I look like I'm fighting it?' she mumbled into her hands. 'Maybe I need another week.'

'That could be arranged.' Raf traced an idle path down her back and Cassie could barely breathe. 'Would you like me to oil you?'

'Would you mind?' She cleared her throat, the catch in her voice giving her away.

'Not in the least. Budge up.'

She shifted across, aware of him reaching for the bottle of factor fifty on the floor. Was he being deliberately loud as he unscrewed the top and tipped some onto his hand, or was it that her every sense was heightened, poised for him to begin. He smoothed gentle circles across her back, working the suncream into her skin, brushing her hair out of the way. She gasped when his fingers slid beneath the strap fastening the bikini around her neck.

Slowly he worked his way down, his hands firm and sure, as though he was imprinting himself onto her soul. Never had her body been touched with so much sensitivity, as though they had all the time in the world and the only thing Raf cared about was her and how he made her feel. She could barely recall her own name as she wondered wildly how he could make so simple a task feel so utterly sensual, until she was almost melting with anticipation and desire. When his finger tugged at the thin bikini strap across her back, she stifled another sharp intake of breath.

'You have a line, here,' he said huskily, a second finger joining the first. 'It seems a shame to spoil your suntan. Would you like me to undo it?'

'Please,' she told him tremulously, the whispered reply making her decision clear. 'I think you're right. It would be a shame.'

Cassie couldn't care less about her suntan. It was all Raf, his touch and how they felt, where they were going, that mattered. How slow and careful he was being, how polite and yet lethal, every brush of his fingers leaving her longing for more. Was she imagining the length of time he was taking to unfasten it? And when he parted the straps and let them fall away, she wondered how the separating of two thin strips of material could suddenly make her feel so naked. He could see no more of her than he had before, and yet she felt totally undressed and entirely aware of his every ragged breath. Even the sun couldn't compete with the heat he was generating in her body. She felt scorched, branded. *His*.

'I think you're good now,' he muttered. He found the bottle again and tightened the lid. 'I should go and make us some lunch.'

'What if I don't want you to go?' she whispered.

'I don't want to go either,' Raf told her hoarsely. 'But I promised I'd wait until you were ready. I want you to be certain and maybe this isn't the right moment to decide that. Not when you're lying here almost naked and I don't want us to stop.'

She swallowed, caught between desire to have him continue and a tiny voice telling her he was right. That she might act on this moment and regret it before the day was out. And she wanted to be certain, too. No regrets. She needed reason, not her body clamouring for more.

'So it's not just me who feels this way?'

'You want me to prove it?' He leant over to place the words in her ear.

'How would you do that?' Cassie muttered distractedly.

'I'll show you, when you're ready.' He dropped a kiss onto her shoulder, and she was already ruing reason and sense.

'I just don't think I can mend my heart a second time, Raf,' she whispered.

'I don't want you to have to mend your heart again, I promise. And for what it's worth, I think we can work it out. I want to work this thing out, so you and me can find a way to be together. But we take it as slow as you need.' The lounger shifted as he stood up. 'I'll be inside when you're ready to eat.'

After lunch he disappeared, telling her he had to work. She napped in her room after another swim, opening her bedroom door to a knock after she'd woken and showered.

'You forgot this, when we were at the market.' Raf held out something soft wrapped in tissue paper, and she took it, tearing it open. Inside was the rose-patterned dress she'd found this morning, and she laughed.

'You went back to get it for me? Why?'

'Because you loved it and I think you'll look beautiful in it,' he told her softly.

'Thank you.' She held it against her body, tilting a hip. 'I do love it, even more than I did this morning.'

'You're welcome. I'm going for a shower. I'll see you at dinner, yeah?'

'Absolutely. And it's my turn to make it.'

There was no doubt what she'd be wearing tonight. Throughout their friendship they'd shared the usual celebratory gifts, but he'd never chosen one like this before.

One so intimate and meaningful, that he wanted her to wear. An idea fell into her mind as she closed the door to change, wondering if she dared see it through.

Chapter Eighteen

Cassie had only brought one pair of heels, and they tapped a beat steadier than her heart as she crossed the terrace. The skirt of her new dress floated around her bare legs, the creamy rose pattern highlighting the suntan dusting her skin. After her shower she'd dried her hair, run her hands through it then added perfume and lipstick, unsurprised by the danger and desire glittering back in the mirror.

Raf was sitting with a glass of white wine in one hand as she approached, his hungry gaze drinking her in. He stood when she reached him, and she spun around, offering a slightly self-conscious twirl to show off the dress.

'You're stunning. It looks incredible on you. I knew it would.'

'Thank you, I totally love it.' Her heart slammed inside her chest at that heated look.

Was it wrong to want someone so completely, when she'd loved and been loved before? Nothing could alter her love for Ewan or diminish its significance and foundation in her life. She'd learnt the hard way that life was short and that love, longing and feeling this way about someone else might not come around again. Shaken by admitting the inescapable truth she'd been trying to deny for months, her limbs were trembling. Maybe she and Raf really would find a way, and it would be okay. For now she was free of her life in London and all that held her steady there. Here, it was just the two of them.

His hands went to her shoulders and he dipped his head, letting his kiss and then his lips linger against her cheek. 'Let me get you a glass of wine.'

She missed his closeness the moment he turned away, lifting a bottle from a cooler and pouring her a glass before topping up his own. His fingers skimmed hers as he passed it across and heat curled through her. With every single look, every touch, she was moving their unspoken conversation on, making her decision and her desire for him clear.

'I'll bring dinner.' She took a sip of wine, savouring the taste on her tongue, before setting the glass down and turning to the kitchen. She halted when he caught her hand.

'Can I help?' Other than his thumb tracing a lazy circle on her palm, he wasn't even touching her, and still she quivered as his gaze fell to her mouth. Taking this so slowly seemed to heighten each sensation, every second both a promise and a torment of waiting.

'There's nothing to do. I left everything in the slow cooker earlier.'

'I just like watching you,' he murmured, and Cassie was mesmerised by the tiny flecks of gold in his eyes. 'Is that okay?'

In truth it was a very different question, and she nodded. Raf was testing her again, finding out how far along she was on the path they were treading. She cupped his cheek with a palm, his gaze never leaving hers as he pressed a kiss against it. Heat pooled in her body, reminding her again how it felt to have his mouth on her.

'You do the table.' She freed herself and walked inside, taking deep breaths to settle her racing pulse. She sliced bread from the loaf they'd bought that morning and heaped chicken, chorizo, tomatoes, olives and peppers onto plates. Raf helped her carry everything outdoors, and when they were sat opposite one another, he touched his glass to hers.

'What are we celebrating?'

'You. Me. Us being here, together. Healing.'

A flare of anxiety brought a shaky note to her voice. 'Maybe it is being here, in this house with you, that's making me better.' A tear caught on the corner of her eye. 'I don't want to lose this feeling, Raf. To go back to being sad again.'

'That's why we take this slow.' He took her hand across the table. 'I don't want to go back to a place where we pretend we don't feel this way either. And I can't promise we have all the time in the world, but for now it's just us, and we'll keep it that way until you're ready for more.'

'And what about when you're ready for more?' she whispered. 'What if that time never comes for me?'

'Cass, it's already here,' he said simply. 'I want everything with you.'

It was impossible to avoid the honesty in his eyes, a look she'd never seen before. At home she'd spent months trying to avoid him, telling herself time and again that her feelings for him weren't real, couldn't matter, and now his were laid bare in that unwavering gaze. 'Promise me it won't change anything for Isla and Rory. I can't do this if I think one day you might walk away from them.'

'You have my word.' He raised her hand to his lips. 'I promise. Nothing could ever alter my love for them.'

They began to eat and Cassie loved how he tucked in, mopping up the sauce with the bread they'd bought, the simple tasks of togetherness that felt so profound. 'I am learning to enjoy feeling happy again, and not to feel guilty or sad when those moments come. That there is still joy to be found even when living with loss.'

'Exactly that.' Raf's smile was a pensive one. 'I don't think there'll ever be a day when I don't miss my mum. Even though it was so long ago, it totally defined our lives and we live differently because of it.'

'Are you happy, Raf?' She realised with dismay that she'd rarely thought to consider this question. He'd always carried an air of sadness; it was just another thing that had made him so popular with the fans. That hint of vulnerability on show without his ever fully revealing it. 'I'm sorry for assuming you had everything you wanted, with the band and the travelling. Did it make you happy?'

'Happy enough.' He paused, fork halfway to his mouth. Cassie was finding it almost impossible to stop looking at it, holding on to the memory of their kiss, desperate to make another one. 'I think when you're busy, you just keep going. There wasn't much time to dwell, and I guess I liked it that way. I'm happy when I'm with you.'

'Me too. And I'm glad you feel that way. Happy. How is it that time can pass so quickly when doing so little? I feel incredibly lazy, the sun really is doing its work.' And Raf; he couldn't have been more considerate. She stretched, aware of him watching, alighting that blaze on her skin again.

'Good. That was the whole idea of coming here.'

'Really? The only reason?' She raised a brow, loving the smile spreading across his lips at her tone. She hadn't flirted in so long and it felt wonderful to play that game, to dance on the edge of desire with him. With just a look he made her feel both totally safe and wildly out of control.

He cleared up after they'd eaten and they settled on a sofa to watch the sunset, the sky blazing with shades of orange and yellow. Cassie topped up their glasses with the last of the wine, aware her exhilaration had nothing to do with alcohol. It was all Raf and the way he was making her feel. They had two more days and nights, and she wanted to savour every moment. He'd set up a playlist on a speaker, and she stood up, holding out her hand.

'Dance with me?'

He was on his feet too and his arm went across her back, fingers folding tightly around her hand. She felt the muscles beneath his shirt, heady with the freedom to explore, as they danced slowly to a new rhythm.

'Can I ask you something?'

'Of course.' He bent his head to reply, lips skimming her ear.

'Have you recorded your song, the one you played the other night?' She was certain he would – he had set up a studio in his house. He nodded.

'So would you play it for me now? I understand if you'd rather not. If it's totally private and just for you.'

His reply was to raise her hand and kiss it again as he stepped away. His phone was on the table, and moments later, she heard the opening chords and the lyrics he had already planted in her heart as his voice filled the perfumed night air.

Cassie wrapped her arms around his neck, holding every line, every note close as she listened again to the song he'd written for her. She understood how rarely he allowed himself to feel vulnerable, to open himself up to more hurt. His arms were around her too, their bodies finally touching, reducing every millimetre separating them until there were none left, and she was pressed against him. One arm was across her back, the other in her hair, holding her steady. She tipped her head back and couldn't do anything other than follow the certainty in his gaze, his heart slamming against her.

'Are you sure, Cass?' He smoothed away a tear with his thumb. 'I had no idea I was going to feel this way until Australia, and then I knew it was you. I know neither of us was looking for this. I've spent months trying to pretend it's not real, and I can't do that anymore.'

'Same,' she whispered. 'Whatever happens tomorrow and the day after and the one after that, I want this with you, Raf. I want you.'

Was he teasing her now on purpose, making her wait for his kiss as his beautiful mouth curled into a smile, running a finger down her cheek? She caught it between her lips and heard his sharp intake of breath as his arm on her back tightened. After all these months, she couldn't wait another minute. She placed both hands on his head and dragged his mouth to hers.

It was like no kiss she'd ever experienced before, and Raf perfected it. It was everything, the way he was holding her, keeping her close when she was no longer certain she could stand on her own. His mouth, slow and hurried and insistent all at once, his tongue finding hers and making her moan, yearning for more. His song for her was over, their dance only just beginning, and she had no idea where she ended and he began.

He pulled back with glittering eyes and her quick laugh at the bewilderment and joy in them was almost a sob. The rush of desire, the longing and the pleasure, the promise of so much more. It was everything in this moment, and so was he. His lips were pink and swollen from their kiss, and her fingers were on the buttons of his shirt. She undid the few that were fastened, parting the white cotton to stare at the kneeling warrior offering his sword to an angel.

'This is how I think of you.' She laid a palm on the tattoo, the brush of hair rough against her skin, the silver cross nestled close. 'Defending those you love.'

'Cassie,' he murmured. Both hands went to her face, and the way he'd said her name was enough to set her confidence soaring again. She moved his hands to her shoulders and lower still, her breasts tingling in anticipation of his touch, almost screaming when his palms brushed against them. It wasn't enough, she needed more, and she told him so as she pulled his head down to whisper into his ear.

'You're so greedy,' he muttered, and she laughed.

She wanted to hold that look in her heart forever, to always remind her of this moment. She touched a finger to her own face, her skin tender where his beard had brushed it. Heart clattering, she took his hands and led them to the bow tied at her waist. She loved the dress because it was pretty and he'd bought it for her, had thought to go back and bring her his gift.

'I'm going to swim. Do you want to join me?' Slowly, she helped him untie the bow, swallowing nervously as the dress parted. Underneath she was naked, and he dragged in a sharp breath. She watched the surprise and pleasure rush into his gaze as it dropped to drink her in. She almost closed her eyes as she slid the straps from her shoulders and let the dress pool at her feet. But she couldn't. She needed to know everything he felt and could no longer hide, to draw on his certainty when her own might let her down.

At the steps she glanced back as she undid her heels and slipped them off. Raf was hurrying to join her, his shirt and shorts discarded on the terrace. She began to swim, the cool water dissipating some of the burning heat in her body. He quickly caught her up, tugging her backwards until she was against him. His hands were on her breasts as her head tipped onto his shoulder, his lips roaming hungrily across her neck. He was all angles and firm, hard against her bare skin as he explored every curve, and Cassie was lost all over again. It could only be him, and the words she confessed to say so were a breathless whisper.

'You're the strongest, best person I've ever known,' he muttered against her ear, and she gasped as his hand followed the curve of her stomach lower. 'You're incredible, and I'm going to make certain you feel it.'

Moments later she was shuddering in his arms, and through the haze, as he held her in the water, she was crying. Quiet little gulps that soon became great heaving sobs as tears poured down her face, and her body shook against his. Raf held her tightly, his arms the only thing keeping her upright. He lifted her easily, carrying her from the pool. He laid her gently on the still-warm grass, her skin super sensitised as the blades brushed against her. He drew her close, warming her with the heat of his own body tucked around hers, soothing her with quiet murmured words and his hands, until gradually her cries faded away.

'I'm sorry.' She hiccupped, burying her face against his chest. 'I have no idea where that came from.'

'Hey, it's totally fine. Please don't ever say you're sorry. And I think I do.' He eased back, and she was ready to cry again at that look. 'It was your body's way of letting go, of freeing yourself from the stress and the worries. You needed it.'

'Is that your professional opinion, Dr Jones?' The shock of her emotions pouring free the way they had was slowly receding, and she was wholly conscious they were naked, his beautiful body facing hers. She raised a brow as his smile slowly widened, and Raf propped his head on a hand.

'It is. And I recommend as many repeats as you feel are necessary.'

'You do?'

'Absolutely.'

Cassie laughed as she leant over him. His hands caught her waist to pull her on top, and she kissed him, dizzy with release and longing and more. 'Well, in that case…'

–

When she woke hours later, the night dark and silent, she was in her bed, the white curtains fluttering against the open doors. She reached out, wondering if she was dreaming, until her hand found the warm body sleeping beside her. But Raf was real, and this time her tears were happy ones as she looked at him in wonder. They'd lain on the grass until they were cold and then he'd carried her to the outdoor shower, warming them both beneath the hot water. They'd snuggled together on the terrace, with Cassie wearing his shirt, and when it was finally time for bed, he'd asked if she wanted to sleep alone. Her reply had been to take his hand and lead him to her room. She'd fallen asleep with his arm around her, her head on his shoulder, and it had been perfect.

She couldn't go back to dating apps after this; it would be like dropping a pin on a map blindfolded and expecting to land on paradise. Until they'd kissed in Australia, she had never dreamt the first time she made love after her marriage might be with Raf, but now she knew it could never have been anyone else. He had been incredible. So tender and thoughtful, and he'd made it all about her and her pleasure. Holding her afterwards as she'd cried in his arms, shocked by her own emotions, the promise he'd made to care for her children always. She couldn't stop touching him, and she smiled when a pair of gorgeously brown, sleepy eyes opened.

'Sorry, I wasn't trying to wake you on purpose,' she whispered. 'Just checking you're real.'

'Totally real, in your bed, and entirely yours.' He gathered Cassie close, holding her against his chest. 'And I'll still be here when you wake up tomorrow.'

In the morning they made love again as the sun rose outside. The heat seemed to have seeped into her very bones, leaving her replete, almost weightless. She had slept so well, and they swam before sharing breakfast on the terrace. She couldn't bear to think of this interlude ending, of having to go home and pretend they were merely old friends. Going up to bed in separate rooms instead of falling asleep after making love wherever they lay. But family life beckoned, and only the thought of seeing her children made returning so soon feel bearable.

They had intended to stroll down to the market again, but the idea was abandoned when Raf fell asleep on a lounger and Cassie loathed to wake him. They had one more day after this and she wanted to savour every single moment. To swim and make love and sleep and read and touch him. To let him know what he meant to her and how afraid she felt of what lay ahead on their return. But those words weren't for now, and she pushed them aside.

When the car arrived to return them to the airport early on Saturday morning, they held hands all the way home. The sun had vanished when they retrieved their bags after the flight and made their way out to another waiting car. She had seen how normal a life he tried to live, and he didn't often take advantage of the privileges that came with his position. Like now, being able to climb into the back of the car and hide from reality a little longer.

'Are you sure you don't want to stay in town with me?' Raf squeezed her hand. They'd flown into Heathrow this time as he had a meeting arranged with his manager, who took care of the band's business interests. 'I'm sorry, the timing is terrible, but there's some stuff we need to go over, and this was as good a time as any.'

'No, I think it's better that I go home. And I've promised to meet Isla and Rory at the airport. Fiona offered, but I'd like to be there.'

Had she really just referred to Hartfell as home? It certainly felt like that, although anywhere could be home if her children and Raf were with her. The car would be dropping him off before driving her back up to Yorkshire. He had insisted, even though she'd said she could get the train. And the separation would place a little bit of distance between them, if they were going to keep private the feelings they had finally confessed in Majorca. He would return to Hartfell tomorrow, and they would begin the process of trying to find a way to be together.

'You haven't changed your mind, about us?' There was a note of alarm in his voice, and she shook her head slowly.

'No, but we need more time, Raf,' Cassie told him gently. 'Time to get used to this, and to work out how we're going to tell our families.'

It was her family that worried her most. How her children would react to Raf's changed role in her life, even if it might not make much difference to theirs. And most especially, how Fiona and Gordon would feel about him stepping into a role their adored son had occupied for so long. Her stomach swooped every time she thought of trying to find the right words and break the news.

Once they'd kissed goodbye and Raf had disappeared into a building across a street in Pimlico, Cassie was desolate as the car made its way north. After the heat and the sun and the views in Majorca, the gloomy grey clouds blotting the sky seemed to match her mood perfectly, despite the excitement of seeing Isla, Rory and Flynn again. The pleasure of Raf's company and the care she'd basked in already slipping away. She wanted him here still, at her side, assuring her they would be okay and would find a way.

She fell asleep on the long drive, her heart lifting when she woke and realised she was already in the Dales, Hartfell not far away. Once she reached the house, she thanked the driver as he helped with her bag and let herself in. It was utterly silent without Raf, Isla and Rory, or Flynn padding from room to room and making his quiet presence felt. She switched the coffee machine on, thankful that someone, probably Fiona or Pippa, had thought to leave fresh milk in the fridge. She had an hour before she needed to leave for the airport.

At the table she sat down with her coffee and pulled out her phone. It was still in flight mode and she switched to Wi-Fi, watching the notifications piling up. Surprised to see four missed calls from Raf, she smiled. He must be missing her as much as she was him. She went to voicemail and played his only message, alarm sharply spiking at his tone and the few words he'd recorded.

'Hey, Cass. Call me when you get this, okay? I'm fine, but we need to talk.' A pause. 'And please, don't go online until we've spoken. Trust me, yeah?'

Sweat had already broken out on Cassie's brow, and her palms were clammy as she fought for calm. It couldn't be her children; she'd just seen the notification from Jas about their flight and that they were on their way. She hit the return call on Raf's number as dread lodged in her mind. The engaged sound came and the call cut off, and she tried again, battling tears of worry. What if something had happened, like before…

But it couldn't; he'd simply said not to go online, and he sounded okay, unharmed at least. She brought up a browser and her finger hovered over it, temptation lingering. She should trust him; he had always looked after her. But he still hadn't called back, and she hurriedly typed his name and pressed enter. It was probably old news, some gossip about an ex he'd rather not expose her to.

The images were the first thing her blurred vision took in. Her and Raf, that day in the market, hand in hand and laughing as he adjusted her sunhat, his palm on her cheek. Another one, when he'd tugged her against him and stopped just short of kissing her, the longing in his gaze she saw perfectly captured in her own. They looked like lovers, even though they hadn't made love when these photographs were taken. A couple in love, their every gesture exuding a togetherness she hadn't even fully realised herself. Her betrayal was laid bare for the world to see. And far, far worse, her children and everyone she loved. Her phone hit the floor as she shoved her chair back, retching as she rushed to the downstairs loo just in time to throw up.

Chapter Nineteen

Every warm feeling had vanished as Cassie drove to the airport, numbed by the revelation about her and Raf, and what it meant for her family. He had tried again to speak with her, and she'd listened dully to his second voicemail, his assurance that Vanessa, as Jonny's partner and the band's publicist, was on it. But Cassie knew how these things worked; she had too many years of experience. There was only one thing she wanted to do – deny, for all she was worth. To convince her children that the photographs had somehow lied and she hadn't been trying to exclude them from an attempt to make a life with Raf in place of their father.

Nausea was still churning in her stomach when Isla, Rory and Jas appeared in Arrivals, and she pasted on a bright smile that faltered the moment Rory's chilled gaze met hers. She'd been desperate to speak with them before they found out, and it was clear that impossible hope had gone, and she hurried towards them. Like almost every other teenager, her own were permanently online, and even if they hadn't seen the images for themselves, someone else, friend or foe, would likely have alerted them. Their mum and Rory's adored godfather, holding one another like lovers and kissing in the street as though they didn't have a care in the world. Photographs did that, she'd found. Froze a single frame and created an entire story around it. There was a beginning and a middle to hers with Raf, but now she had no idea what the end might be.

'You all look wonderful!' Cassie rushed forward anyway, feasting on the sight of her children and Jas safely returned, their suntanned skin and the healthy glow they carried. Isla submitted to a brief hug before she wriggled away, staring at her phone. When she held out her arms to Rory, he walked straight past her. Her beautiful boy, whom she'd nurtured and loved and held through every triumph and tragedy, loathed her now, and her vision was suddenly hazy with tears.

'I'm so sorry, Rory,' she whispered to his back as people pushed by. 'I never meant to hurt either of you.' And so it had begun. She had no idea how she could put right her mistake.

Jas embraced her, telling Cassie gently not to worry too much, that he would come round. Cassie nodded. Jas hugged Isla and Rory goodbye, and it pierced Cassie's heart to watch Rory hold the young woman, the embrace he refused to allow her. Jas was getting the train back to London, and she disappeared into a sea of people, just one more traveller heading home.

They trooped back to the car without a word. On the drive home Cassie asked about their holiday, the fun and adventures they'd had. Only Isla shared some details; Rory was plugged into ear buds and ignored every word. They desperately needed to talk, but she wasn't about to attempt it in the car when she had to concentrate on traffic and couldn't clearly read their body language. At the house he was even more disappointed to realise that Flynn wasn't home as Pippa was due to return him this evening. He and Isla went straight to the fridge once they'd dumped their bags, and Cassie asked them to sit down.

'Isla, Rory, we need to talk. Please.'

'Do we, though?' It wasn't like Rory to be so scathing, and her heart ached for him.

'Please, Rory. It's important. Could you take your ear buds out, please?'

He scowled when Isla nudged him, and the chair scraped across the stone-flagged floor when he dragged it from the table. He perched on the edge as though he might flee at any moment, still staring at his phone. Isla sat next to him with Cassie opposite; she wanted to be able to see their faces. She'd gone over and over what she might say in this moment, but none of those words had stuck.

'I'm so sorry about what you must have seen, about me and Raf. But I promise, it's not what you think.'

'You don't actually know what I'm thinking, Mum. And it doesn't matter what you say.' The ice in Rory's gaze was unfamiliar, and she was chilled by it. 'Now everyone knows you betrayed Dad with his best friend, even if you say it isn't true.'

'Rory, those pictures… They're not the whole truth, I swear.' But weren't they, though? It was her greatest fear about Raf, that she'd never reconcile her feelings for her husband's friend and allow herself to live them. She'd been calling it betrayal herself for months.

'Your dad and I loved each other, and I'll always love him.' Her words caught on a sob. 'Nobody can ever change that.'

'Forget it. There's nothing you could say to make this better.' Rory shoved his chair back and leapt up, snatching his phone.

She stared after him, his feet clattering along the passageway. She covered her face with her hands as Isla stood up too, braced for another angry exit. But tears began to fall when she felt her daughter's arms go around her shoulders.

'I'm so sorry, Isla.' Cassie hiccupped. 'I didn't plan any of this. I wasn't expecting it.' She raised her head, swiping at the blotches staining her cheeks. 'And I swear, the very last thing on my mind was to ever hurt you or Rory. You're my heart, both of you.'

'It's okay, Mum. I get it.'

'Is it okay, though? What if Rory always hates me after this?' Rationally she didn't imagine he would, but right now that time felt a very long way off.

'He'll come around, don't worry,' Isla said calmly. 'It was pretty obvious to me and Harriet how you and Raf feel. You're always so awkward around each other, and Harriet said she's never known him not have a girlfriend this long.'

'Seriously?'

'Yeah.' Isla shrugged with all the insouciance of any fifteen-year-old unconcerned about a parent's love life. 'But Rory didn't see it coming and he's put Raf on the same pedestal as Dad. In his eyes they can pretty much do no wrong.'

'And so I'm the bad guy,' Cassie said faintly. 'He's right about that. I'm the one who's married.'

'Was married,' Isla corrected her kindly. 'I'm sorry, Mum, I know that's a horrible thing to say.'

'But it's true,' she replied sadly. 'Even though it's taken me a long time to get used to it.'

'You just fell in love again, that's all. You're not a bad guy, and we still love you.'

Cassie gaped as Isla let her go. She'd barely even allowed herself to think such a thing, much less have it pointed out by her own teenage daughter. But it was there, wedged now between her and her son, no matter how much she wanted to pretend otherwise.

'There wasn't anything between us before Australia, Isla, I promise. Only one unexpected kiss when we were away that I've been trying to forget ever since.' She took a deep breath. 'But whatever I feel, I can't share my life with anyone who doesn't fit, or Rory can't accept. You and Rory come first, always, and I never wanted you to find out this way. I've let everyone down.'

'Mum, seriously, stop talking crap! Yeah, we would've preferred to hear it from you, but it doesn't matter what anyone else outside the family thinks. You deserve to be happy, both of you.' Isla grabbed an apple from the fruit bowl and went to the door. 'And anyway, if we could choose our own stepdad, Raf would be the only one we'd want. Rory just needs to get his head around it and then he'll be fine.'

'Sweetheart, I think it's too late for that. And we probably all need to get used to seeing less of Raf.' Cassie looked around the kitchen she'd come to think of as home, reminded too of the village and the community she'd fallen in love with. And Flynn, he would be home soon, and she would have to leave him here as well. But this was a dream, a summer interlude, and they had to go back. And now, with weeks of the holiday still to come, they'd have to return early because she couldn't stay here in Raf's house, not after this. They'd have to cut short their summer, something else Rory would hate her for.

'Why?' Isla flashed her a grin. 'Harriet told me what you said to Pippa last year, about grabbing love with both hands when it comes around. Why should you be any different? We already love Raf like family.'

Then she was gone, taking her optimism and her sense with her, leaving Cassie feeling more confused than ever. But her children's happiness and security were the lifelines she needed to cling to, and their feelings came first. Always.

She still hadn't spoken to Raf; there didn't seem to be anything to say. She was the one at fault, the one with children, and he'd done nothing other than be wonderful to her when she didn't deserve it. She ignored the new messages from Fiona; there was no one she wanted to talk to, no one who could truly understand what she'd done. Majorca seemed like a dream already, the hours afterwards turning into a nightmare. Pippa had called three times, and Cassie was dreading having to speak with her eventually. The end of whatever it was she had shared with Raf was going to alter their own friendship, one which had endured more than thirty years. Perhaps it couldn't survive this.

Later she was curled on the sofa in the television room, staring blankly at the screen and wondering when might be the right time to put pizza in the oven and call Rory down for supper, when Flynn ambled in. He spotted her and trotted straight over, resting his huge head on her lap as his tail wagged madly. His cheery welcome and quiet care were her undoing, and when Pippa followed a moment later, Cassie was sobbing as she clutched him, tears soaking his shaggy grey coat.

'Cassie! Oh sweetheart, come here.' Pippa clambered onto the sofa too and folded Cassie into her arms. 'Hush, it's okay. Please don't cry.'

'It's not okay,' Cassie muttered, still stroking Flynn's head as her breath came in stuttering little gasps. 'I've really messed up, Pippa, and now Rory can't even stand to be in the same room with me.'

'He's a teenager and a boy trying to process his mum's feelings about someone who's not his dad, it goes with the territory.' Pippa raised Cassie's chin and passed her a tissue. 'Darling, you're allowed a life of your own, a private one that doesn't include them.'

'But not with their dad's best friend,' she said dully. 'I've let everyone down, and Raf and I, we hadn't even... I mean, in the pictures.' She hesitated. There wasn't much left that felt private anymore. 'Nothing had really happened when they were taken. It was after...'

Their feelings had finally burst free that evening, when he'd opened her heart and made it his, had made her soul sing again. It wasn't only making love and how unselfish he had been; Raf had revealed all of his own heart too, and she understood him in a way she never had before. The song he'd written for her and played as they'd danced, his vulnerabilities and the sadness he carried over not having children of his own. The life he'd made travelling the world, never standing still long enough to let anything hurt him after the woman he'd loved before had betrayed him. And the losses he lived with, just as Cassie did.

'I did wonder, but then I decided I was wrong,' Pippa said quietly. 'But I've never known Raf to even think of buying his own home before. Every time the house was mentioned he asked me if I thought you'd be happy here and would use it for holidays. It's obvious he chose it for you, Cassie. And your children.'

She opened her mouth and Pippa help up a hand. 'And no, I don't think it's all because of Isla and Rory, and he was just being kind. There's the way he looks at you and how you always seem to be trying not to look at him. I didn't see it until we were all together for his birthday. I'm sorry for encouraging you with Jago, and Raf and Allegra. I can't believe I was so blind. It's wonderful that he's making a life here, and I don't think he's planning to do that with someone who isn't you.'

'And you don't mind, how we feel?' The moment of hope about their being together was gone as soon as the words left Cassie's lips. They couldn't be together. Not now, after this.

'How could I possibly mind about my best friend and my brother falling in love?' Pippa laughed softly. 'Two of my most favourite people in all the world, and whatever happens, I know he'll always be there for you, and Isla and Rory. I want you both to be happy.'

'I can't do it if Isla and Rory aren't happy too,' Cassie said quietly. 'My happiness doesn't come at their expense.'

'You've had a nasty shock, Cass, and you need some time to process it, just like Isla and Rory. Please stop being so hard on yourself. You couldn't have known that someone would take pictures and splatter them online.'

'But it's happened to Raf before, and I should have been more careful. I wasn't thinking.' Cassie's head was in her hands again, eyes reddened and swollen. It hurt to be reminded of those carefree hours in Majorca, how it seemed they had left the rest of the world behind for a time. And those images proved that they hadn't, they'd been perfectly visible to anyone who had taken an interest. She looked up at the sound of footsteps, hoping to see Rory, and her stomach clenched as Fiona appeared. Beyond her children, her beloved mother-in-law was the one person she dreaded hurting the most.

Pippa squeezed Cassie's hands and stood up. 'I'll be at home if you need me, and I'll be checking in regularly. If you don't answer the phone, I'll come and find you,' she said firmly. 'I love you and there isn't a single thing that will ever change that.'

'Love you too,' Cassie muttered. She attempted a smile as Fiona said hello to Pippa and came to sit beside her. Flynn was sticking close, his head heavy on her feet.

'Darling, are you all right?' Fiona took her hands. 'I'm so sorry for what you're going through.'

'It's all my fault,' she said faintly. Fiona's usual comfort and concern was almost too much. 'I should never have gone away with Raf. I should have put Isla and Rory first and gone to Italy with them.'

'I think we need to get a few things straight,' Fiona said firmly. 'You're a wonderful mum and you spend most of your life putting your children first. So please don't let me hear you say otherwise. I know what growing up was like for you, with parents who constantly let you down, and never once have you done that to Isla and Rory. And yes, I've seen the photographs. But more than that, I've seen time and again how much you love and care for your children.'

Fiona eased back and her hands went to her lap. 'And nothing could make me doubt that you loved Ewan, and he loved you for the time you had together. Or that you've stopped loving him because you've fallen in love with someone else.'

'Fiona,' Cassie said helplessly, wanting to refute that last part. 'I'm not...'

'Of course you are,' she said softly. 'But the love we have for others isn't finite, it doesn't depend on how many people we have in our lives, as though there's only so much to go around. You didn't love Isla any less when Rory was born, your love simply grew to encompass him as well. And I think it's the same with Raf. You mustn't worry that people might assume you no longer love Ewan because of how you feel about Raf.'

Flynn nudged Cassie's leg, and she tried to smile. Just having him close was such a comfort, and he hadn't budged from her side since he'd come home.

'I know that Ewan was single-minded in pursuit of his career. I'm aware that you supported him fully and sacrificed your dream so he could pursue his. He was driven and brilliant and wonderful, and he loved you all very much.' Fiona wiped away a tear, leaning forward to smooth Cassie's hair from her face. 'But this is another sign that you're healing, and a very good one. Healing doesn't come at the expense of loving the person we lost any less, but by being able to accept their place in our lives is a different one and, slowly, we move on.'

'I don't want you to think there was ever anything between me and Raf before.' It was this worrying Cassie the most, Rory's anger over her betrayal still so raw. 'Neither of us saw it coming, I promise.'

'Nothing could ever change how I feel about you, and quite honestly I think Raf is the only person I can trust to love you the way you deserve. So don't fret about those pictures. They're a reflection of your heart and you don't have to hide it. You grab at happiness when you can and hold on to it for all you're worth. Isla and Rory will be fine, and they'll be leaving home in a blink. And when they do, I'll be thankful that you have Raf to stand at your side.'

Cassie sniffed too, swiping at her face with the tissue again as a tiny seed of hope began to bloom. 'So are you saying you would support us, if Raf and I could be together?' she asked tentatively. It was more than she'd dared hope in the distressing hours since she'd seen him this morning.

'Of course we'll support you, because we love you, and you absolutely have our blessing.'

'Fiona, I…' Cassie couldn't even find the words, except the only ones that mattered. 'It means the world, and I love you too.'

'Would you like me to speak with Rory? Or Gordon will, if you think it'll help?'

'I'd love that.' She gulped. 'He's always been so loving, and this feels… horrible. Raf and I, we planned to take our time and get used to the idea before we told anyone.'

'Well, that plan has vanished,' Fiona said briskly. 'I'll have a chat with Rory and see if I can help him understand. When things are calmer, he and Isla could come and stay for a couple of days now their rooms are finished. It would give you and Raf some time to talk things through.'

'I think they'd love that.' But not yet. She couldn't be without her children until she'd done everything possible to fix the fracture in her family. 'Thank you, for everything. For being wise and wonderful, and loving us the way you do. I found my true home when I met you, and our family is better because of you.'

'I'm so thankful to have you as my daughter.' Fiona leant down and they shared a hug. 'It's how I've always thought of you, and I couldn't have wished for a more wonderful one. Now let's work out how we fix this.'

Chapter Twenty

Cassie sank back on the cushions once Fiona had gone, her mind spinning with the events of the past few hours. So much had happened, and she was incredibly grateful for Pippa and Fiona's understanding and support, and Isla's practical sense. But Rory was hurting the most, and until she could put that right, there could be no thought of anything else. Raf was due home tomorrow and by then she could well be packing up and heading back to London if Rory refused to stay under the same roof.

She got up and Flynn clambered to his feet, watching her. 'Let's go for a walk, hey? I always think better when I'm outside.'

She didn't need his harness for a stroll around the meadow, and after a few days away, it was as though she was seeing everything for the first time. The house solid and firm at her back, guarding them. The garden beginning to change with late summer and the approach of autumn, the intense shades of golden yellow rudbeckia and paler heleniums, the bright splash of scarlet dahlias. Even the plants reminded her of Majorca.

Was it really only this morning that she and Raf had made love before they'd left the villa and flown home to a storm? Nausea rose every time she thought of their feelings being exposed in the way they had. The hurt it had brought her children, the shock it had generated. Without him here it was as though a part of her was missing too, and she glanced up at the house as Flynn raced around, praying that Rory would eventually find a way to forgive her.

After the conversation with Fiona, Cassie was also reminded of Raf's flying visits to London in between band commitments, how he had often been the one who remembered to ask about the important meeting she'd had at work, the event she'd attended, or how Rory had got on in a test, the new pony Isla was riding at the stables. For all Raf's fame and glory years with the band, around her kitchen table he had been himself, the boy she'd watched grow into a man who loved and defended his family. He had always understood her, had been there to see her through almost everything.

She hadn't loved him like this, not then. She'd loved Ewan and had made her home with him; they had encouraged and loved their children together. This was a love which had grown over time, and she and Raf hadn't been able to nurture it, not yet. She treasured his sensitivity and his understanding of her children, and how he strived to make them happy, to stand alongside them too. How he loved with a strength and depth that made her feel secure and seen, cherished and understood. There could be no other for her now; it was a certainty which brought a rush of sadness that theirs might never flourish, not if her son wouldn't accept it. She couldn't be a buffer between them, balancing one against the other. For this to work, the four of them needed to stand together. She needed to talk with Rory again and hoped that this time he might listen.

The house was silent when she returned, as though it had been stripped of life and laughter, and she longed to have them back. She wanted to gather her family around her, with Raf part of it too, and hold them close, remind them every day how much she loved them. To watch her children flourish and fly and be at their backs when they needed her. Isla's boots were abandoned under the table, and that meant she had returned. Cassie went to the fridge. A good meal went a long way to fixing things in her world, another lesson she had learnt from Fiona. Then after pizza she would ask Rory if he would like to talk.

The door from the boot room flew open and Flynn barked in surprise as Raf bounded into the kitchen. The box in her hand slid to the floor when he shoved the fridge door shut and gathered her in his arms. He looked wonderful and troubled, and still somehow happy, and the tears came again as he held her tightly.

'Cass, I'm sorry,' he rushed out. 'So sorry you've been dragged into this shit. I should've known better, I should've remembered it could happen. I was just so happy, and I wasn't thinking.'

She wanted to tell him it was okay, but it wasn't because their actions had hurt her children and sent Rory storming to his room. 'Isla and Rory...' she mumbled. 'It's them I'm worried about.'

'I know.' He drew back to look at her, warm hands cupping her face. 'But we'll sort it, I promise.'

She wanted to ask him how. Raf was the person Rory loved and respected the most outside of their immediate family. Or he had, until a few hours ago.

'How are they?'

'Isla's okay. She's being pragmatic and kind, which is so lovely of her.'

'She's your daughter, that's why,' Raf muttered, his eyes narrowing. 'And Rory?'

'He won't speak to me. I think he hates me for betraying his dad with you.'

'He doesn't hate you,' he said gently. 'He's hurt and he didn't see this coming, any more than we did.'

'But we should've known better. Not been so obvious in public.' She'd seen enough images of Raf down the years with various girlfriends, pictured hand in hand and laughing, the photographs revealing an intimacy very like their own. Was she making a huge mistake, falling in love with him? Would this be over in a few months and she'd have shattered her children's trust for no reason? Her mind was swirling with doubt, and Raf kissed her forehead. Much as she loved his certainty and his strength, it was harder to think clearly when he was so close. She drank him in, inhaling the scents that had filled her heart these past few days.

'I would never have chosen this way, but I'm glad it's out there, Cass.' He kissed her eyelids, her cheeks and then her lips, soft, gentle kisses quite unlike the ones they had shared before. 'Because I can't hide this forever, and I don't want you to have to, either.'

'But what are we going to do?'

'We're going to talk, all of us, is what.' Flynn was nudging him and Raf smiled, bending briefly. 'Hey, Flynn. Sorry for ignoring you. I'm glad to be home as well.'

'I thought you weren't coming back until tomorrow?'

'This couldn't wait.' He glanced towards the stairs. 'They're in their rooms?'

'Yes. I haven't seen Rory since we got back from the airport.'

'Right. I'll be back soon.' He squeezed her hand. 'Don't go anywhere.'

Cassie set about making supper once Raf disappeared; she couldn't sit still. To her surprise, he was back in a couple of minutes, Isla and a mutinous-looking Rory behind him, before she'd put the pizzas in the oven.

'Family conference,' Raf announced, pointing to the table. 'Sit down. We need a conversation, and I think it's best we do that together. No phones.'

'Since when did you get so bossy?' Isla grumbled, but Cassie caught the slight smile her daughter offered him as she left her phone on the windowsill, and her heart lifted a smidge. But Rory wouldn't even look at her once his phone had joined Isla's, and Raf laid a hand on her arm as she moved towards Rory. The shake of his head was so minute she wondered if she had imagined it.

'So here's how this goes.' Raf waited until everyone else was seated and then he pulled out a chair, next to Rory and opposite Cassie. She realised he hadn't sat beside her on purpose, avoiding the two of them facing her children like a wall. Rory was pale and her heart ached for him, wanting only to hold her lovely boy and tell him she was sorry, that all would be as okay as it ever could be without his dad.

'You can ask your mum and me anything you want, and we promise to give you the truth, okay?' Raf's gaze drifted to Cassie. 'But there are some things which are private, and they belong just between us. But we will be absolutely honest. And I want to be clear from the start.'

He laid a hand flat on the table and Rory's eyes flickered up. 'Your mum loves you both more than anything in the world, and she has never lied to you about what those pictures were suggesting. Not once.'

'Suggesting?' Rory's single word was laden with scorn. 'Do you know how many messages I've had about them already? What am I supposed to say?'

'Rory...' She went to stand up, and Raf laid a hand on her arm.

'I am sorrier about how you and Isla found out than I can ever say, Rory,' he said gently. 'It's happened to me before, but then it didn't matter so much. I'm sorry I failed all of you. I should have been prepared for it and protected you better. But I'm not sorry you know how we feel, even if that's hard for you to hear.'

'So it's true, then? When did it start?' Rory's eyes were pools of ice now he'd been confronted with feelings and a situation he hadn't seen coming. 'Between you and Mum?'

'Honestly, I'm not even sure.' Raf glanced at Cassie, and he raised a shoulder. 'But I'd say it was when we were in Queensland last year that I realised my feelings had changed, and I thought your mum maybe felt the same.'

'So what happened?' Rory was watching Raf, and she offered him a faint smile when his gaze wandered to hers.

'We were talking on the second night when the four of us stayed at the beach,' Raf explained. 'Talking about your dad, and how much we missed him and wished he was there. We were both feeling sad and we shared a hug. We've done that loads of times, and I had no idea it would feel so different. Then we kissed, once. And that was it, until this week.'

'Seriously?'

Cassie was expecting more scorn, but there was a hopeful note in Rory's response, too.

'You haven't been...?' He fell silent and Isla jumped in.

'Together all this time and lying to us?'

'Nope.' Raf leant forward. 'And the reason why not is partly because we just couldn't get our heads around feeling the way we do, when we both love your dad.'

He placed a hand over Isla and Rory's. 'But mostly it's because your mum made it very clear that you come first, and she couldn't ever be with someone either of you wouldn't accept. And she didn't see how you would accept me, as your dad's friend. So yeah, for the past nine months we've been trying to pretend we're just friends and there won't ever be more. That's how much she loves you, how much she strived to protect you from anything else that might hurt you. And then, while we were away, we talked some more and decided our feelings deserved a chance, that maybe we could find a way to tell you and hope you might be okay with it.'

Raf huffed out a breath. 'She's amazing, your mum. I know you kind of know that, but maybe you don't realise how much. How she copes without your dad and takes such incredible care of you and checks in with everyone else to make sure they're all right.

'So we totally understand that you're hurt and shocked, but please realise that your mum is, too. And I don't think she deserves the silent treatment, Rory. You can't understand the truth if you're not prepared to listen. Beyond those we love, no one else's opinion matters.'

At this Rory's eyes drifted to Cassie, and she leapt up when she saw the tears glistening in them. She hurried around the table and pulled him into her arms, his head falling to her shoulder as he clung to her.

'Oh, Rory, darling. I'm so sorry. I never wanted to hurt either of you.'

She hadn't realised that Raf had stood too, until she felt his hand on her back and her own tears came when she saw his hand on Rory's back, too. She sniffed as they slowly drew apart, and she returned to her chair.

'I wanted it to be true,' Rory whispered, his eyes glued to Raf. 'Because if you and Mum were together, then maybe you wouldn't always have to leave us, and we could stay here. There's no one I love in London, other than Jas, and she's leaving too. But I was scared it wasn't real when I saw the pictures. You always told us not to believe that stuff.'

Raf exhaled as Cassie swiped her eyes, and he reached across to grip Rory's hands. 'I'm not going anywhere, buddy, I promise,' he said softly. 'Whatever happens, I'll always love you and Isla and be there for both of you.'

'Do you love Mum?' Isla was always direct, and Cassie held her breath. They hadn't said these words out loud, not yet, but everything they had shared, especially in Majorca, felt exactly that. A passionate, long-lasting, life-affirming love she had never expected to find again and now couldn't imagine living without.

'Truthfully?' Raf smiled as he let Rory go, his eyes landing on Cassie's. She was already reading his reply in them, and her heart lifted at the unspoken words he'd shared time and again these past months. 'Truly, madly, deeply, for the first time in my life. Is that how the saying goes?'

'So we're good, then?' Isla jumped up and grabbed her phone. 'It's just that I'm meeting Harriet and Alfie at Young Farmer's, and I've got to get going.'

'Wait, that's it? The conference is over?' Cassie's words came on a short laugh. Dare she believe this might all be real and her children would be okay?

'I'm cool with it.' Isla shrugged. 'But just keep the ick stuff to a minimum when we're around, yeah? You're both pretty old to be, like, kissing and stuff.' She mimed sticking her fingers down her throat, and this time Cassie did laugh, even as her gaze went to Rory, still sitting.

'You haven't said it back, Mum,' he said seriously.

'Said what?' She was trying to keep up, but it was hard after a day such as this one.

'That you love Raf too.'

'Rory's right, you haven't.' Raf sat back, and her stomach dipped when he grinned. There was confidence and amusement and more dancing in his eyes, and her smile turned into a laugh she couldn't restrain. 'So go on then, say it. If it's true and you mean it.'

She wanted to tease him for a bit longer, but it wouldn't be fair on Rory, who was staring at her hopefully. She hadn't realised quite how much her son looked to Raf for guidance, and how his life was flourishing with Raf in it. She couldn't be the one to take all that away from them, and now she didn't have to. It felt amazing, to look at him this way and not wear a disguise, to dismiss feelings neither of them had expected. And now she understood it wasn't the fear of having Raf in their lives in every way possible that had frightened Rory; it was the dread of living without him.

'I love you back,' she said softly. Her hand found his, and he gripped it as the cheeky grin widened. 'Truly, madly, deeply.'

'So does that mean you're officially our stepdad?' A smile spread across Rory's face. 'Like, for real?'

'I think it does, Rory, yeah.' Raf laughed as Rory jumped up and came around the table. He let go of Cassie to hug her son, and she was crying again, swiping away

277

tears of happiness. 'So you'd better get used to me asking you about homework and stuff.'

'I don't think you can help me with homework.' Rory let go, and his gaze was serious before he grinned. 'You always told me you were shit at school and that I'd better not copy your example.'

'Rory!' But Cassie was laughing as well, her glance darting between the two.

'What? It's true, he did say that.' Rory grabbed his phone. 'I think it's pretty cool too, having a famous rock star drummer for a stepdad. Can I take my bike and go with Isla, Mum? I can eat there.'

'Yes, you can,' she told him softly. 'Ride safe, remember the rules and that I love you.'

'Love you too.' Rory snatched up his cycling helmet, and at the door he paused, looking between her and Raf. 'Both of you.'

Suddenly this was Cassie's life, and she loved it. Her children safe and happy, close by with old friends and new. A place in the landscape she'd come to love, with adored family on hand she could watch over, and Flynn at her feet. The promise of studying to begin a new career, however long and difficult the road ahead would be to achieve it. And Raf, getting up and coming around the table, tugging her upright to hold her.

'That went better than I expected,' he murmured against her hair. 'I was prepared for a battle, but they really do seem okay with you and me.'

'I love how that sounds. You and me.' She eased back to look at him. 'But what will we do? You're here, and I have to be in London for Isla, Rory and school. We can't leave yet, not with her GCSEs coming up.'

'I think for now we have to commute. Maybe there's a way we can spend some weekends and the holidays here, and I'll come down to London and work from there whenever I can. If that's okay?'

'It's more than okay. I'd love it, and I think Isla and Rory will too. We can talk about what happens when she leaves school next year.' Cassie paused. 'As long as it works out best for everyone. I want to be here, Raf, with our family and friends.'

'So do I. And I'm sure we'll find a way. I don't want to lose you.'

'Neither do I. Have you asked Flynn how he feels about living in London?' The wolfhound had nudged between them, his head pressing against Cassie's thigh. 'I think he's trying to tell me he wants to come too. I hope he doesn't mind small spaces.'

'I think as long as we're around, he won't care where he lives.' Raf's gaze was intense again, and she recognised it. She had seen it so often these past few days. 'Ginormous dog notwithstanding, you do realise we're temporarily alone?' His hands went to her thighs, and he lifted her onto the table. 'And if you love me half as much as I love you, we should make the most of every minute.'

'Agreed. And I do love you, so much that I can hardly even believe it.' She wound her arms around his neck, pulling him close as Flynn backed away.

'I might need you to prove it.' Raf couldn't stifle a groan when she kissed him, his hand in her hair.

'I could make your favourite dinner tonight.' She tipped her head to one side, as though pretending to be serious.

'Nope. Not hungry, at least for steak. Some other way?'

'Breakfast in bed?'

'No, it's my turn. You brought me breakfast this morning and then we...'

'I remember,' she whispered. 'I won't ever forget a moment with you.'

'Tell me what's in your heart, Cass.' The seriousness had returned, and she kissed him, wanting him to be certain, to know how she truly felt.

'You,' she whispered. 'You're in my heart. You're amazing, and I intend to spend a very long time reminding you how much I love you.' He hadn't been her first love, but he would be her last. There would never be room in her heart for another like this.

'I love you too,' Raf said in wonder. 'I'm going to tell you that every single day and show you all the ways I mean it.'

'Promise?'

'Promise. Starting right now.'

Acknowledgements

Book one was the dream, and I still have to pinch myself that Book ten is out in the world! It really does take a team, and I'm thankful for the support, advice and encouragement I've received. Cassie and Raf's journey has been very special to write, and I knew as soon as they appeared in *Finding Home in Hartfell* that they had a story to share. Both characters arrived on the page almost fully formed, and I couldn't wait to plan their romance and help them find their way to a happy Hartfell ending.

I'm very grateful to my agent Catherine Pellegrino, editor Emily Bedford, publicist Kate Shepherd, and the wider Canelo team for all you do to encourage my writing, produce the books and help share them with readers. Thank you to Hannah George and Diane Meacham for illustrating and designing the gorgeous cover, and bringing Cassie and Flynn so perfectly to life. Jamie Barbakoff narrates the books beautifully; thank you for making my characters leap off the page.

Writing for and connecting with readers who love romance is a joy, and I'm very thankful for everyone who reads my books. I hope our wonderful genre with love at its heart brings you much happiness. Thank you to bloggers, reviewers and readers for sharing our books, and the admins and members of fabulous Facebook groups bringing us all together. Shout out to Chick Lit and

Prosecco, Riveting Reads and Vintage Vibes, and The Friendly Book Society, brilliantly bookish places to hang out. Cassie and Raf spend some time away from Hartfell, and my thanks go to Karen Henderson for suggesting Majorca. It was an inspired choice!

Thank you to Cass Grafton and Sarah Shoesmith, always ready to offer support, encouragement and a good laugh. You make everything so much more fun and we always have the best time when we're together (we need more!). To the Thursday night RNA group, and the Lightfooters, spending time with other writers is invaluable and inspirational. Susan and Victoria, keep writing and embracing the joy it brings you.

To Stewart and Fin, thank you! You make all the difference in the world to mine, especially when I'm so often immersed in a fictional one. I very much appreciate all the help, support and space you give me.

To Becca and Nicky, both mums-in-a-million. We've shared so much with our families down the years, and I have many happy memories of the fun we've had together. It would be impossible to name them all, but our Grizedale adventures, miniature trains, too much chocolate cake and New Year's Eve remain highlights. Thank you for reading my very first book, and lugging that huge file around, especially on a soaking Lake District weekend! I so appreciate your love and support, and we're blessed to have you in our lives.